"A quietly building, sinister, creepy tale. Wright has a unique imagination."

—Dean R. Koontz,
author of *Strangers*
and *Phantoms*

I've learned one thing at least:

The dead don't look forward. They don't plan for the future. They don't put money away for their kids' education. They don't take pictures, or decorate their houses, or read horoscopes, or fill calendars up with events. They don't brush their teeth or check their clothes for signs of wear. They don't write letters, or bad checks, or poems. They don't paint, they don't dust, and they don't wax their cars. They live only in the present and in the past. The past is their present.

It's the only way to tell the dead from the living, you see.

Because the dead don't look where they're going. They look only where they've been . . .

Look for all these Tor books by T. M. Wright

CARLISLE STREET
A MANHATTAN GHOST STORY
THE PEOPLE OF THE DARK
THE PLAYGROUND
THE WAITING ROOM

T.M. WRIGHT

The Waiting Room

A TOM DOHERTY ASSOCIATES BOOK

This is a work of fiction. All the characters and events portrayed in this book are fictional, and any resemblance to real people or incidents is purely coincidental.

THE WAITING ROOM

First printing: August 1986

A TOR Book

Published by Tom Doherty Associates
49 West 24 Street
New York, N.Y. 10010

ISBN: 0-812-52760-7
CAN. ED.: 0-812-52761-5

Printed in the United States

0 9 8 7 6 5 4 3 2 1

With love and thanks to my mom—
MARIEANNE AUBIN

Acknowledgments

For her much-needed letter of encouragement, my thanks to Stacy Horn. For his continued support, my thanks to Jeff Zaleski. And, as always, my gratitude to my editor, Harriet P. McDougal.

And one person deserves acknowledgment merely for being the marvelous woman that she is—Barbara Doherty.

PART ONE

At the Edge

ONE

My name is Sam Feary. I have a friend named Abner W. Cray. Sometimes people call him "Abner Doubleday," either because they think it's funny or because they're hard of hearing and they really believe that's what he's called. He hates it, though.

Abner and I have known each other since we were kids in Bangor, Maine. I'm a year and a half older, probably fifty I.Q. points smarter, and I'm not nearly as clumsy as he is with women. Take that stupidity with his cousin Stacy, for instance, and the unholy mess he made of things with Phyllis Pellaprat, which, of course, he couldn't have helped—when the love bug bites Abner, it bites him hard, right through the skin and into the blood. It happened more than once in Bangor, when we were in high school together.

* * *

I came to Manhattan, and I stayed here, because I like it. I like people—all kinds of people. Everyone's interesting as far as I'm concerned, everyone's got some great story to tell, even if he's not aware of it. So I came to Manhattan, I got myself a job with a construction company, set myself up in a small apartment on Second Avenue, near 11th Street, bought myself a pet boa constrictor—which has since gone the way of the carrier pigeon—met a woman named Leslie, whom I rapidly fell in love with, and started to live.

I like living. I get a kick out of touching and tasting, out of going into an Italian deli—there's one not far from here—and taking a giant whiff of whatever gritty aroma wafts my way. And I like to dance, though I'm the first to admit that I've got three left feet and fifteen big toes. And except for country western, I like music, too—pop, rock, classical (if it's not too sleepy). If it's got a beat, I'll listen to it and enjoy it. There's very little in this world that I don't like, in fact. Except the *New York Post*, and the memory of Idi Amin and Joe Stalin and Richard Nixon (because he got me into so much damn trouble in Viet Nam), and commercials for Charmin toilet paper, and a lone fly buzzing me while I'm trying to eat, and two radios playing different stations at the same time, and the smell of peanut butter sandwiches mixed up with the smell of ironing.

I had to grow up with that. In Bangor. I had to come home from school at lunchtime, because the school I went to had no lunch program, and invariably I'd get fed peanut butter sandwiches and milk while my mother finished up her morning's ironing. I didn't think much about it while it was happening. I think I may even have enjoyed it—those two smells mixed up together. I started hating it later, in Nam, I think. I'm not sure why. Maybe I had a thing for my mother, I don't know. Maybe I had a thing for peanut butter sandwiches, or fresh ironing, I don't know. I'll probably never know, because what I've learned about myself over the years is this: There's a stranger living inside me, and sometimes he's a damned ignorant bastard.

I had no idea Abner was here, in Manhattan, when I got here. The last time I'd seen him, I was two days away from catching a Greyhound bus to Parris Island, in South Carolina, where some asshole D.I. was going to try and "mold" me into a Marine. Abner was drooling over his cousin Stacy then; he was going on and on about her "incredible body," and I remember saying to him, "Christ, Abner, she's practically your sister, and here you are talking about putting it to her."

"Putting it to her?" he asked. I didn't know then that Abner was a virgin. I thought that anyone older than fourteen had a constant hard-on and was lying in wait for whoever happened to back into it. "Put *what* to her, Sam?"

"Your thing," I answered. "Your little ding-dong. You know—put *it* to her, have *sex* with her."

"With Stacy, Sam? Naw. She's too smart for that. She's smarter than I am, for sure."

Abner was fifteen then, maybe sixteen. And it

wasn't that he was homely, or smelly, or stupid. He was just plain scared of girls. Especially girls like Stacy. This was 1965, remember, a full ten or fifteen years before people finally figured out that, male or female, *everyone* likes to get it on. In 1965 all of us guys *knew* that only men liked to get it on, and that it was the full-time job of women either to prevent it or to grin and bear it. So there was Abner, fifteen or sixteen, horny, and scared. And there was Stacy, fifteen or sixteen, smart, stacked, and enticing, which, as far as poor Abner was concerned, added up to obscene intimidation.

Abner and I broke into a mausoleum once, when we were kids, shortly before I got called up and shipped away to Viet Nam. Breaking into the mausoleum was his bright idea right from the start. He said something about wanting "to see how the dead ticked," which, I told him, was just about the dumbest thing I'd ever heard anyone say. "The dead," I told him, "*don't* tick anymore, Abner."

He shook his head, squinted, pursed his lips, tried to look befuddled. It's a pose he uses quite a lot, especially when he realizes that something incredibly stupid has just come stumbling from his mouth. Then he explained, "Well, I guess 'tick' isn't the right word, is it, Sam? But it really would be a neat thing to do. I mean . . . you could bring that cat skull you've got—"

"It's not a toy, Abner. That cat was my friend."

"Sam, you dug her up, Jees—*you* dug her up—"

What could I say? The cat was named Flora, and I

really did love her, if only because the original Flora was a girl I'd taken to a couple of horror movies and had fallen hopelessly in love with because of the way she clutched at me in panic. Then she moved from Bangor to Oshkosh or Hoboken or some such place, and I was devastated. The cat itself was pretty much just a cat; she was nothing special (and it comes to me that my father once pointed out that Flora was a male, which, because the cat had long, thick black fur was not something that was easy to spot, and since he had a soft, feminine face, I assumed that *he* was a *she*).

I said to Abner, "I dug her up only because we were close. If we do this thing, if we break into this mausoleum, Flora stays home. Okay?"

He shrugged.

But, at last, I did bring Flora's skull, if only so Abner wouldn't sulk. And I brought some candles, too, and a dozen Mallo Cups, because I had something like a craving for them then, which has since vanished. I have no real cravings anymore. I have needs, and desires, and passions. I'm pretty much like anyone else.

We all grow up. We lose our craving for Mallo Cups, we stop being afraid of thunder, we turn out the night-light, we go down into the cellar to change a fuse, we peek into the attic, and we end up being proud of ourselves for it. We say we're adult and rational, we say there's really nothing to be afraid of anymore besides IRS audits, slippery roads, and canned vichyssoise. But I know one thing about that damned ignorant bastard living inside me: I know that he's about ready to piss in his boots every time the fuses blow, and that if he's got to move around with me on some dark street, then he'd just as soon curl up and go to sleep.

Even now.

Even after all this time with my friend Abner W. Cray.

Even after so much black water has passed under the bridge.

Right up front, let me tell you a little of what this story is about, so you won't come back later and say I'm perverse or mixed up or that I've got a memory like a sieve. This story is about *people,* it's about *love,* it's about *friendship*. That's what it's mostly about.

But it's about traffic flow, too. The same kind of traffic flow you'll find on I-490 or Route 66 or on the New Jersey Turnpike. Traffic flow. Getting people from one place to another without too much hassle and delay. No one's got it down to an exact science. Sometimes it works, but most times it doesn't. And you know why, of course. It doesn't work because of *people*. On the expressways and the turnpikes it would work just fine if none of those cars had *people* in them, if each car were programmed to go exactly where it should go. But those cars do have people in them, people with brains and souls and aches and pains and likes and dislikes and habits, et cetera, et cetera. So when everything is moving along beautifully, one of those people decides he's going to go rent a videotape before heading home. But the video rental place is in Weehawken, and Weehawken is off that exit there, coming up at fifty-five miles per hour, and only one hundred feet away. And he thinks, *Hell, there's still time*. So he jams on the brakes and swings into the exit lane like Mario Andretti. And behind him, the poor slob who's been following a bit too close has fishtailed and been hit broadside by a semi. The traffic flow didn't work. *People* screwed it up.

TWO

I worked in construction for two months, in January and February this year. I never actually built anything, because buildings usually don't get built in the winter. I dug some trenches for sewer pipes, I operated a forklift, I hauled bags of cement from one place to another. And I helped demolish an ancient red brick apartment building on East 80th Street.

It was an ugly building, old and rotting, the red brick was a streaky dark brown, most of the windows were gone. Raised letters in the cement over the front doors read "THE MILFORD," though the *F* and the *O* had weathered away nearly to nothing, so the guys I worked with started calling it "The Mill Road," which they clearly thought was interesting and catchy.

We had to stop work after the second day when a man they sent through the building to look for transients found a body in an eighth-floor apartment. No one got upset about it. The body had been there, we were told, for quite a long time. It was mummified, in fact, because the apartment was dry and cool and faced north, so sunlight never touched it. One of the guys I worked with, a fat man named Lenny who had a red tattoo on his left arm which read "RASPUTIN EATS IT" ("I don't know how it got there," he told me. "I was in this whorehouse in Louisiana, and when I woke up, there it was—I never did find out who this Rasputin guy is.") said that they were always finding bodies in old buildings. "Usually they're winos, you know. Your bums and your basic trash. Sometimes they ain't. Sometimes they're guys the mob's gotten to, and sometimes they're these old farts who keep on living in a place even when the rats have run off."

The body they found was the body of a young black woman who was dressed in a long black silk dress and white mink cape, as if she'd been planning an evening on the town. She was sitting in a kitchen corner, knees up, head down, left hand in front of her knees, clutching her right wrist. She was holding a purse that turned out to have a couple of hundred dollars in it. She had the purse in a strong death grip in her right hand. ("I tried to take it from her, you know," said the guy who found her. "But I could tell—she didn't want me taking it, so I let her have it a little while longer.")

"Junkie," Lenny said.

"Yeah?" said a guy named Allen, who was also fat, though not quite as fat as Lenny, and who wore sleeveless T-shirts no matter what the weather. "D'joo see her, Lenny? D'joo see her?"

Lenny confessed that he hadn't seen her, though he wished he had, and that's when the foreman came over and told us to go home, that he'd call us when we could start work again.

It was while I was on my way back to my apartment for a long, relaxing shower and a shave to get ready for my date with Leslie that I saw Abner. Leslie and I had a "talk-it-out" evening planned: dinner first, at a quiet Italian place on East 81st Street, then a long leisurely walk down Fifth Avenue, then back to my place. We were having some trouble then and we had agreed to try to get to the bottom of it. I was walking on Second Avenue near 38th Street; he was across the street, coming out of a little Greek restaurant, and was swiping at his chin with the back of his jacket sleeve. "Hey, Abner!" I called, because I recognized him right away. Hell, I hadn't seen him for nearly twenty years, but he had the same quick, stiff walk, the same *I'm watching you over my shoulder* look that he'd had then, when he was going on and on about his cousin Stacy. He's kind of an odd-looking guy; his brow is low and heavy, his hazel eyes deep-set, his nose long and straight, his lips large. And though he should, by all rights, look Neanderthal, he doesn't. His girlfriends in high school invariably described him as "poetic-looking" and "intense." I always thought "poetic-looking" and "intense" meant *screwed up*. I'd say that described him then, and describes him now, although, I'll admit, it's a vulnerable, lovable kind of screwed up. I think I've always felt *protective* of him, like he's some nerdish little brother whose ideas of the world around him are naive at best and self-destructive at worst.

He looked in my direction when I called to him. He stopped walking, his mouth fell open, and he stared wide-eyed at me.

"Abner, it's me," I called. "It's Sam Feary!"

He ran off, east, toward 39th Street. I watched him, flabbergasted, and when he was out of sight, I whispered, "Christ, same to you, fella," because, of course, I had no idea of the mess he'd gotten himself into.

Lenny told me, when we were called back to the building on East 80th Street, that the black woman they'd found huddled in an eighth-floor kitchen had been there for years, that when they'd lifted her up off the floor she'd started to fall apart, "first her arms, you know, 'cuz they tried to pick her up by her arms, and then her legs, 'cuz they tried those, and then they'd got her by the back and didn't hold her head up so it fell off . . ."

"Gimme a break, Lenny," I said.

"No," he protested, "it's true. Course, I'm not saying that her arms and legs and head fell right off, plop, onto the floor, but they were hanging there pretty loose, you know—"

"Name your sources," Allen cut in. He reads lots of newspapers.

It took Lenny a couple of seconds to figure out

what Allen meant. Then he said simply, "Cops, two cops."

"Which two cops?"

Lenny shrugged. "Cops got names?" he asked. "Two cops I heard talking, that's all."

Allen grimaced. "It's pretty disgusting," he said, which surprised me because he looked like the type who'd find nothing at all disgusting. Then the foreman came over and told us we could start earning our pay again.

We were sent up to the eighth floor. It was the foreman's idea of a joke because the building was going to be blasted, which meant that practically all the work had to be done in the basement, on the foundation.

"Gotta rip out the wiring up there," the foreman said with a wide, shit-eating grin.

"What the hell for?" Lenny asked.

" 'Cuz the city says so," the foreman answered. "Gotta rip out the fuse boxes in all those apartments up there and save 'em—" He stopped; he could barely keep himself from breaking into a laughing fit. He went on, "Comes straight from the mayor's office, boys."

So we tromped up to the eighth floor, which I thought was okay—ripping out fuse boxes was lots easier work than hammering away at cement foundations. And of the three of us who got sent up there—Lenny, Allen, and me—only Lenny let on that he'd rather be somewhere else.

"Yeah," Allen said, "like on the moon, Lenny?"

"Florida," Lenny said. It was late February and very cold, and Lenny talked often about going to Florida.

When we got to the eighth floor, Allen asked, "You guys know which one it was?"

Lenny nodded sullenly to the right. "Must be that one down there," he said.

An apartment door was standing open at the end of the hallway. Around it, on the floor, plaster dust and chunks of plaster that had fallen from the ceiling—it littered the hallway everywhere else—had been swept into several neat piles.

Allen said, starting for it, "Dat must be da place," and Lenny, staying put, said:

"No reason we got to start there. No reason we got to go in there at all, Al."

"Allen," said Allen, "not 'Al'!"

Lenny ignored him. "No reason we got to be up here, either, you ask me. That limp-dick foreman wants some fuse boxes, we can get 'em on the seventh floor, no reason we got to be up here."

Allen was halfway to the apartment now, and walking quickly, nearly swaggering, so the hammer and chisel and half-dozen screwdrivers on his utility belt swayed left and right.

It smelled of antiseptic in that hallway, Lysol, I guessed, because the smell had that cloying bitter-sweetness to it, and, underlying it, the smell of flies.

"Stinks," Lenny grumbled. "Smells like garbage up here."

I called, "Let's go down to seven, Allen, okay?"

He stopped, looked back, grinned a flat, macho kind of grin: "No dead black woman's gonna keep me from doin' *my* job!"

To which I said, "I'm very impressed, Allen."

Lenny grumbled yet again that the hallway smelled like garbage, and added, "How's anybody know she didn't have some kind of sickness? You know, like Legionnaires' disease, or . . ." He stopped, thought a moment, went on, "Like Legionnaires' disease" —stopped again and shook his head slowly, eyes closed.

I called to Allen, "We're going down to seven, Al."

"Allen," he corrected, glancing around at us.

"Sure. Macho Allen. We're going down to seven."

The image he made in that hallway, his body stiff and still, left arm up slightly, right arm straight at his side, legs apart, feet firmly planted on the floor, and a window at the end of the hall letting dull February afternoon light in, was of an oversize plastic replica of a man, like a prize in a cereal box, caught in lazy clouds of white plaster dust.

"C'mon," I called to him, "let's tell that limp-dick foreman"—I liked Lenny's phrase—"to put it where the sun don't shine."

And Lenny, who despises euphemisms, no matter how unsubtle, corrected, "Up his freakin' *ass!*"

Allen said nothing. He continued to stare at us, that flat, macho grin on his mouth, clouds of plaster dust swirling fitfully around him.

I turned toward the stairway to the seventh floor, glanced back at Lenny. "C'mon, Lenny," I said.

"Somepin's wrong," Lenny whispered.

I started down. I said, "He won't stay up here alone, Lenny," and I heard, "Yes, he will." I looked back. The stairway wall was between me and Allen; I could see only Lenny. I guessed that Lenny was still looking at Allen, asked, "Did you say that, Lenny?" and he said once more, turning his head very briefly to look at me, "Somepin's wrong, somepin's real wrong!"

I took a long, slow breath. I called to Allen, "We're going down to seven, Al. You can stay here if you want."

And I heard, "He will."

"Somepin's wrong, Jesus Christ, somepin's wrong!" Lenny whispered.

I asked him, "Did you say that, Lenny?"

He turned to me. "Jesus, Jesus!" he whispered. I could see fingers of plaster dust in the air around him and I said tightly, urgently, "Come *on*, Lenny," and started back up. I stopped a couple of stairs from the top, reached for him.

He screamed.

I cursed.

And I heard his scream shut off abruptly as the plaster dust around him grew thick and smothering and he struggled for his breath within it.

He stumbled through it to the stairway, lurched forward. I reached, caught him.

Then the plaster dust began to settle and Allen appeared at the top of the stairs, cheeks puffed out like a blowfish, face red. He took several stiff, quick steps down, sat heavily, and let his breath out. I continued to hold on to Lenny, who was hacking up plaster dust and trying to curse at the same time.

Allen said, through intermittent coughing, "I felt it coming, you know"—cough—"in through that window, that little"—cough—"wind, and I thought" —cough, cough—"*Shit, it's so damned*"—cough— "*dry up here this stuff's gonna be everywhere,* so I thought I'd better . . . come back—"

Lenny cut loose with several very loud, coarse coughs, then cursed mightily.

Allen glanced at him. "He okay?"

"Sure," I said, "why don't we go down to seven?"

"I think we'd better tell that foreman," Allen said, "to stick it"—cough—"where the sun don't shine."

"Up his freaking ass!" Lenny said.

But we never did. We went down to one, found the foreman, and told him there were no fuse boxes on the eighth floor. He shrugged, "Course there ain't. You think the riffraff around here's gonna leave stuff like that?" And he laughed.

"Up yours," Lenny whispered, but not loud enough that the foreman could hear him.

Two days later, the Milford fell, reluctantly, after the fourth load of dynamite was touched off.

The trouble Leslie and I were having—which hadn't gotten resolved the night before because we were both unwilling to broach it out of fear, I think, of where it might lead—had to do with her father, who stayed with her in her loft apartment on East 73rd

Street. He was a quirky middle-aged man with a number of ailments plaguing him.

We were lying naked in my single bed, pleasantly exhausted from lovemaking, and had been engaging in light conversation that I hoped would eventually lead to more lovemaking. After a while, the conversation turned somehow to her father. She said, "He's not easy to handle, but he's fun most of the time."

And I said, "Maybe he should be somewhere that he can be taken better care of, Leslie."

Leslie riveted me with a cold stare and said, "He's my *father*, Sam. He's *family*, and from where I come from we take care of our own."

"So do we," I protested feebly. "It's just that—"

"I never realized you could be so uncaring, Sam," she cut in. "I don't know why I never saw it before. I'm glad I see it now."

"Hell, I'm not uncaring. I was just making what I thought was a rational suggestion."

"Oh, rational, smational! That's just a euphemism for *let's do what's expedient. Let's shuffle the old folks off to where they aren't going to be such a bother—*"

"He's not old."

She sighed. "And that's another thing: Whenever we get into an argument, you try to change the subject. I don't like it. Arguments should be hashed out, they should be brought to a conclusion—"

"We aren't having an argument, are we? If we are, I wish we'd stop."

She said nothing.

"Leslie?" I coaxed.

She sighed again.

I said, "I like the way your chest heaves when you do that."

She grimaced. "That's a stupid thing to say at this point."

"At *what* point, for God's sake?"

"In the middle of a discussion."

"*Discussion?* I thought it was an argument!" I chuckled. It was distinctly the wrong thing to do. She got up abruptly from the bed and started putting her clothes on. "What are you doing?" I asked.

She looked back at me. "I don't sleep with people who have ice for blood."

"I don't have ice for blood. I have blood for blood."

"Always the funny man," she quipped. She leaned over, picked her bra up from the end table, and put it on with her back turned. I said, "You don't have to turn away from me, Leslie."

"If your attention's going to be only on my heaving chest, then yes, I do."

"Well, okay," I said, feeling grimly playful—hoping it might, somehow, get her back into the bed—"my attention's on your bouncy bottom, how about that?"

She said nothing.

"Leslie?"

She turned her head. "This is a side of you I've never seen before, Sam, and I don't know if I like it. I'm going to go home now. Call me tomorrow. We'll talk." And while various futile protests stumbled from my tongue she silently finished dressing and left the apartment.

THREE

When I was growing up in Bangor, I had a white mouse named Sparky. I kept it in a big wire cage that had a gerbil wheel in it, a water dish, and a dish for food. Sparky grew up in that cage, and when he got to be an old mouse and I knew he was about to kick off, I took him out of the cage and into a farmer's field. I was doing him a favor. I was giving him a taste of the wide-open spaces before death came along and gobbled him up. After all, there were probably ten thousand of his cousins in that field, and how many of them, I asked Sparky, would want to die in a damned wire cage?

But when I let him out of it, he spooked. He froze. He wouldn't budge. And at last I figured out why—he wasn't just *Sparky the white mouse*. He was *Sparky the white mouse who lived in a wire cage with a gerbil wheel and a food dish and water dish. That* was Sparky's identity. And I'd tried to take it away from him.

It's kind of what the EL-HI Construction Company did on East 80th Street when that rotten old building came tumbling down. They pushed a lot of scared and shivering Sparkys out into the street.

Which was nothing new. People have been blasting buildings and tearing them down and burning them up for a long, long time.

And interrupting the traffic flow.

Everyone's got to have a place to live, you see. Not just to keep the rain away, and not just to put furniture and drapes and knickknacks in, and not just to repaint and have friends over, but because people are happy having walls around them and roofs above them. It's one of the things that make them who they are, and sometimes, after death has gobbled them up and all the friends have gone away, it's just about the only thing—besides their habits, like turning the TV on at seven-thirty, or making meat loaf and mashed potatoes on Thursday, or having a favorite chair to sit in, or calling Mother on holidays and on every second Saturday, or peeling potatoes, or fixing cars. Habits are comfortable things, at first, like a pair of soft suede shoes. Then they become things we need, then they become passions. And, after it's all done, they become a part of us, like our hair and fingernails.

And, like our hair and fingernails, exactly like our hair and fingernails, they last just about forever.

* * *

The second time I saw Abner, I was on my way to the unemployment office. It was the middle of March but still pretty cold in the city, so construction had ground nearly to a halt. I was on Second Avenue, and he was again across the street from me, coming out of the same Greek restaurant I'd seen him come out of several weeks earlier. He was wiping his lips with the back of his sleeve, as he had the first time I'd seen him, and again I called to him, "Hey, Abner. It's me. Sam Feary!"

He stopped, turned his head, looked wide-eyed at me, just as he had that first time. Then he shook his head, slowly at first, as if there were some kind of old engine inside him that he was cranking up, and then faster, more furiously.

After thirty seconds of this, he ran off.

I was pissed. We'd been friends, for God's sake. Sure it had been twenty years earlier, but so what? Twenty years, forty years, it didn't matter. I was one old friend calling across a New York City street full of strangers to another old friend, and I was not about to be ignored. If he was going to run off, I sure as hell was going to find out why.

So I went after him.

I lost him momentarily in the crowds on 42nd Street, but I saw him again, a couple of moments later, in a cab going west, slowly, because a traffic jam was in the making.

I watched as he leaned forward in his seat and his eyes settled on me.

And because I was very close to him, and could see him clearly, I muttered, "Good Lord," because it was hard to believe that it was Abner Cray I was seeing in that cab. What I was seeing was like a skinny caricature of Abner Cray, as if he'd decided that eating was passé. He leaned back in the seat, then an opening appeared in the snarl of traffic, and the cab shot forward into it, which ignited a deafening flare-up of shouted curses and blaring horns.

"Goddamn maniac cabbies!" one of the drivers yelled.

"You wanna kill someone?!" shouted another.

And the cabbie stuck his head out his window and yelled back, "It wouldn't be the first time!" then careened down East 42nd Street.

Let me tell you what I used to believe about death when I went to Nam and while Abner and I were sitting in the Hammet Mausoleum twenty years ago, with Flora's bleached white skull between us, the yellow-orange light of six candles flickering on the walls, and both of us on the verge of being terminally spooked:

I believed that death was *it!* The end. Zilch. Limboland. I believed that if a truck fell over on me—*splat!*—then maybe I'd feel a second's worth of incredible pain, but I wouldn't feel anything else because suddenly I'd be beyond pain and feeling. There'd be a stinking, gooey mess on the sidewalk that some poor slob would have to scrape up and shuffle onto a stretcher, but "Sam Feary" would be nothing but a name that someone, a couple of years down the line, would have trouble remembering.

Sometimes I think how really pleasant it would be

if all of that dreck had turned out to be what really happens when the curtain comes down.

Abner was never a classic nerd. Even in high school he knew enough not to wear white socks with black shoes, slide rules baffled him, and he wasn't abysmally clumsy, although, after gym class when he was putting his jeans on, they usually had a hole in the knee that he'd get his foot stuck in and he'd hop about, on the verge of a fall, until he found a wall to steady himself against. But at heart, he was a nerd. His view of the world was nerdish. He was convinced that as complex as it was, as baffling and unfair and unjust as it seemed to be, there was a niche somewhere in it for him, and because it was his *right*—as a creature of the universe—he would find that niche and fill it. And once he'd filled it, the world and its complexity and injustice could pass him by and that would be all right. He'd be comfortable, he'd be set.

I believe that he still thinks that way, though he's not so passionate about it. He used to be a photographer, for instance, which was why he came to New York several years ago, to do a big photo book on all that was wonderful about Manhattan. Now he shrugs and says, "Hell, there's just too much to photograph, Sam."

The tumbledown beach house on Long Island, where Abner is now, was owned by Art DeGraff. Art went to school with Abner and me in Bangor, twenty years ago, and I thought he was a slime-ball right from the start. He was a great actor and had lots of charm, but he smiled too much, as if some invisible layer of mud had made his smile stick on his face.

Art married Abner's cousin Stacy in 1975. It broke Abner's heart, and nearly killed Stacy because, after they were married, she learned that beneath his stiffly smiling exterior, Art liked to beat people up, women especially. Abner said that Stacy called it a "character flaw," which made him smile sadly and made my blood boil. Whatever it was, it gave Stacy a lot of pain.

The beach house on Long Island has fifteen rooms, five on the first floor, seven on the second, and three in the attic. It's a very big place, at least one hundred years old, and when the wind off the ocean is strong enough, it shimmers and shakes and complains so loudly that you have to shout to be heard above it.

For a while, Abner lived there. Madeline, too. You'll meet Madeline by and by.

There have been several fires in the house. One, in 1943, was started by a hobo who broke in one frigid winter night and tried to keep warm by building a campfire in the middle of the living room floor. It killed him and blackened the ceiling, but the house survived. In 1962 a family of four who'd driven up from North Carolina and had no place to stay broke into the house and set up housekeeping. It was late fall, and they were sure that no one was going to be using the house for a while—all its doors and shutters were locked, a thick tangle of dead weeds surrounded it, and the nearest neighbors were a good mile off, blocked by a stand of trees—so they unloaded what few pieces of furniture they had in their rattletrap pickup truck, put up curtains, and made ready to wait out the coming winter.

Two days later three of them died when the wood stove in the living room cranked out carbon monoxide as they slept. The youngest of them, a six-year-old boy named Frankie, survived, no one has ever figured out how.

In 1970 the house was left to Art DeGraff by his Aunt Carol. She'd inherited it from her Aunt Bernice ten years earlier. Aunt Carol also died at the house. She'd been leaning against an attic window frame when it gave way and she fell thirty-five feet to the ground. She weighed close to three hundred pounds, so no one blamed the window frame. And it wasn't the fall that killed her. She died several days after the fall when a fat embolism broke free of her fractured right leg, made its way to her heart, and stopped it cold.

No one, not even Abner, maintains that the beach house is a happy place, if it can truthfully be said that any house, all by itself, is happy or unhappy. But it is a place to *be*, it has walls, several dozen of them, and roofs, three of them, and it certainly must have its hidden charms, too, because whenever I was there, it was awfully crowded.

I met Leslie the day my boa constrictor died, so I was in a pretty foul mood. I have a tendency to grow very attached to people and pets, and though that boa constrictor had been a dismal conversationalist, he was loads of fun to have hanging around.

I was on my way by taxi to Queens and the possibility of construction work (I had a '68 Chevy Nova that was continually in for one repair or another; I have since given it up). On the corner of East 74th Street and Park Avenue, the taxi stopped. I leaned forward and tapped on the Plexiglas partition. The driver opened it a crack.

"What are you doing?" I asked.

"Earning a buck," he answered, then my door opened and a tall, stunning, dark-blond-haired woman of twenty-nine or thirty, dressed in a long earth-colored wool skirt and bulky beige sweater, stuck her head in, said, "Oh, sorry," and started to back away.

The driver called, "Where you going, miss?"

"I'm going to Queens," she answered. She had an air of quiet authority about her. I liked it. It seemed to fit her.

"Where in Queens?" the driver asked.

"Mission Boulevard."

"Uh huh." I could tell that he was fighting to keep his patience. "Whereabouts is that?"

"It's in Queens," she answered, and slid in next to me. She smiled congenially, nodded, said, "Hi."

I nodded back. "Yeah, hi," I said, and found that my foul mood over the death of my boa constrictor was beginning to fade.

"We've established," said the driver, "that Mission Boulevard is in Queens. What I need to know is, is it in Jackson Heights, or Flushing, or—"

"Oh," she cut in, "yes. Sorry. It's in Jackson Heights."

"Thanks," said the driver, and pulled away from the curb.

She nodded at me, once more repeated "Hi," and smiled congenially again. What impressed me most about her at that moment, as she smiled, were her teeth, which looked perfect, her high cheekbones—which suggested that she was Indian, though she isn't—her ruddy, even complexion, and the way her entire face got involved in her small, congenial smile, so I did not doubt for a moment that it was genuine. I found myself rapidly warming to her.

"Hi," I said.

She stuck her hand out. I took it. Her grip was very firm. She let go of my hand and gave me a quizzical look. "You've obviously got something on your mind," she said. "I didn't mean to intrude." She turned her head and looked out the window.

I said nothing. Although I had been drawn to her almost at once, she was clearly very perceptive, as well as very attractive, and that's a combination I've always found intimidating. We rode in silence for several minutes. At last I said, surprising myself, "My snake died." I grinned an apology. "My snake died," I repeated, as if she hadn't heard me. "It was a boa constrictor. I was attached to it."

She nodded. "Old age?"

"I think so. It was hard to tell. He got . . . listless. He wouldn't eat. And he died."

She said, "It could have been a virus. Boa constrictors in this climate are plagued by viruses. Did you get him to a vet?"

I shrugged. I smiled. It was a nervous smile because, of all possible topics, my first conversation with this stunning, perceptive woman was about snake viruses. "He went too quickly," I said. I chuckled, embarrassed. "I sound like I'm talking about a favorite uncle. 'He went too quickly.' " I chuckled again. I looked questioningly at her. "How do you know about boa constrictors?"

She grinned. "I know about frogs, too, and toads, and salamanders. It's my job. I teach natural history." She paused. "And it's a . . . consuming interest, as well."

"A naturalist in Manhattan, huh?" I said.

She shrugged. It was a slow, graceful, enticing gesture. "Yes," she said. "No apologies."

"None required," I said, which seemed to bring the conversation to an abrupt and uncomfortable halt. I stared straight ahead, through the Plexiglas partition, and grinned vapidly until the conversation resumed several minutes later.

She asked, and I heard immediately that her air of quiet authority was gone, "Do you think we have to go through a tunnel?"

I looked at her. "I think so," I said. "You're new to the city?"

"Yes," she answered. "Relatively so." She paused. "Shit!" she breathed.

"You don't like tunnels?" I asked.

She shook her head. Her straight, shoulder-length, dark blond hair moved freely; she brushed it back from her face. It came to me then how strong and sensual she looked, and what a contradiction that was to the conversation we were having, to the vulnerability she was showing me. "No," she whispered, gaze straight ahead, "I don't like tunnels. I keep thinking they're going to . . . cave in, especially with so much weight on them." She looked at me. She had very expressive dark blue eyes—expressive, at that moment, of gathering anguish—and every few seconds, as she talked, her mouth broke into a quick, nervous grin. She was sitting very straight in the seat, her hand clutching the armrest, and when she finished a sentence she turned her head away and appeared to focus on whatever was in front of the cab. "Haven't you ever thought that—going through a tunnel, I mean"—she looked away—"that it was going to collapse?" She looked pleadingly at me. I wasn't sure if she wanted me to confirm her fear with a similar fear of my own, or if she wanted me to tell her she was being silly.

I said, "No. Never."

She turned away, grinned nervously, looked back, grinned again. She cocked her head a little, which made her look girlish. "Don't you think there's a bridge or something?"

We headed down a ramp that led to the Queens Tunnel. "Too late," I said.

"Shit!" she said. She sat doubly erect in the seat now as we entered the tunnel. Her hand gripping the armrest turned a bright red. Her other hand found mine and grabbed it as if in panic.

I told her, "We'll be through the tunnel in a couple of minutes. And besides, it's been here for quite a few decades and it hasn't collapsed yet."

Her eyes seemed to be glued on the road ahead,

and on the white tunnel walls zipping past. "It's like someone else's dream," she said. "Like someone's idea of a nightmare—a tunnel that keeps getting narrower and narrower, smaller and smaller, until *you* have to get smaller and smaller, too. But you can't. How can you? So the walls themselves make you smaller, the walls squash you like you're a bug some kid's discovered under a rock." She looked pleadingly at me. I wanted very much to hold her, to reassure her. She said, "I'm sorry."

"*This* tunnel ends," I told her.

"Yes. I know it does."

A couple of minutes later we came out in Queens and I saw that the clouds had parted and that the sky was a cool, pale blue. "See?" I said.

She nodded and let go of my hand.

"My name's Sam," I told her.

"Mine's Leslie Wirth," she said.

"Good to meet you, Leslie." I shook her hand. Her grip was weaker than it had been twenty minutes before. I said, "Can I call you?"

She smiled noncommittally. "Thanks for the moral support, Sam."

"My pleasure."

When she got out of the cab in front of her sister's house on Mission Boulevard in Jackson Heights, I called after her, "You didn't answer me."

She looked back. "About what?"

"About calling you."

"Oh. You're right, I didn't."

"Well," I said, "can I or can't I?"

"I wish you would," she answered, smiled invitingly, and went up the walk to her sister's house.

* * *

I called her three days later. We went to a Chinese restaurant called the Imperial Palace, on East 29th Street, where she made light conversation about an aquarium near our table. A cockroach climbed up the side of the aquarium and we both scowled at it. I didn't know what her feelings about cockroaches were then. For all I knew, she could have jumped up from her seat and run away screaming. But she didn't. She said that the cockroach was gone and that was good. I agreed. If she had jumped up and run screaming from the restaurant I don't believe I'd have anything to write now; I think the whole thing would have ended there. So our first agreement was about a cockroach.

I've always thought that people in love should agree.

After the restaurant we walked in a small park near Second Avenue. There were no streetlamps and the evening was pleasantly cool. My arm slipped easily around her waist, and her arm slipped easily around mine. There was no groping, no uncertainty. It was as easy as our conversation. She told me I had a belly and should get rid of it. I chuckled. I didn't like being told that I had a belly because I was constantly sucking it in and thought no one noticed.

"No I don't," I said.

"Yes, you do. You're out of shape."

I shrugged. "I guess I am," I said, and I found that I didn't at all mind admitting my imperfections to her.

FOUR

The last time I saw Abner in Bangor, I thought he was a lot more than just another of my high school friends, more than merely someone who had written something stupid in my high school yearbook. I thought we'd shared quite a lot during our five years in school together. Hell, we'd grown up together, we had shared the torments and anxieties of the damned (the damned, of course, being those who have to live through the ages of thirteen to seventeen). I'd told him secrets that I'd never have told anyone else, and he had done the same with me. So, in the most important ways, we were like brothers.

After I got shipped off to Viet Nam, I wrote him at least two dozen long, rambling, and drearily philosophical letters about what a "shitty place" it was and what a "shitty war" we were waging there, and he wrote long, newsy letters about goings-on in Bangor and goings-on in his life, his thoughts, his loves, his heartaches.

When I came home, I learned that he'd gone to live in the midwest. I wrote several letters to various addresses his father gave me, but only one was answered, briefly and brusquely, and the rest were returned marked "Addressee Unknown." Inexorably, we fell out of touch.

But when I saw him come out of that little Greek restaurant in New York twenty years later, he was like a lifeline to my past, to a time when I was younger, and happier, more naive, less cynical, more hopeful—to a time when *I* was pretty much of a nerd, too. And the fact that I had such a short glimpse of him then, that first time, made it very dreamlike, almost romantic. Sort of, *This is my brother and I haven't seen him in a long time and here in this big impersonal city we can prop each other up and give each other strength.*

So, when I saw him that second time, when that crazy cabbie roared past me, down East 42nd Street, I latched on to the first thing that might possibly get Abner and me back together again—the name of the cab company. The Wilson Cab Company. And the number of the cab. Number 432.

The Wilson Cab Company was in a cramped and seedy garage on West 61st Street. I talked to the dispatcher, a skinny white-haired black woman named Iris, who was in her late fifties, I guessed, and who kept an unlighted Tiparillo sticking out of the corner of her mouth as she spoke. I asked her about cab number 432.

She asked if I was a cop, gave me a quick once-over, which was the first time she'd looked at me, decided I wasn't a cop, and said that the Wilson Cab Company didn't have a cab number 432. "Used to," she said. "Ten years ago, till it went into the Harlem River one night, and that's the last anybody seen of it in *this* world."

I told her that I'd seen it the day before.

She let the corner of her mouth that was free of the Tiparillo rise in a half grin. "Then it was somebody else's cab, mister," she said.

"Back to square one," I said.

When I take a long look backward, I think that Abner's been into the grim and grisly for quite a while. Like it's a hobby. He used to write poems about it, about death. He used to talk about it, used to hold séances (though I'll have to be fair about that—I think he held those fruity séances because he was trying to make it with some of the women he'd conned into coming along), and I swear that when he talked about death—about going to someone's funeral, for instance, or about what might be going on over there, on the Other Side—he got this tiny, contented gleam in his eye, as if he were eating warm chocolate pudding. And all of his sentences, no matter what grisly thing he was talking about, would end on a little, wispy high note, like someone who lives in Buffalo talking about going to Florida for the winter. There were plenty of times that he spooked the hell out of me.

* * *

I was into the grim and grisly, too. Especially that night twenty years ago that Abner and I broke into the Hammet Mausoleum. Hell, I enjoyed it just as much as he did. I got a real kick out of putting Flora's bleached skull in the center of the cement floor, and setting candles around it, and making ghostly noises at it, as if it were some kind of *link* to somewhere.

We all get into death at one time or another. Some of us shrug it off, or put it in a back pocket, or we lock it up tight in one of the billion tiny rooms the brain has, and some of us don't. Some of us pick at it like it's a scab.

I caught Abner the third time I saw him. I got him by the arm, wheeled him around, and said loudly and happily to him, "Damn, Abner, it's me, Sam! Don't you remember me?"

Then I focused on his face. The way I had when he'd peered at me from the back seat of cab number 432 a couple of weeks earlier. And I said, my voice low and tight, "Good Lord, Abner, have you been doing drugs or what?"

He smiled crookedly, as if it hurt. "Sure, Sam," he said, "something like that."

As I said, Abner's kind of odd-looking. He's not a Quasimodo clone, people don't run screaming from him, but he's no threat to Tom Selleck or Robert Redford, either. It's mostly his eyes. They're too deeply set, and his brow shades them well so he looks like he's been brooding in a cellar for a long time. And his head is large and angular, a little too large and angular, in fact, to look comfortably balanced on top of his long, lean frame. In high school he was into long-distance running for a while and it toned him up, made him look healthy. But he fell, broke his ankle, decided that running wasn't very interesting anyway, and soon got back that sick and brooding look. Some women find it attractive. Stacy did. And Phyllis did, of course. But I always thought he looked like he needed sunlight, and air.

And that third time I saw him in New York, when I caught him, he looked like he'd been on speed for a year or two. His skin was a light gray-pink, his eyes were nearly puffed shut, and he looked like he could have used another fifty pounds spread out evenly on his body. Which is why I asked him if he'd been doing drugs.

"Sure, Sam," he said. "Something like that."

Then I did something impulsive; I tried to hug him—*My nerdish little brother, Gee I haven't seen you in a long time,* and all that. And in return I got an "Uhn" of surprise and a quizzical, put-upon look when I let him go. I shrugged. "Sorry," I said.

"Sure," he said.

He had been coming out of the same Greek restaurant I'd seen him come out of twice before, and I noticed the vague smell of clam sauce lingering around him. I nodded to indicate the restaurant, a half a block behind us. "You've already had lunch, Abner?"

He nodded. "Yeah, lunch," he said just above a whisper, as if his throat were sore. We were standing in front of one of those tiny newsstands that are maybe twice the size of an outhouse and have various men's magazines clipped up under the roof edge. The man behind the counter—short, chubby, and balding—waved us away: "Hey, don't stand right there, yer blockin' my customers, go talk somewhere else."

"Okay," I said, and because I was still holding Abner's arm, I led him to the edge of the curb. "Are you living here, in New York, Abner?"

He shook his head. "No. Long Island."

"Long Island," I said. "You know you look like hell?"

He nodded. "Yes, I know."

I was getting embarrassed. It was clear that he didn't want to talk to me. But I wasn't about to be put off again. "Are you in some kind of trouble, Abner?"

He ignored that. He said, "I thought you died. In Viet Nam."

I put on a big false smile. "Do I look like I died in Viet Nam, Abner?"

He shook his head. "No." He gave me a long once-over. "No, you don't."

"Besides, I wrote you when I got back."

He thought a moment, then nodded vaguely. "Oh, yes. I remember."

"Why'd you drop out of sight, Abner?"

He grinned, again as if embarrassed. "I don't know. I guess I was trying to find myself. Wasn't everyone trying to find themselves back then?"

"Sure. But hell, Abner, I thought we were friends—"

"We were," he cut in, and looked pleadingly at me. "We still are. It's just that, back then—" Another pause; he looked very much at sea. "It's just that I was trying to break away—"

"From what?"

He shrugged. "I don't know. Attachments, I guess. People. I'm sorry."

I studied him for a few moments. He was clearly in discomfort over seeing me, clearly wanted to be somewhere else. "Hell," I said, "that was twenty years ago, Abner. This is now."

"Sure," he said, trying hard to sound enthusiastic.

He was dressed badly. In Bangor he had never dressed well; he sometimes wore striped pants with checked shirts, or forgot to remove tags from new jeans, or wore colors that clashed, and I realized then that it was because he was usually preoccupied or, at least, that he was trying to convince people that he was preoccupied, so he couldn't care less about style. Now, on the corner of 38th Street and Second Avenue that chilly mid-March afternoon, it wasn't a matter of taste or style. He looked like a bum. His faded, shiny brown pants hung from him like paper bags. He carried a soiled and threadbare green cloth raincoat over his arm, his pink long-sleeved shirt had its two middle buttons missing, and his aged Wallabees were separating at the seams. I nodded to indicate all this: "You know, Abner," I said, "if this were Bangor, they'd send you to the Salvation Army for the night."

He ignored me again. "I'm glad you didn't die in Viet Nam. I'm glad you're alive," he said.

"Thanks. So am I."

Around us knots of people moved quickly and

efficiently about, jaywalked with mechanical precision, stepped hurriedly into cabs. New Yorkers move as if they're in a tunnel whose walls crowd their shoulders and whose ceiling is an inch too low.

Abner said, "I've got to get going. There are people waiting for me."

"Sure," I said, and let go of his arm. "Sorry. Maybe you could tell me where you're living, Abner. I'd like us to get together, if that's possible."

He shook his head. "It isn't possible. I wish it were—God, I wish it were, but it isn't."

I got jostled a bit by a woman who used her umbrella as a kind of prod. "Move, please," she commanded, and I stepped away from her. I nodded at her as she bustled on, across 38th Street, using her umbrella in the gathering crowd every few seconds. "Lively city, isn't it, Abner?"

"Don't follow me, please, Sam," he said.

"Follow you? Why would I follow you?"

He shook his head briskly. "I don't know. Of course you wouldn't," and without another word, he hurried across 38th Street, against the light, so several cars had to screech to a halt.

I kept my eye on him. I saw him turn down 39th Street, toward Third Avenue. I followed him.

FIVE

He never looked back. He moved easily through the crowds, as if he'd been doing it all his life. And although I lost track of him now and then, he was easy to spot again because he's at least a head taller than most New Yorkers.

He walked to Fifth Avenue and 25th Street, where he caught a bus. I was a street block behind him, and when I got to the bus stop I asked a young man giving away twelve-exposure rolls of Kodak film—along with invitations to use it at Nash's Nudes in the West Village—where the bus was going.

"Staten Island ferry," he said, and pushed a roll of film at me.

"Thanks," I said, pocketed the film, and, after ten minutes' worth of trying, hailed a cab that would take me to the Staten Island ferry. I'd give the film to Abner as a gesture of apology for following him.

* * *

It was the first time I'd ridden the ferry and I was amazed how crowded it was. I even speculated aloud, to a red-haired woman in her early twenties who was, out of necessity, standing shoulder to shoulder with me at the railing, that maybe it would sink with so many people and cars on it. She smiled thinly, said, "No, I don't think so," and looked away.

I'd been able to spot Abner a couple of minutes before. He was on a lower deck, with his elbows on the rail, his hands folded, and his head down slightly, as if he were in thought. From above he looked less like a bum and more like someone who was just mildly eccentric, as, I think, half the people in New York are. He was standing very still, although every once in a while he unfolded his hands, interlocked his fingers, and brought his hands up, so his forefingers were at his lips. It seemed, at these times, that he didn't look so much in thought as *lost*, somehow.

"I thought it would sink, too," said the woman standing next to me.

I looked at her, surprised. "Sorry?" I said.

"I said I thought it would sink once, too. When I first started riding it. It sits so low in the water, you know." She nodded toward the water. Her long red hair fell forward over her shoulders.

"Yes," I said, "it does sit kind of low in the water, doesn't it?"

She nodded, so more of her hair fell forward. "But it hasn't sunk yet, so I doubt that it ever will," she said.

Her eyes were a light green, like the underside of a

leaf, and they didn't linger long on me. She looked back, at the water. "My name's Serena," she said, and looked at me again.

"Serena," I said noncommittally. "That's a nice name."

"And yours?" she asked.

"Sam Feary," I answered.

She looked away, nodded once, slowly, as if in thought, then looked back at me and said, "Hello, Sam." She looked away again.

I focused on Abner. He was in the same spot, and in the same position, but after a couple of seconds he turned his head, looked directly at me, and appeared suddenly crestfallen, as if he had just gotten bad news. Reading his lips, I saw him mutter, "Dammit all to hell!" then he shook his head and mouthed the word "No!" emphatically at me.

I whispered to myself, "My God, what's wrong with you, my friend?! What kind of trouble have you gotten yourself into?"

"I beg your pardon?" said the red-haired woman with me at the railing.

I looked quickly at her, embarrassed. "No, I'm sorry," I said. "I was talking about someone else, I was talking about him, down there," and I inclined my head to the right to indicate Abner on the deck below.

A small grin appeared on her mouth, then vanished. "Oh," she said. "I understand."

"You really don't," I said. "He's an old friend, he's someone I knew in high school—"

She looked quizzically at me. "I don't know you,

Sam. You don't know me. So there's nothing at all you have to explain.'' She was saying, *Please, leave me alone*. So I did.

And when I looked back at Abner, he was looking up at me, grinning in a flat, sad way, a kind of "I told you so!" grin.

I mouthed at him, "I'm coming with you."

He mouthed back, "Of course you are," pointing stiffly back the way the ferry had come. "That way!"

Twenty minutes later, when the ferry unloaded, I went to where he was still standing, on the lower deck. "I thought you lived on Long Island, Abner," I said.

He nodded glumly. "I do."

"Then why are you on the Staten Island ferry?"

He shrugged. "I was trying to throw you off." He grinned weakly at me. "Stupid, huh?"

I thought a moment. "Yes," I said. "Pretty stupid." I paused. "So what do we do now?"

He shrugged again. "We go back, I guess. And we take the subway to Queens."

"Oh," I said.

And that's what we did.

He had a car parked in Queens. It was a decade-old red Chevy Malibu two-door, with a bumper sticker on the back that read, "This Car Climbed Pike's Peak," and another beside it that read, next to the stylized drawing of a panda bear, "Animals Love You, Too."

Abner nodded at the passenger door. "Get in, Sam."

"Does this thing actually run?" I asked. He ignored me. I got in, watched him slide into the driver's seat, toss his raincoat into the back seat, fish in his pants pockets for his keys, which was difficult because he was sitting down, and start the car, after several tries.

We rode silently for a while through Queens. At last, he said, "One day, Sam, you're going to look back on this day and you're going to say to yourself, 'Why the hell didn't I just let him be?' "

"That sounds pretty melodramatic, Abner."

"Don't interrupt. I'm telling you the truth here. It will probably be something like the way you felt when you came home from Viet Nam. You probably said to yourself, 'God, why didn't I just go to Canada?' or, 'Why didn't I fake some kind of disease at the physical?' It'll probably be the same kind of thing, Sam."

"I try not to look backward, Abner."

"We all look backward." He took a right at Queens Boulevard and Cosco Street, pulled over to the curb, looked earnestly at me. "I'm going to give you the chance to get out now, Sam. I'd advise you to take it."

"No way, José," I said. "If you're in some kind of trouble—"

He cut in, "Let me put it to you this way, Sam. What if you came across a box, some kind of box on the street—no, I'll amend that. Let's say someone mailed you a box with a note that said there was one of two things inside the box, that there was either a spider—" He stopped, apparently to search for the right words, went on, "A poisonous spider, a black widow spider, a brown recluse. Or, maybe, that there was a stack of thousand-dollar bills in the box. But the only way you could find out which one it was was to stick your hand inside. You couldn't just peek in with a flashlight; you couldn't prop the lid open and peek in with a flashlight, you actually had to stick your hand in and *feel*. Tell me, Sam, what do you think you'd do?"

"I'd probably throw the box in the trash, Abner, because I don't know *anyone* who'd send me a box with a stack of thousand-dollar bills in it."

He nodded. "That's good, Sam," he said, "because no one would." His earnest look changed dramatically to one of pleading and concern. "Please, Sam, get out of the car. For your own sake, for my sake, I'm begging you to get out of the car."

I said again, "But, Abner, if you're in some kind of trouble, I want to help you. Just please, tell me, what the hell is going on."

"Hell is a good word for it, Sam." He paused. "So you're not going to get out?"

"No," I said.

SIX

We were on Highway 12 going east out of Queens when a motorcycle cop drew up alongside us and motioned to Abner to stop. Abner nodded, and pulled off the road into a little parking area that overlooked a housing complex under construction. The cop stopped behind the car, swaggered up to the driver's door, and leaned over. Abner rolled the window down. "Something wrong?" Abner asked.

"I dunno," said the cop. "Mebbe, mebbe not." He was a typical New York cop. He had short black hair, a face that was flat, expressionless, and astoundingly average—except for a bright red J-shaped birthmark on the right side of his jaw—and his tone was clearly designed to announce that the only friend he had in this world was the .38 police special strapped on his hip. He nodded at me and said to Abner, "Who's that?"

I began, "It's none—"

Abner put his hand on my arm, glanced at me, and whispered, "Let me handle this, Sam. Please." Then he looked at the cop. "He's just a friend, Officer. Could I ask why you stopped me?"

"Sure," said the cop. "You can ask. Go ahead and ask."

I couldn't believe what I was hearing. I leaned forward, so the cop had to look at me. "Hey, buddy, if you stopped my friend for a *reason*, then tell him the reason, but if you stopped him just for the hell of it—"

Again Abner put his hand on my arm. "Sam, please—I know how to handle these people—"

"What do you mean—'these people'? This guy just wants to hassle us, Abner—"

"Please, Sam, I'll handle it—"

"You wanta get outa da car," said the cop. I looked at him. I saw that he'd straightened, unbuckled his holster, had his hand on his .38. I could see only his midsection, from his waist to the bottom of his neck. I looked at Abner. "What the hell's going on, Abner? What'd you do, murder someone?"

"No," he said. "But I think we'd better get out of the car."

"Abner," I said, "he's got no *right*—"

"*I* know that, Sam. *You* know it. But *he* doesn't know it—"

"Oh, Good Lord!"

The cop bellowed, "Get *out* of the car. Now!"

"Why?" I bellowed back.

Abner shook his head as if in disbelief. "Sam, don't get him upset."

The cop leaned over again. He patted his .38 slowly, menacingly. I saw that his face was very pale, as pale as snow, and that the J-shaped birthmark was bright red, as if it were actually a slit in the skin. "You bad-mouthin' me, boy?"

I shook my head. "No, I'm just asking why we've got to get out of the car. You have to give us a *reason* for stopping us, don't you know that?"

"Sam," Abner said urgently, "he *doesn't* know that. He doesn't know much at all. Now, if he wants us to get out of the car, I think we should get out of the car—"

"Just him," the cop said, and nodded sharply to indicate me.

I said again, "Oh, Good Lord."

"Now!" the cop bellowed, and straightened once more, his grip hard on the .38.

I got out of the car, slammed the door, peered over the roof at the cop. "Now what?" I said, and heard a tremor of fear in my voice.

"I don't know," the cop said. "I don't know," he repeated, clearly confused now.

"Huh?" I said, also confused.

"I don't know," he repeated, appeared to be lost in thought for several moments, then swaggered back to his motorcycle, right hand slapping the holstered pistol again, head moving from side to side in time with his swagger. He got on the motorcycle and roared off west, toward Queens.

* * *

"Next time," Abner began, and I interrupted, "Next time I'm going to get that asshole's badge number and I'm going to sue the goddamn city for goddamn harassment, *that's* what's going to happen next time!"

"He could have killed you," Abner said.

I stared disbelievingly at him. "What in the hell for?" I asked.

"Because it's part of his job."

We were well out on Long Island now on a narrow, all-but-deserted dirt road that paralleled the ocean. Although I couldn't see the water, I could smell salt air. Abner was driving very slowly. I said, "It's part of his job to *kill* me, Abner? What kind of crap is that? Cops don't just kill people without reason."

"Yes, I know that, Sam. But sometimes they do kill people. Sometimes they have to."

"In self-defense, sure, or to stop someone from killing someone else, sure—but it's always a judgment call, Abner—"

"Precisely." He gave me another *I told you so* kind of grin. "You've got your hand in the box, Sam," he said. "You've got it in up to the elbow. But it's not too late to pull it out. I'll stop the car and we can say 'Good-bye, it's been nice seeing you again,' and that'll be it. You can go back to your apartment. You can go back to worrying about money, women, whatever it is you worry about, Sam, and you'll be okay. But you've got to get out of the car, and you've got to get out now."

I shook my head.

"Think about it first, Sam."

I shook my head more briskly.

"You're making a mistake," he said, and turned down a rutted lane then up a little rise. The ocean was in front of us. He brought the car to a halt and nodded to indicate a rambling, tumbledown beach house about a hundred feet in front of us. "We're here," he said.

"Good," I said. "Now maybe I'll find out what kind of crap it is you've gotten yourself into."

"Sam?" he said, and I noticed that his tone had changed, had become conciliatory.

"Yes?"

"I'm glad you're here, Sam. I need a friend. I really do desperately need a friend."

The first kiss that Leslie and I shared was in the parking garage behind the Imperial Palace. I had tried for a first kiss in the restaurant. I had put my hands on the sides of her head and had drawn her closer to me over the table. But she'd turned gently away. I thought a couple of things then. One was that she didn't want to kiss me because I'd been eating Chicken Garlic. But so had she, so I discounted that possibility. Then I thought that she was simply being cautious, that the sort of kiss I wanted from her was the sort of kiss that she had reason to withhold unless and until the moment was right.

The moment was right thirty minutes later, in the parking garage, as we walked hand in hand to my car. I stopped, turned to her, and we had a long, passionate, and hungry kiss. We *were* hungry for each other. That was clear then, as we kissed. It had been clear over the Chicken Garlic. It had been clear three days earlier in the taxi. But nothing, of course, happens instantaneously.

She said, when we stopped kissing, "Our first kiss."

She's not always beautiful. There are moods and personalities within her that transform her. But she is beautiful most of the time, and sometimes, for a minute or more, I find myself looking into her face and I hear myself saying at last, as if in awe, "You're so beautiful!" I think she doesn't know how to react when I say that. She likes it when I say it, and she has said of herself that she's "pretty nice to look at," but I think it's possible that I embarrass her with my spontaneous declarations of her beauty. So, occasionally, I want to snatch the words back.

Once, when we were in the car and she was driving, I studied her profile. It was not the profile I expected after looking into her face. It was strong, and forward, and resolute, and if someone, I thought, were to make a caricature of it, that caricature would probably look much like the profile of an Easter Island stone. It was a contrast I hadn't expected.

I don't think I *grew* to love Leslie. I think it happened all at once, and over time I grew to understand exactly *why* I loved her. The times we had together confirmed the good sense I had to love her in the first place. Which leaves the question of whether my love for her has grown deeper. I don't know if that's a legitimate question. I think love latches on and grows more tenacious, but I think that right from the beginning it is what it is, deep or not, and the deeper it is from the beginning, the more tenaciously it sticks.

SEVEN

When Abner and I were growing up, he never gave me good advice. It's true that I rarely asked for his advice; why ask for advice from a nerdish-but-lovable-little-brother type? That's the type I gave advice *to*. But there were a few times when, out of adolescent desperation, I did go to him for advice. Once I asked him which girl to ask to the freshman hop.

"Belinda Becker," he said. "She likes you."

That was what I wanted to hear, because I liked her and had all kinds of fantasies about her; but when I called her she said, "Drop dead, weasel!"

Another time he advised me to see a movie called *The Blob*, which he swore was just about the greatest thing since ice cream. I paid good money to see it, and I thought it was the worst thing since visible nose hairs. So I didn't grow too fond of Abner's advice. That's one reason I stayed put when he advised me to get out of the Malibu—his advice had always been so lousy.

He was also intriguing the hell out of me.

He drove the last hundred feet to the house.

"Yours?" I asked. We got out of the car and walked toward the beach house. It sat virtually alone on the beach, and though it did indeed look "tumble-down" it didn't look abandoned. It looked very comfortable, at least from the outside. The wide, wraparound porch had something to do with that look. I've always liked porches; they're great places to sit and listen to crickets and peel apples.

"No," Abner answered, "it's not mine, it's a friend's—it's Art DeGraff's. Do you remember him?"

I nodded. "I remember he was an asshole. What's he doing these days?"

Abner had his hands in the pockets of his shiny brown pants, and his head down. I saw him smile slightly, as if at some secret. "Looking backward," he said, and didn't elaborate.

We were within fifty feet of the house then. My eyes were on Abner. I heard, "Hello, Abner." I looked toward the house. A tall woman in her early twenties was standing in the doorway. She was wearing very tight jeans, a loose-fitting long-sleeved white blouse which she filled wonderfully, and I said to Abner, my eyes glued to her, "Who's *that*?"

"That's Al," he answered.

" 'Al'?"

He nodded. "Her real name's Allison, but she likes to be called Al—I call her Al."

She stepped back from the doorway and closed the door. I glanced at Abner. His head was still lowered. He stopped walking and looked sadly at me. "She's not what she appears to be, Sam."

"Who is?" I asked.

He continued looking at me for a few seconds, then he said, "No one. Not me, not her. No one."

I smiled broadly, as if I knew he was trying to be coy and cryptic. "It sounds like you're lost in a world of confusion."

"No," he said, "not quite yet. Soon, though. The signs are there, I'm making plans—I'll tell you about them sometime."

"You worry me, Abner." I added, "Of course, you always did."

He stared at me; his sad, pleading look changed to a look of resignation, as if he'd been expecting steak and potatoes all day but was getting carrot salad instead. Then he started walking again, his head down, hands in his pockets, and I said, as we stepped onto the porch, "We've got quite a bit to talk about, Abner. We've got a lot of years to catch up with." I spoke casually, cheerfully, the way I would have if we'd just that moment happened upon each other and were going to have dinner to hash over old times. "I mean, we haven't seen each other in twenty years—"

"Twenty years," he said. "So what?!"

"Sorry?"

"Two hundred years, a thousand years—"

"I don't understand, Abner."

"It *is* a world of confusion, Sam. You're right. I can see that."

"Good for you," I said, and added, "Abner, I think you've gone over into Munchkin Land. Why don't you let your big brother Sam help you back?"

"No," he said, his tone suddenly clipped, and deadly serious. He looked questioningly at me: "Munchkin Land—that's from *The Wizard of Oz*, isn't it?"

"I think so," I said.

He shook his head, frowning a little. "No," he repeated, "it's not Munchkin Land." He opened the front door of the beach house. "And you're not my big brother."

It was a very large room I entered; "the great room," Abner called it. There were at least a hundred photographs on the walls, some in black and white, some in color, most of them five by seven or eight by ten, some larger. Abner told me he'd taken them for the photographic book he'd once planned to do—"About Manhattan," he said. Indeed, most of the pictures had a nice Manhattan flavor to them. "They remind me of who I am," he said.

"Sure," I said, "I guess we all need that." I was still feeling the sting from his "And you're not my big brother" remark.

There were at least a dozen plants in the room, although there was very little direct sunlight because the two windows faced north. Several of the plants were of the large, floor-standing variety that would have dominated a smaller room. Abner said they were "a kind of fern" and went on to give me their scientific name, which I can't remember and couldn't spell if I did. Some of the others were in small clay pots that had been hung from the ceiling on lengths of decorative reddish-brown twine. I recognized some of these; one was a nerve plant—so named because its leaves curl up when touched—and another was clover, which I like because it's so simple. The plants gave the room a slight tangy smell, "the smell of the earth," Abner said, "a good smell, a *real* smell."

A huge gray stone fireplace took up half the north wall. Several large, brightly colored throw pillows lay in various places around it.

"The plants don't live long," Abner said. "About a week, most of them, then I've got to throw them out and buy new ones."

"Don't they need more light?" I asked.

He nodded. "Yes. That's one of the reasons they don't live long."

"Then why have them at all?"

He answered simply, in the same vaguely pleading tone he'd used earlier, "Because I need them, Sam. Because they're alive."

When I was growing up, there were a few words that I regularly used to describe Abner W. Cray. "Nerd," of course, fit him well. But he was also a pretender, and an actor, like Art DeGraff, though, unlike Art DeGraff, Abner is just about the gentlest person I've known.

He was an actor when he was holding one of his séances, for instance, and wanted to impress one of the women there with how sensitive he was. He'd sit down with someone he hardly knew, get this earnest and *interested* look on his face, and let the other person talk, and talk, and talk. I supposed it was either because he had precious little to say or because he thought that if he kept quiet, and didn't offer anything of himself, he'd be less vulnerable. But most of the people he *listened* to thought it was because he was especially interested in them, and especially sensitive, and especially caring.

So there in his tumbledown beach house, surrounded by his photographs, his plants, and his brightly colored throw pillows, I suspected that *Because I need them, Sam. Because they're alive!* was only an example of what I'd first seen twenty years earlier—an Abner W. Cray pose, a way of demonstrating his incredible sensitivity. But I was wrong.

"Why do you live here, Abner?" I asked. He'd led me through the great room, down a narrow hallway—also festooned with his photographs of Manhattan—and into the kitchen, which was, oddly, at the beach side of the house. I thought, following him, that the inside of the house, in stark contrast to the way it looked outside, had the same dead-end *feel* to it as that mausoleum we'd broken into twenty years earlier, like a still life of stale beer. I couldn't imagine anyone, even Abner, actually wanting to live in it.

"It's safe," he answered. "For now, it's safe, and I can live here. Alone, if I want."

The kitchen was tidy, which surprised me—I'd always thought of Abner as a slob. One wall, opposite four large windows and a door that faced the beach, had an upper row of freshly polished knotty-pine cupboards on it, a stainless-steel double sink below, more knotty-pine cupboards to the left of it. At the center of the room there was a small table with a white enamel top and wooden base, painted white, and three old ladder-back chairs with cane seats. A rounded-top General Electric refrigerator, circa 1960, stood next to the sink, and a huge, battered gas stove was kitty-corner to it. The side of the stove next to the outside door—the door that led to the beach—was badly chipped, and I guessed that the door hit it every time it was opened. There was a cream-colored cereal bowl in the sink that had a spoon in it, a little milk, and some remnants of what looked like Rice Krispies.

I sat in one of the ladder-back chairs. It wobbled. I hoped it would hold me. Abner stood in front of me, at the sink, with his arms folded in front of him. I asked him, "What do you mean, 'alone'? What about that woman I saw—what was her name? Al? What about her?"

"She doesn't live here. She's a guest."

"Oh," I said. "It must be nice to have guests like that."

"I've got lots of guests here. I've got at least a dozen guests. Maybe you'll meet some of them." This seemed to amuse him.

I stared at him for a few moments, then I said, "Where, Abner?"

"Where what?"

"For God's sake, where are your guests?" I held my hand up, palm out, as if stopping traffic. "Sorry,

Abner. It's just that I hate to see a friend . . . teetering on the edge—"

"The edge of what, Sam?" He was clearly confused.

I sighed. "Abner, I'm sorry, but maybe I'd better go."

"Go?" He shook his head. "You can't go, Sam. They won't let you."

Another sigh. " 'They' won't *let* me? Who's 'they,' Abner?"

"My guests, the people in the house."

"Abner, Christ!" I pushed my chair back noisily. The racket seemed to jar Abner because he stiffened up. I stood, glanced first at the door to the beach, then toward the hallway that led back to the great room. "There are no 'other people' in this house!"

"Yes, Sam, there are. They live in the walls. Most of them. Except Madeline, of course. She lives upstairs." He grinned flatly.

Again I stared at him, and for a moment I felt an incredible urge to slap him around, as if that might shake the rocks out of his head. Instead I said, "Abner, you need help, probably a lot more than I can give you." Then I turned, went quickly down the hallway, to the great room, and out the door.

I had to walk at least three or four miles until I found a bus stop, but I was back in my apartment early that evening.

EIGHT

He called soon after I got back.

"Sam? I'm sorry, I guess I was spooking you a little, wasn't I? It's just that . . . how do I explain this? It's just that when you get used to a thing, when a situation, no matter how bizarre it is, becomes a real part of your life, you take it for granted, and you talk about it as if *everyone's* life has the same sort of situation in it. Am I making any sense? Tell me if I'm making any sense, Sam?"

"You're not making any sense, Abner."

"Okay." He paused. "Okay. Tell me what you don't understand."

I sighed. "Listen, Abner, we share some . . . interesting memories. We went to the same high school, we did some stupid things together. We were friends—"

"I thought we still were friends, Sam."

"Sure. Sure we are." I didn't know how to continue. It was clear that Abner was in some kind of trouble. Whether it came from outside him, from something in that house, or from within, didn't matter much to me then. I'd assumed that I was going to renew acquaintance with a close friend from high school, that we'd have some good times together, and that that would be that. I didn't expect him to be carrying the kind of emotional baggage he seemed to be carrying. I had my own emotional baggage, and it was damned heavy—hell, I thought I was losing the woman I hoped to marry. In retrospect, I think all that goes a long way toward explaining why I ran from his house. But there was this, too: He was right—he'd spooked the hell out of me. "Sure we're friends," I went on, "but Abner—"

"Abner Doubleday," he cut in.

"Abner Doubleday? What are you talking about?"

"Abner Doubleday, remember?—Abner W. Cray, Abner Doubleday—the two sound pretty much alike, don't they?"

"For God's sake, Abner—"

"Sam, I just wanted to warn you."

"Abner, I know where you're staying. Just give me some time to get my own life squared away, then—"

"Sam," he broke in, "listen to me. They don't like people . . . knowing—"

That was it. "The only thing *I* know, Abner, is that I want to sit back, watch some football, slug down a few beers, maybe send out for a pizza—"

"They won't let go of you, Sam."

"Maybe *they* won't," I cut in, "but you sure as hell better, pal," and I hung up. Half a minute later, I called him back to apologize, to give him a good long chance to talk—maybe that was all he needed, someone to talk to—but after his phone rang a good two dozen times, I gave up. "Damn!" I breathed, and decided I'd try to find my way back to the beach house in the morning.

The L.A. Rams were playing the Dallas Cowboys that evening, but the cable system was on the fritz, so all I got was colored snow and a play-by-play that sounded like it was being broadcast from a fishbowl. I listened anyway, and in the middle of the game I heard a knock at my door. I thought it was the super or one of the other tenants, because no one gets in my building without being buzzed in.

"Who is it?" I hollered.

"Sorry?" I heard. It was a woman's voice.

"I said, 'Who is it?' "

"Oh," the woman called back, "no one. I need to come in to your apartment."

"Why?"

"To use the phone?"

"Is that a question?"

"Sorry?" she called.

I sighed, got out of my chair, went to the door, put my hand on the knob, and hesitated. "Do you need to use the phone?"

"Yes," she answered quickly, and crisply, as if she had just then decided that that was what she needed to do. "Yes, I need to use the phone."

I looked through the security peephole in the center of the door. I saw only the left side of her face, a swatch of red hair. "Are you one of the other tenants?" I called.

"Sorry?" she called back.

"I said are you one of the other tenants?"

"Oh. Yes. I am. I'm one of the other tenants."

"I don't believe you."

Silence.

"I said I don't believe that you're one of the other tenants."

"I'm not."

"You just said you were."

"I'd like to come in and talk with you, if that's okay."

I hesitated, looked through the peephole again, saw the same thing—the right side of her face, a swatch of red hair, a bit of her eye—green, I guessed. "No. I'm sorry," I called. "Maybe you could ask the super, down on one—how'd you get in, anyway?"

"Through the door," she answered. "Don't you remember me?"

I looked again through the peephole. She'd stepped further to her right and back a bit, so I could get a good look at her. "We were on the ferry together, do you remember?"

Again I hesitated, then I said, "Yes, I remember. What do you want?"

"Only to talk."

I turned the knob and opened the door until one of the chain locks stopped it. "Okay—talk."

"I'd like to come inside." She nodded to indicate my apartment. "Could I come inside?"

"How'd you find me?" I asked.

She answered simply, "I looked. I found you." She nodded again to indicate my apartment. "Could I come inside? I can't talk to you out here. I need to come into your house. Please, tell me I can come into your house."

I didn't like the sound of that. It sounded half like a plea, half like a threat, and I told her, "Find the super, he's on one, you can use his phone."

"I don't know the super. I know you."

I shook my head. "No, you don't."

"I do," she said. "Your name's Sam." She stepped closer to the door, put one hand on it and one on the frame, and stuck her face into the opening so only her left eye, part of her nose, and the left side of her lips were visible. She whispered, her voice suddenly very low and coarse, "Let me into your house, Sam—tell me I can come into your house."

The phone rang.

She glanced quickly toward the noise, as if she'd been startled.

I backed away from the door, toward the phone. I called again, "Find the super, he's on one, he'll help you."

She was gone.

I hesitated, took a couple of steps toward the door, and called, "Hello, miss, are you there?"

The phone continued ringing. I looked at it and snapped, "Hold on, for Christ's sake!" It rang again. "Goddammit!" I went to the door, looked through the opening, saw nothing. "Miss?" I called. Still nothing. The phone rang again. "Blow it out your ass!" I yelled, then went and answered it.

It was Abner.

"Listen to me, Sam, please listen to me."

"No more bullshit, Abner. Let's just let the whole thing rest overnight, okay, then tomorrow I'll—"

"It won't rest, Sam. *They* won't rest, no one rests!"

"Abner, did you send her here? Was it some kind of dumb joke?"

"Send who? I didn't send anyone there. Who was there?"

"That woman from the ferry. Is she part of your scheme, Abner, like the cop, and the woman at the house—"

"You mean Al? What about her? Was *she* there?"

"No, she wasn't here. The woman from the ferry was here—"

"That redhead, you mean? She was there, at your apartment, Sam?"

I shook my head in disbelief. "Good Lord," I whispered.

"Sorry, I didn't hear you, Sam—what'd you say?"

"I said *bull*shit, Abner. I said you're full of *bull*-shit! And when you've unloaded it, *then* we'll talk—"

"No, Sam, please, trust me—"

I hung up and took the receiver off the hook.

The cable reception got back to normal a half hour later, and I settled grumblingly down to watch the end of the football game—guilt and bad feelings pushing through me like a fever. The Cowboys won, but that didn't cheer me up at all, because I kept telling myself things like, "Some friend you are, some big brother you are,'' and, ''The guy needs your help, for God's sake,'' and, ''What if he ends up *doing* something to himself?'' and, ''You're just afraid of getting involved, admit it.''

I admitted it. In Nam I'd gotten involved a lot more, it turned out, than I should have. For one reason or another, I was one of the lucky ones who didn't spend half their time being homesick, or depressed, or strung out. I'd told myself that if I was fortunate, I'd make it through to the end of my tour of duty, but that along the way I'd have to bide my time, count the days, do what I was told, within reason, and eventually that miserable war would be behind me. But there were plenty of guys who didn't do that, and I was the one they chose to talk to. I was a big-brother figure, I suppose—not only am I big physically, I also look a good ten years older than I really am. They told me what they thought of the war and what they thought of themselves for getting involved in it—and opinions on that score varied widely. They told me about their lives back home, about their girlfriends (and some of them about their boyfriends), about Mom and Dad and little sister. After a while, I got awfully depressed just from the sheer weight of their agony. At last I said *No more*, and forced myself to climb up out of the pit they'd dragged me into.

That's the way it seemed with Abner, too, there in his dismal Long Island beach house. He was someone drenched in his own pain, someone who was reaching out to me—big brother Sam—telling me to listen, to lift him up, out of the world of confusion he'd gotten himself into.

I went to bed feeling like I was being slowly pinned to a wall by a semi.

I woke at just past three-thirty that morning, feeling ravenous. It came to me that although I'd planned on sending out for a pizza during the game, I never had, so my poor stomach had staged a minor revolution.

I threw back the blanket, swung my feet to the floor, and sat up.

I sleep naked, and this late March night was damned chilly, so I reached for my pants, which were on the back of a chair near the bed. I heard low, suppressed giggling from the far corner of the room.

It was very dark in the room—the only light was the diffused yellow glow of a streetlamp four stories below—but I hurried into my pants, muttered, "Christ's sake, Abner, this is going too far," switched on a reading lamp over the bed, and looked at the corner where the giggling had come from.

There were two young girls, fourteen or fifteen, both in knee-length pink taffeta gowns, each with a blue corsage in hand, standing very stiffly and solemnly between the bookcase on one wall and the radiator on the other, and I said to them, my voice rising in pitch because they'd surprised me, "Who the hell are *you?*"

Their mouths opened in unison. Two soft, suppressed giggles came out, but their bodies remained stiff, as if everything but their lips had been painted there, on the beige wall. And again their mouths opened, again two soft, suppressed giggles danced about in the room.

Below, on the street, a car horn blared.

Above me, in an apartment rented by a guy I knew worked the 8:00 P.M. to 2:00 A.M. shift, a radio was switched on, and a late-sixties protest song filtered down through the ceiling.

And from the corner, where the two young girls in pink taffeta stood so very, very stiffly, I caught the odor of waterlogged, decaying wood. I whispered at them, "Who in the hell *are* you?"

From above, the sixties protest song grew a little louder.

And the two girls in pink taffeta melted into the wall like ice.

NINE

I called Abner's number again from the kitchen phone; he answered on the first ring. I heard him say sleepily, "Yes? Hello," and I screamed at him, "Goddammit, Abner, who *are* these people?"

"Sam? Is that you?"

"Damn it, Abner—I wake up . . . I wake up, and I turn the light on, and there are these two *girls* in my room, and they're *giggling* at me—"

"Sam, I'm sorry; I warned you—"

"I'm coming over there, Abner, right now, and we're going to hash this out."

"You're coming here, to the house?" He sounded incredulous, happy. "That's great, Sam. Really. I'll make some coffee for you, we'll talk, we'll talk . . . Sam, this is very good news, I need a friend here—"

My anger began to fade under the influence of his

sudden good feeling. "Sure, Abner," I sighed. "I'll be there as soon as I can."

"Great." A pause, then, "Sam?"

"Yes?"

"Do you remember the way here, Sam? To the house."

"Good Lord, Abner, of course I do." It was my pride speaking, and it spoke far too soon.

"Then I'll be waiting for you," Abner said.

I was on the subway an hour later. It was not quite five in the morning, and the train was all but empty, except for a young Puerto Rican couple necking in front of me, an older man in a stiff gray pinstripe suit in the seat to my right, and a red-haired woman at the rear of the car, seated facing away from me.

I was tired, I was hungry, and my head had started to ache shortly after I'd left the apartment. (I'd dressed like a madman, and didn't realize until I was on the street that my jacket was buttoned crookedly, that my shoes were untied, and that I'd forgotten to put underwear on.) I busied myself with reading some of the transit advertising—"Join the Coffee Generation," "Join the Pepsi Generation," "Read *The Me Generation*." I whispered that "generation" seemed to be the word of the hour.

"Sorry?" said the man in the stiff gray pinstripe suit.

I shook my head and explained that I'd been talking to myself, that I hadn't meant to disturb him.

He smiled. He had a round, smooth pink face, high cheekbones, and big, watery hazel eyes. He was thin, and his Adam's apple bobbed as he talked. "Oh," he said in a creaking, high-pitched voice, "what was it that you were saying?"

I thought of telling him it was none of his business, but he seemed harmless enough. I raised my chin to indicate the transit signs above him. " 'Generation,' " I said, "seems to be the word of the hour."

"Does it? Why's that?" His congenial smile became quizzical.

Again I indicated the transit signs over his head. "I was talking about the advertising up there, above you."

He leaned my way in his seat and craned his head around to look at the advertising. "Hiram Walker?" he said. "I don't understand." He straightened, looked at me.

I forced myself to smile. My headache was gathering strength. "No, no, I mean . . . if you look again, you'll see that some of the advertising has the word 'generation' in it—"

"It's thirty-eight years, you know," he cut in happily. "A generation is thirty-eight years. Most people don't know that. I know it. I'd guess that we're"—he pointed quickly at his chest, then quickly at me—"a good generation apart—"

"Yes, sir," I said; I was growing annoyed with him. "I suppose we are."

"But I don't see what it's got to do with the advertising." He looked again. " 'Be a Pepper'? What's a Pepper?" He looked back at me. "What's a Pepper?—I know what salt is." He chuckled to himself.

I nodded. The headache was very bad now; I put my hand to my temple.

The man said, "You talk to yourself quite a bit, do ya? I had an aunt once who talked to herself from morning till night, nonstop—she talked about her *life*, she talked about her children, she talked about her lovers—I guess she probably had as many lovers as a dog has fleas—and she talked about all the Presidents she'd seen come and go, 'specially Hoover, 'specially Roosevelt—Teddy, not Franklin Delano—"

"Please," I cut in sharply, "I'd rather just sit quietly."

"And she talked about her houses, and she talked about her"—I closed my eyes; I realized he was going to rattle on for quite some time—"and she talked about her cats, she had plenty of cats, and she talked about everything under the sun from morning till night—"

"If you don't mind . . ." I stopped; I was on the verge of shouting.

"And she talked about sin, and she talked about God, and she talked about—" He stopped suddenly. I heard a harsh, gurgling noise. I opened my eyes, looked.

The red-haired woman looked back; she was standing behind him, her eyes wide, hands hard on his throat, and he was groping crazily in the seat, eyes as wide as hers.

"Love," she shrieked, "is sacrifice. Love is giving, and taking. *Now* do you love me, *now* do you love me?"

The Puerto Rican couple vaulted from their seats, ran to the car ahead.

The man in the gray pinstripe suit went limp under her hands.

It was only then that I realized that the woman was the same woman I'd met on the ferry, the same woman who'd knocked at my door.

I threw myself across the aisle at her, caught my groin on the seat edge, tumbled over so her heels were near my mouth, grabbed her by the ankle, yanked hard. She fell toward the window, hit it with the side of her head, and crumpled so her thighs fell across my arm, so her stomach went into my shoulder and a gust of foul air escaped her.

I grabbed my groin and launched into a fit of panic-ridden cursing that continued a good minute or two, until, at last, I pushed myself to my feet and saw that except for the body of the man in the pinstripe suit—who had fallen over the seat, mouth open wide, feet on the floor—the car was empty.

The train stopped moments later.

TEN

It was clear that the man in the pinstripe suit was dead.

A well-dressed black man in his early thirties got on. He saw the man in the suit, gave him a quick once-over, and glanced questioningly at me.

"Bum," I managed, "dead drunk," and shrugged. The man shrugged, too, then turned and found a seat at the back of the car.

Minutes later, I was on East 57th Street and looking for another subway entrance so I could get to Queens. The Manhattan sky was a still, dark gray, only a little lighter than the old man's pinstripe suit, and the air had a grisly cold snap to it that smelled vaguely of car exhausts and tar.

I heard, from behind me, across the street, "Hey, up yours!"

And, "Yeah, up yours, too! *You* get the fuckin' heavy one!"

I looked. Two garbage collectors, a beefy white man and a tall, muscular black man, were arguing over who was going to pick up which garbage can. A yellow garbage truck waited several feet away, a plume of gray exhaust billowing around it. I called to them, "Hey, where's there a subway entrance?"

The beefy white guy called back, "You just come outa one!"

"I know. I want to go to Queens; I need a different one." It still hadn't dawned on me that I didn't know precisely how to get to the beach house. I thought a moment, added, "One that doesn't smell so bad."

Both of them laughed shortly. "Shit, my man," called the black guy, "they all of them smell, you know, but you go on down to West 60th Street and you'll find yourself one that maybe smells a little *different*."

"Yeah," I called, "sure, thanks—I hope so." I was beginning to look and sound like a complete ass. "Thanks again," I called. They stared blankly at me a moment, then got back to their argument about who was going to lift which trash can. The truck driver leaned on his horn for a couple of seconds. They continued their argument. The truck driver leaned on his horn again. The argument continued.

I called, from fifty yards down the street, "For God's sake, why don't you both pick it up?!"

In unison, they turned, leveled their gaze on me, and started walking very slowly in my direction. The truck's gears meshed, and it lurched forward several feet, gray exhaust billowing around it like a cloud.

"I was only being helpful," I called. "I was only trying to be helpful."

The white guy, the black guy, and the truck all continued slowly, methodically in my direction.

I turned and ran. When I'd made it to Fifth Avenue, I looked back briefly and saw that they were still coming my way. I looked up Fifth, saw a cab coming, and hailed it. It pulled over. I got in.

"Queens," I told the driver.

He turned, looked at me. "It's a big place, mister."

"So's the moon," I said.

"You're a real card."

"Somewhere near the ocean, then. North of Queens, near the ocean."

"It's your quarter," he said, put the flag down, and closed the Plexiglas partition between the front and back seats.

A good forty-five minutes later, the cabbie pulled up in front of a small shopping plaza, turned in his seat, and said, "This okay, fella?"

I shook my head. "No. I'm sorry. I'm going to a house on the beach somewhere. This isn't the beach."

He nodded to indicate the meter, which read $22.70; it clicked over to $22.90 as I watched. "You gonna be able to *pay* me, mister?"

"Of course I'm going to be able to pay you."

"You wanta check and make sure?"

"I don't need to—" I stopped, realized that I'd cashed my last payroll check three weeks earlier, had put most of it in my savings account, and had lived quite frugally ever since. I sat up straight and looked at the meter. "How much is that, now? That's $22.90?"

"$22.90. That's right." It was clear he was losing his patience.

I checked my wallet, found three tens and two ones in it. I sighed, relieved, handed him the three tens, told him to give me a five and keep the rest. "This will be okay, right here. Which way's the ocean?"

He inclined his head to the right. "That way. Just keep walking—you can't miss it."

"Thanks," I said, and got out.

I have a lousy memory for places—streets, roads, houses—so it didn't surprise me very much when, an hour later, I found myself walking the shoulder of a four-lane highway flanked by industrial buildings. The highway looked like it might lead to Abner's beach house eventually, but could, I thought, just as easily lead to Pittsburgh.

It was nearing eight o'clock; the sun had warmed things up, and the highway was taking on its morning rush of traffic—cars were moving past in increasingly greater numbers and in increasingly tighter knots.

I knew the ocean was close by, maybe within a couple of miles, because I could smell it when the wind picked up.

I tried to recall any landmarks I'd noticed when I'd ridden with Abner. I remembered little except the run-in with the motorcycle cop, getting out of the car, peering at him over the roof. I remembered something large and red behind him. A billboard, perhaps, or some kind of unlikely building. But now when I glanced about, I saw nothing even remotely like it and I cursed myself for having too much pride to get directions from Abner.

That's when a Nassau County sheriff's car pulled up just ahead of me, and a tall, lean, very powerful-looking cop got out and sauntered toward me. When he was a couple of yards off, he nodded and said, "Good morning, sir."

"Morning," I said.

He stopped an arm's length away. "Could I see some identification, sir?"

"Could I ask why?"

He nodded again. "Yes, sir. A man roughly answering your description was seen prowling around some back yards a few miles away."

I shrugged. "Well, it wasn't me."

"I'm sure it wasn't, sir, but if you could please show me some I.D."

I got my wallet out and handed him my driver's license. He glanced at it. "You are Samuel L. Feary?"

"Yes."

"Could you come to the car with me, Mr. Feary?"

"Am I under arrest?"

"No, sir. Could you please come to the car with me?"

"If I'm not under arrest, why should I come to the car with you?" I could hear the high nervous whine in my voice, and I realized that he could hear it, too. I put my hand to my temple. "I'm sorry. I'm not feeling very well," I said, and realized that I sounded stupidly melodramatic.

"Yes, sir. Now, if you come with me, please—to the car."

I nodded at my driver's license. "Can I have that back?"

"Yes. In a minute." He held his hand out, took my arm. "Please, sir."

I walked with him to the car; he opened the back door, asked me to get in. I looked at him. "Can I sit in front?"

"No, sir."

"I still don't understand—"

"Please, sir." He pushed gently at my arm; I sat in the back seat. He closed the door. There were no door or window handles in back; a wire screen separated the back seat from the front.

The cop got in, left his door open, and said, "We'll just be a few moments, sir, then I'm sure you can be on your way." He called in my name and address. While he waited, I said, "I'm looking for the ocean; I'm going to a beach house on the ocean." I heard again that high nervous whine. "And I'm afraid since I've only been in this area once before—"

"Yes, sir. Hold on just a moment."

I cursed under my breath, said, "Were you in Viet Nam, Officer?"

"No, sir. I was too young."

"Well, for Christ's sake, *I* was in Viet Nam—"

"You'll have to be patient, sir. Please. I don't want to cuff you."

"*Cuff* me?! Why in the hell would you want to cuff me—"

A woman's voice over the radio said then, "Samuel L. Feary,'' spelled my name, gave my address, added, ''Nega-file, Jack.''

The cop said, ''Thanks, Vera,'' got out, opened the back door, smiled flatly at me, said, ''I'm sorry for tying you up, Mr. Feary. You can be on your way now.''

I got out, tried hard to look angry. He apologized again and drove off.

I turned and looked back the way I'd come. Where the road met the horizon, and all but obscured by a cloud of its own exhaust, I saw that damned yellow garbage truck moving very slowly my way, and two men walking just as slowly in front of it.

ELEVEN

I called Abner from a public phone a mile from where the cop had stopped me. Across the highway from the phone booth was what looked like some kind of military installation—an early 1950s fighter plane, painted red, stood in front of it, on a pedestal. I was breathless from running, and Abner noticed:

"Why are you all out of breath, Sam? What's wrong?"

"Abner, where's the damned beach house?"

"What are you—lost? Where are you calling from?"

I had seen a highway route marker. "I'm on Route 14. Where's that?"

"It runs through Nassau County."

"Abner, there's a garbage truck following me!"

"Why would a garbage truck be following you on Route 14, Sam? Are you driving, do you have a car?"

"Christ, Abner—"

"Is it a county garbage truck, Sam? Can you see the words 'Nassau County' on the side of it? What *color* is it? The county trucks are blue, you know." A pause; he continued, "Why would it be following you, anyway? Garbage trucks don't follow people—"

"It followed me here from Manhattan, Abner."

"It's a Manhattan garbage truck? Does it say 'Manhattan DPW' on it, Sam? Is it yellow?"

"Oh, what the hell does that matter, Abner?"

"I guess it doesn't, Sam; I was only trying to be—"

"Just tell me how to get to the beach house, okay?"

"No, tell me where you are, and I'll come there, I think that's a better idea. I've got the car—did you say you have a car, Sam? You don't have a car, do you?"

And the operator cut in, "Your three minutes are up, please deposit another quarter or your call will be interrupted."

"Dammit," I said, "everybody's so damned polite," and I fished frantically in my pocket, found a quarter, and deposited it. Abner said: "Where on Route 14 are you, Sam?"

I told him about the military installation across the highway and about the early 1950s fighter plane, painted red, which stood in front of it on a pedestal. Abner said, "I know exactly where you are, Sam. Sit tight. I'll be there in ten minutes." And he was.

He looked better. He was wearing a white turtleneck sweater, clean but faded jeans, brown Hush

Puppies. He looked scrubbed, and rested, too, as if he'd just had a shower and shave after a good night's sleep.

We pulled away from the phone booth. "You're not serious about this *garbage* truck, are you?" he asked.

"A lot of shit's been going on, Abner."

"It sounds like it." He gave me a big, broad smile. "I mean—a *garbage* truck?"

"Abner, what are you into?"

He gave me another broad smile. "Remember the mausoleum, Sam? In Bangor. Twenty years ago. Did you think that was fun?"

"We were kids, Abner. And we were stupid. We aren't kids anymore."

His smile altered slightly. "Who the hell ever grows up, Sam?" He came to a stop at a flashing red traffic light, and started through, though there was a car closing on us. "Jesus Christ!" I breathed, and he stomped on the accelerator. The car closing on us braked hard; Abner whispered, "Gross overreaction, if you ask me."

"Dammit, Abner," I yelled, "where'd you get your license, at K mart?"

We were going seventy now. He eased off on the accelerator, let the car slow to fifty-five. "You asked what I'm into, Sam," he said. He glanced at me, a look of dead seriousness on his face. "This is what I'm into, Sam: I'm into reality. I'm into *existence*."

"Oh, give me a break," I snarled.

"I know, I know, it sounds corny, it sounds half-baked, it sounds half-assed, but Sam—listen to me

. . ." He stopped for another light, though just barely. "In the past six months, I've done more actual *living* than I'd done my entire life. That's no exaggeration."

"What is it you're into, Abner—cocaine, heroin?"

"C'mon, Sam, you know I'd never touch that stuff."

He turned down the dirt road that led to the beach house, and I saw that I'd actually gotten pretty close, that my memory hadn't become total mush after all.

He stopped to let a girl of ten or so cross in front of us. When she was across, she smiled, mouthed "Thank you," and disappeared over a dune that crowded up to the road.

"Polite kid," I said as he started up again.

"Uh-huh," he said, and then the beach house was in front of us. He smiled oddly at me. "I'm sorry, Sam—I warned you once, so warning you again just wouldn't do any good." He parked, got out of the car, and started for the house. I followed.

When we got to the door, he looked questioningly at me. "A garbage truck, Sam? Are you sure it was the same garbage truck each time? Maybe there were *two* garbage trucks, one in Manhattan and one here, on Long Island."

"Let's go inside, Abner."

He stopped in the doorway. "Did I tell you that I've fallen in love?" He sounded as if he'd just discovered a fifty-dollar bill tucked in his pants pocket. "That's the good news."

"Let's go in*side*, Abner. Please. We have to talk."

"The bad news is that she's temporarily . . . inaccessible."

"I feel for you."

He added offhandedly, "Because she's dead."

I said nothing.

"Her name's Phyllis. Pellaprat. Pretty name, huh? And she's here, you know." He nodded toward the inside of the house. "I'm just not sure where, exactly. I've looked. Hard. I guess I've got to look harder. Maybe you can help me. Do you think you can help me find Phyllis?"

"Sure, Abner. Sure I can. But let's go inside now, okay? Let's talk."

"Because once I find her," he rattled on, "I've got this little place up north. In Vermont. It's a place I've been working on, you know—"

"Abner," I coaxed, "inside, okay? Then we'll talk."

"Oh," he said, as if catching himself in a belch, "sure, I'm sorry." And we went inside, into the great room. That morning it had an odd, vaguely shimmering quality about it, as if hundreds of fireflies had been let loose in it and each one had found a hiding place.

He led me through it into the kitchen again and motioned for me to sit at the table. I did. He sat across from me and said expansively, "I don't know about you, Sammy, but I've always thought that kitchens are the friendliest part of a house—"

"I like to be called Sam, Abner. You know that."

He shrugged. "I thought I called you Sammy in high school. I guess I'm wrong."

"Abner, listen to me." I hesitated.

"Yes?" he coaxed.

"Abner, there are no dead people in this house. There's you, and me, and . . . and whatever her name is—"

"Al?"

"Yeah. Al."

"And Madeline, too. Don't forget Madeline."

I nodded wearily. "Yes, and Madeline, and you and me."

"And Phyllis," he said happily. "And quite a few others. They come and they go. They're here. Now. In this house. Sam, they live in the walls—"

"There are no dead people living in the walls, goddammit!"

He looked quizzically at me. "Did I say 'dead'? They're not dead, Sam. Not the way a tree is dead, or a leaf, or . . ." He stopped and thought a moment. "What's 'dead'—do you know? Am *I* dead, Sam? Or am I alive? Can you tell just by looking at me? Can you say, 'Yes, Abner is alive because he's sitting at his kitchen table and he's talking to me'?" He paused. "Sam, it's not that simple, nothing is that simple."

"Abner, *you* know you're alive."

He nodded. "I do now. Right now. While we're sitting here talking. But in a half hour, an hour, I probably won't be so sure—things change."

I interrupted, sniffing. "Abner, what's that smell? It smells like something's burning." I went to the hallway that led to the great room, sniffed again. "It really does, Abner; it smells like something's burning." The photographs on the walls of the hallway—photographs of people, mostly; portraits, candid shots, some in color, others in black and white—were shimmering like a lake on a sunny day because of a dim and erratic light coming from the great room.

Abner came up behind me and put his hand on my shoulder.

I said, "What's wrong here, Abner? For God's sake, what's wrong here?!" The photographs changed then. Their top and bottom edges peeled free of the frames and curled inward, as if from heat, and one by one they dropped to the floor of the hallway. In their place I saw the dim suggestion of color, as if the walls were bleeding, as if there were gallons of paint in various colors being spilled behind the plaster.

I felt Abner's grip strengthen on my shoulder. "Forgive me, Sam," he said.

TWELVE

Walls are made of plaster, furring strips, nails, paint. Only mice and squirrels live in walls.

Walls can't bleed people the way a madras shirt bleeds colors.

But the walls of that beach house did. I saw those colors puddle up in various places on the floor, I saw them come together, I saw arms jut out, feet, legs, faces—while the great room erupted in flames beyond, the walls bled their people and built them up again. There was a man of thirty dressed as if for a wedding reception who rose up from the floor like bamboo, and a fat woman of forty or forty-five who wept soundlessly, her shoulders heaving; near her, a young boy dressed in white, and standing alone where the hall opened onto the great room, a blond girl of ten or so, the same girl who had crossed in front of the car.

"Forgive me," Abner said again. "I can't predict these things."

I turned open-mouthed to him. I wanted to tell him, *We've got to get out of here, the house is burning down around us,* but I couldn't; it would have been like yelling, just before the truck rolls over, *My God, there's a truck rolling over on us; what are we going to do?*

Because I was sure there was nothing we could do, sure that it was inevitable that the house was going to burn down with us in it. All of us. Abner and me. And the people who had been bled out of the walls. The house was going to burn down and destroy us all and there was nothing I could do about it.

Then Abner asked, "Are you worried?" very casually, as if he were asking if I'd had my dinner. "Don't be worried," he went on, "or frightened. Enjoy it. We are being *entertained*, Sam. These are actors here, showmen, enjoy it, they *want* you to enjoy it—if you don't, they won't like it, and they'll hurt us." Over the frenzied roar of the flames pushing out of the great room and down the hallway, Abner's voice was calm and confident, like the voice of someone who feels it is his right and his duty to be a spiritual guide to others. He put both hands hard on my shoulders now, as if to hold me there, in that house, while it burned. He grinned broadly, as if he'd told me a joke.

"Let go of me, Abner," I said, my voice low and threatening.

"They're enter*taining* us, Sam. You've got to enjoy it."

Perhaps, I thought, he couldn't hear me above the rush of the flames. I yelled, "Goddammit, Abner, get your hands off me!"

He let go.

And I turned and ran past him to the door that led to the beach. I pushed on it; it wouldn't open. I pulled on it; it opened, and I ran from the house, toward the ocean. When the waves were licking at my feet, I stopped and looked back.

The ocean side of the house had a fresh coat of white paint on it and what looked like new black shutters at all the windows. There were half a dozen windows on the first floor, three on the second, and two, longer and narrower than the others, in the attic, where the roof peaked severely. I thought for a moment that I'd run farther than I'd supposed, and that I was looking at some other house. Then Abner appeared in the kitchen doorway and stood silently in it, his hands in his pockets, his body framed by the flames rising behind him.

I yelled, "Abner, get the hell out of there!" The flames danced brightly behind him. I yelled, "Don't do this, please don't do this!" The flames reached around from inside the house and embraced him. I fell to my knees. The ocean lapped at my feet. "Don't *do* this to me, Abner!" I pleaded. "You're my friend!"

He yelled back, hands cupped around his mouth to be heard over the noise of the flames, "Of course, I'm your friend. And you're my friend. We're two friends. Together. For life!"

"Sure we are," I called. "Friends for life, yes—Abner and Sam! Friends for life!"

"Thank you, Sam," he called, and walked back into the house and closed the door.

Within a minute, the flames visible through the windows were gone.

I got off my knees and sat on the sand facing the house, with my legs straight and my arms folded in front of me, my head down. The headache I had had earlier began to creep back. *Tricked me, didn't you, Abner?* I thought. *Abner and Sam, friends for life!* I thought. Maybe. The necessary elements were there—a common set of memories, a sort of gruff affection and concern. But whether we'd eventually turn out to be "friends for life" was something that only time could decide. He, I realized, was using whatever feeling existed between us as a sledge; he was using it to hammer me into place there at his tumbledown beach house. I sat on the sand and wondered when I'd get up and move away from the incoming tide. I couldn't blame him; I understood why he was doing it. Very simply, he was in trouble. He needed a friend. And I was willing to fill that role. But still, as my headache grew, so did my anger.

After a couple of minutes, I yelled, "Damn you, Abner!" and hunkered forward on my rear end, away from the tide. "Damn you!" I screamed again. He reappeared at the back door of the house and wandered out to me, hands thrust into his pockets, a stupid grin on his mouth.

He stood above me for a few moments. That stupid grin went away. Then he said secretively, as if he were playing some game of cops and robbers, "The coast is clear, Sam."

He was standing to my right, level with my ankles, his hands still in his pockets, his legs together, one knee bent slightly. I knew he'd be easy to knock over, so that's what I did. I tripped him and he toppled over onto his side, then rolled to his stomach, so his face was in the sand.

It was an impulsive, useless thing to do, but I realized that anything he might say to me would be bullshit, that he couldn't explain what had happened in his house. He might as well have tried to explain how life began, or how to cure the common cold.

So I tripped him. It was the same as slapping him around. It was designed to give him a good, gritty taste of what I saw as reality. And, futile and stupid as my action was, it made me feel worlds better, for a moment anyway.

I jumped to my feet, pointed stiffly at him, though his face was still turned away from me, and screamed, "What the hell do you mean *The coast is clear*? This isn't some stupid game. You sound like you want us to go up on some building and piss off the roof together, for Christ's sake!"

He turned his head and looked up at me. Sand caked his cheek because the beach was wet. He spit out some of the sand, and that same stupid smirk appeared on his mouth again. He said, "Can't get your hand out of the box, can you, Sam? It's stuck in there, isn't it?" He started to push himself up. I put my foot on his back, kept him down.

"Abner," I said, "you're not getting up until you tell me what happened in that house."

He let himself fall to his belly again, turned his face up to me. His smirk was gone. In its place was a mixture of pleading, desperation, and resignation, like the expression of someone bleeding to death inside a squashed car. He said, "Reality happened, Sam. Reality happened!"

THIRTEEN

I took my foot off his back. He hesitated, pushed himself to his feet, and got that damned smirk on his face again.

I said, "I don't want to hear any more crap from you, Abner."

"You always were a lot more physical than I am, Sam."

"Sorry," I managed, my voice quivering with anger. "I wasn't trying to hurt you. I was just trying to get your attention."

His smirk altered slightly. "You couldn't hurt me." He brushed at the sand on his pants. "Maybe you could have once upon a time. Twenty years ago. Six months ago. But not now." He brushed the sand off his white sweater. He found a smear of dirt on the cuff. "Dammit, Sam, I just washed this sweater."

"Abner"—I pointed at the house, my arm shaking—"I don't give two flying fucks about your sweater! I want to know who those *people* are, I want to know what happened in there!"

He studied the smear of dirt. "I told you what happened." He looked at me. "Reality happened." That smirk appeared yet again. "It's awfully cold out here. Let's go back inside."

I was still pointing shakily at the house. I let my arm fall slowly, incredulous. I said, "I'm not going back into that house. Do you think I'm a moron? I'm not going back into that house."

He shook his head. "Sam, I've told you, they won't allow you to—"

I jabbed his chest suddenly with my finger. "And what I want from you, my *friend*, is for you to call them off. You got that? Call them off! Now!"

"Good Lord, Sam, they're not like dogs, they're people. I don't have any say over what they do or don't do—"

"I don't *believe* you, Abner." I jabbed his chest again. "I think they're your pets, they're your gruesome little pets, I think they'll beg for you, roll over, fetch, play dead"—he grinned at that—"and I think you can tell them when to rise up"—I lifted both hands palms down—"when to lie down, and when to hang around and look spooky."

"I don't think they're going to like this one tiny bit, Sam. I'd watch what I said, if I were you." It was hard to tell if he was joking.

"Is that a threat, Abner? A threat directly from the spooks themselves? I'm impressed. What are they going to do? Are they going to have a garbage truck run me down? Are they going to send two little dead girls into my bedroom to embarrass me to death? Tell me, Abner, Mr. Abner Spook-keeper, just what are they going to do?''

He shook his head. ''You're babbling, Sam. It's understandable. I babbled, too, in the beginning. It's a defense mechanism. You try to fight the impossible with nonsense, but then, after a while, you learn to accept, and to enjoy . . .''

''Listen to yourself, Abner. You sound like a damned religious fanatic.''

''Sam, please—just come back to the house with me, I need you at the house.''

''Call them off, Abner.''

''I can't 'call them off.' I don't even know what that means. Even Madeline couldn't 'call them off.' That's really *stupid*, Sam—it's unkind, too—''

I hit him on the jaw. Hard. With my open hand. He fell backward, sat down hard on the sand. His hand went up, he cursed, he massaged his jaw while I stood above him shaking my head in disbelief at the violence that confusion and fear had coaxed from me.

Then, from behind the house came the kind of deep and resonant noise that I had heard only hours before—the low, ominous, monotone rumble of a truck engine.

What could I do? I sat down close to Abner on the beach, my back to that noise. I took his hand away from his jaw, studied the bruise that was starting there, and said, ''Sorry, Abner. I didn't mean that.''

I paused. "Well, yes, I did. But I don't anymore." He grinned sadly. Behind us, the roar of the truck engine grew louder. I glanced back quickly, then looked at Abner again. "Tell me what the hell is going on. Please, Abner. I need your help here."

"Yes," he said, "and I need yours."

"Okay, then we'll help each other. Like when we were kids. Remember? When one of us got into trouble, the other one was always there to help. Like when . . ." The rumble of the engine stopped abruptly. I hurried on, "Like when you were writing all those dumb, unsigned love notes to Mrs. Singer in American history and I said I wrote them. Remember that?" I glanced nervously around at the beach house, then back at Abner. "Remember?" I coaxed.

"Yeah, I remember," he said; his brow furrowed. "Why'd you do that, anyway?"

I flashed him a quick, falsely magnanimous smile. "So you wouldn't get into trouble, of course." It wasn't really true. I had something of a crush on Mrs. Singer, myself, but my letters, which went unsent, were not nearly as poetic as Abner's. "So now you can return the favor, Abner. Just, please, call these . . . these *people* off, okay?"

He shrugged, began, "I told you, Sam, I can't just 'call them off.' You don't seem to understand—"

"Hello!" we heard.

Abner and I looked back at the house.

From around the side, a man dressed in brown appeared. He had a small package in his arms, and when he saw us sitting on the sand, he held the package up, yelled, "Hey, is one of you guys named"—he looked at the package—"named Cray?"

Abner yelled, "Yeah. That's me." He stood. "I'm Abner Cray."

The man in brown yelled back, "UPS."

Abner called, "I'll be right there," and loped back to the house.

FOURTEEN

I watched him take the package, gaze briefly at me, look at the package, go into the house through the kitchen door, and close the door behind him.

I waited a long time for him to reappear at the door.

People passed me on the beach. There were a few joggers hooked up to Sony Walkmans; there was an old man in baggy pants, a threadbare shirt, and shiny red sports coat who was moving very slowly, metal detector poised inches above the sand. He stopped once, fifty yards from me, dug frantically in the sand, and appeared to come up with some coins, which he stuffed into his pants pocket. There was a boy of nine or ten who was trying mightily to get a huge, wedge-shaped kite into the air. The kite had the words "Star Wars" on it. Eventually, it plummeted nose-first into a sand dune and the boy tucked it under his arm and walked off with his head down and an air of defeat about him.

I guessed that it was close to eleven o'clock and that I'd been sitting alone on the sand for at least an hour, hunkering forward every few minutes to get away from the tide. I looked at Abner's house. Jets had laced the tight blue sky with contrails that seemed to erupt from the roof. At the house's foundation, a mangy gray tomcat sniffed about, paused in midstep, looked up with its mouth open, then ran off.

"Abner?" I called. No reply. I stood, brushed myself off, and called "Abner?" again. Still no reply. I took a couple of tentative steps toward the house. I called yet again, got no reply, and whispered to myself, "Good Lord, he's a big boy, he can take care of himself," though I wasn't at all sure I believed it.

I stopped. I realized that the smartest thing for me to do would be to avoid the house altogether, to walk north or south on the beach until the house was well out of sight.

"Abner, dammit!" I called.

To my right, I heard, "You just watch your language, there, young man," and when I looked I saw a chunky silver-haired woman in her sixties. She was wearing a silky blue dress, black high heels, and a fur cape, and she was moving over the sand with painful slowness behind a large and incredibly fat black dog. The dog was on a leash that the woman held quite taut in her fat right hand.

"Sorry," I said.

"Yes, I'm sure you are," she snapped.

I turned back toward Abner's house, called to him again, again got no reply, cursed beneath my breath, and heard the old woman shout piercingly, "I heard that!"

I took a few quick steps toward Abner's house to put more distance between her and me. "Let's talk, Abner!" I called.

Silence.

"Are you all right in there, Abner?"

Silence.

I took several more steps toward the house, so I was just inside its shadow. I studied the windows; I saw no movement. The headache that had come and gone earlier in the morning returned dully, as if a seed had sprouted inside my skull.

I went the rest of the way to the house, grabbed the knob on the back door, turned it, pulled. The door was locked. "Shit!" I whispered, and put my face to one of the four square windows in the door. The kitchen was empty. I tried the door again, in vain. I stepped back, looked up at the windows on the second floor, looked right, left, called, "Abner, open up!" I waited a few moments, then stepped back, away from the house, went around to the side, and stopped at a window near the front of the house. I peered in at the bedroom beyond; there was a twin bed with a blue quilt on it, a four-drawer chest, a black metal floor lamp beside the bed, a braided oval rug. The room was empty.

I knocked on the window, called to Abner again, and went around to the front door; but it, too, was locked. I knocked on it. "Let's talk, Abner," I called, and when, yet again, there was no answer, I stepped back and gave the door a good, hard kick just below the knob. It didn't budge. I kicked it again. Nothing.

"Dammit!" I breathed, and kicked the door again, and again, and again, until, at last, I heard a loud cracking noise and saw a slit appear in the frame. I stepped back, muttered, "Good!" and kicked it once more. It held. And I realized, finally, that it opened outward, so breaking it down from the outside was going to be pretty close to impossible.

I heard the lock being worked from the other side.

"Abner?"

The door opened a little; a chain lock stopped it. It closed; I heard the chain lock being worked.

"Abner?" I said again.

It opened all the way. Abner appeared, looking bewildered.

I said, "Well, for God's sake; it's about time!"

He silently fingered the door frame where it was cracked, shook his head, said, "Why do you want to break into my house, Sam? You're going to wake Madeline up."

I began, "I don't want to wake *anyone* up, I just want to talk . . ."

He interrupted, stepping back through the doorway and extending his arm toward the inside, "Okay, okay, we'll talk. You don't have to break my door down just so we can talk."

I went inside.

* * *

He led me through the great room—which was whole—down the narrow hallway, where all the photographs were intact, and back to the kitchen, where he motioned me to sit down at the table, which I did.

I said, while he washed a bowl, a spoon, and a glass that he collected off the table, "Just tell me that this whole thing is some elaborate trick you're playing, Abner, and I'll go home a happy man. Can you tell me that?"

He had his back turned at the sink. He ran some water; it sounded as if he was scrubbing the inside of the glass with a dishcloth. He said, "This whole thing is an elaborate trick, Sam. I cooked it up because we were once such damned good friends and I knew you'd appreciate it." Then he turned halfway, so I could see him in profile, held the glass up, studied it for a few seconds, and put it in a dish drainer next to the sink. He smiled a wide, flat smile. "But that's not true at all," he added, turned and started on the bowl.

"Abner," I began, "there's an old man lying dead on the subway—"

He cut in, "There are probably a hundred old men lying dead on the subway. It's part of the charm of New York." He turned his head, looked questioningly at me. "How long have you been in New York, Sam? A couple weeks? A month?"

I shook my head. "Quite a bit longer than that. I know about New York, Abner. I know some people think it's a rat hole. I don't. I like it."

He smiled again, amused. "Good for you. I'm glad you like it. Go on liking it. See everything in it precisely the way you want to see it. Tell yourself that *this* is real, and *that* is real, and if something falls from a building—if a gargoyle falls from a building and goes *clunk* on some guy's head and lays him flat, tell yourself that that's real, too, and all that has to be done is for some poor slob to come and scrape the guy up and the matter is taken care of. Maybe it is, and maybe it isn't. No one can say. Not even the guy who went *splat!*" His small amused smile had changed halfway through his monologue to something like grim bemusement. "Do you understand that, Sam, what I'm saying to you? Do you see what I'm saying?"

I nodded. "Yes," I said.

He looked pleased. "Good. Tell me what you understand."

"Okay." I paused for effect. "I understand that your hand's stuck in that box, too, Abner. I think you've got both feet in it, in fact, and both legs, and your chest and arms, and pretty soon your head's going to disappear into it. Then you'll be lost in it, and no one will be able to find you."

He said nothing for a good minute or more. Then he said, "I want to show you something, Sam." He opened a cupboard over the sink, pulled out a thick black notebook, and then handed it to me. I opened it. The title page read, "A Version of Events," and, on the next line, "By Abner Cray."

"What's this?" I asked.

"Just what it says," he answered.

"Uh-huh," I said. " 'Abner Cray'—you don't use the 'W' anymore?"

He shook his head. "No. It's that Abner Doubleday thing, Sam. Besides, the 'W' stands for Wilson, after my Uncle Wilson; and I hated my Uncle Wilson." He smiled a little, as if embarrassed. "Actually, Sam, it's a book manuscript. Kind of a . . . ghost story, I guess. I sent it to my editor, the one who signed up the photo book." He shrugged. "She sent it back. It's what the UPS man brought me. She says she doesn't believe a word of it." He chuckled. "For God's sake, she thinks it's fiction."

"Sorry," I said.

"It's all right," he said. "I've been having second thoughts about trying to get it published, anyway. As a matter of fact, I don't even want you to read it. Maybe someday, but not now. Now I'd like you to read just the first paragraph, okay?"

"Sure," I said. I flipped through the notebook; "A Version of Events"—and I still haven't read more than the first paragraph—occupied about six hundred single-spaced, handwritten, lined pages. I opened to Chapter One. I read:

"Go, answer the door, peer through the little security peephole at whoever has come to call. You see a face, a smile perhaps, a pair of eyes. And they tell you—open the door. Or they tell you—do not open the door. But if you have shut yourself up on the wrong side of that peephole for too long, they tell you very little. Only what is within arm's reach, not what is above, or below, or to the sides, or behind that smiling face."

I looked up at Abner. "Okay," I said. "I've read it. What does it mean?"

He stuck his hand out; I gave him the notebook. He put it back in the cupboard. "It means," he said, "that for the first time in your life you're peering through the little security peephole, Sam. It means that at last the door is going to be opened for you and you're about to step through."

Leslie and I would both deny it, but I think that we play lots of games with each other. It's something that can't be helped. People play games. People are sly, they try to peek around the edges of their intentions and the intentions of those they love and they have a hell of a time focusing. So they play games. They believe that the games will tell them what's real and what isn't.

This was one of the first games I played with Leslie. We'd been seeing each other for no more than a week, and I started to make a habit of saying to her—with a kind of mock, light spontaneity—"I love you to pieces." I was playing a game. I was trying to tell her that I wasn't really in love with her—how *could* I be in love with her after only a week? It was preposterous. Things just did not happen that way. It was illogical, irrational, and immature. So I said, "I love you to pieces," which doesn't, of course, mean "I love you." It means, "Hey, baby, I'm *crazy* about you!" and yet it still uses that magical word—the word *love*. What I *wanted* to say was, simply, "I love you," but that would have required some response, and regardless of the moments we had danced through in our short time together, I could not have said that her response would not have been anything more than "I think you're special," or perhaps a lingering gaze and a hand to the cheek. I would have felt like a damned fool.

She quickly caught on to the fact that I was playing a game. After the third or fourth time I'd said it, she sighed and said, "I know, I know—it doesn't mean you love me!" And she grinned. I said to myself, "You damned fool!"

FIFTEEN

Abner announced, "I'm in love, Sam, and the woman I'm in love with is somewhere in this house. Maybe she's in the walls. I don't know. I don't know how accurate that is." He paused. "I've seen a whole world in these walls—I've seen a whole world behind these windows and doors, Sam. Sometimes I've walked into it, into that world, looking for Phyllis. And sometimes it's come here, parts of it, into this house. Like today." He smiled happily. "Like this morning." He stopped, as if waiting for some comment from me. I started to say again—not really believing it—*No one's here, Abner*, but when I got as far as "No one's," he interrupted: "And this world, Sam, is wherever we aren't looking, wherever we can't see, wherever we choose not to see. It's in the walls. It's behind the doors. It's beyond the windows." He was on a roll now. "Until we break the walls down, or look out the windows or open the doors. And then what we see, and what sees us, depends solely on who we are."

"Oh? Are you special, Abner?"

"Yes," he answered at once. "You could say I'm special. On the second of January it was two years since my . . . initiation."

"I'm happy for you."

He smiled. "You know, Sam, you're holding up pretty well under the circumstances." He glanced at the door that led to the beach. "But do you think you could do me a favor?"

"A favor?"

He shrugged. "I'd just like you to go to that door"—he nodded at the door that led to the beach. "Open it. And step out. Could you do that?"

I glanced at the door, then at Abner. "Why?"

He smiled once more. "Sam, you're going to have to go out one of these doors sooner or later."

I looked at the door again. I looked at it a good, long time. Then I stood. "I don't like any of this, Abner. I don't like anything I've seen here. I don't like anything you've said. And I don't like this. I don't like the way it feels."

He shrugged. "Of course you don't. It's kind of an acquired taste." I said nothing. He grinned and added, "That's a joke, Sam."

"Oh?" I said. "Ha, ha." I screwed my courage up, strode to the door, pulled it open, and stepped out.

Abner told me later that I screamed, though I don't

recall it. I've screamed only once before, that I remember, and that was in Viet Nam, when a soldier walking a couple of yards to my right through a rice paddy stepped on a Claymore mine. I screamed then, out of desperation, out of the agonizing knowledge that I had to exist in a world where the ground I walked on could blow up beneath my feet.

And I screamed outside Abner's back door for the same reason that I would have screamed if my skin had been stripped from my flesh. Because what I had known as reality—even after all that had happened earlier in Abner's house—evaporated around me, and I was wrapped in something strange, and cold, and terrifying.

I saw the beach, the ocean, the dunes, tall grasses here and there, a bright midday sun in a tight blue sky. I heard the screech of gulls, the low grumble of traffic from somewhere far in front of the house. I smelled the salt air, the slight underlay of dead fish.

But I saw it, heard it, smelled it as if it were at a distance, as if it were removed, the way a caterpillar inside a grimy glass bowl probably experiences the world. And what lay between me and the reality of gulls and dunes and traffic was a place of confusion, a world of stillness and panic where there were a thousand people, ten thousand people, all moving about as if in slow motion, as if their feet were stuck in the earth, as if each of them were playing a part in someone else's nightmare.

And I knew this, too, watching them: I knew that *they* were the reality, that the dunes, the gulls, and the traffic were no more than the sugar coating on a sucker that has a steel ball at its center.

I said, "My God, my God, Abner, this is *hell!*"

And Abner, who had come up behind me, said, "Don't be an ass, Sam. What'd you do in Viet Nam—find religion? This is just what is, it's no more than what is. I can't help it if this is the first time you've opened your eyes."

SIXTEEN

Imagine being digested. Imagine being inside the belly of some beast.

And imagine other people are in there. It doesn't matter, does it? A hundred thousand people. A million people. Ten million people. It doesn't matter. The stomach juices of that beast still sting and smell and eat the flesh away.

Imagine that the air itself is alive with the stomach juices of that beast; imagine that the air is a dark greenish yellow, and imagine that it smells like the men's room at Grand Central Station.

"This is what *is*," Abner said.

"No," I whispered.

"Sure, Sam. Sure. Look at it, take a long, hard look at it."

"Take a look at what? My God, I don't know

what I'm seeing. For God's sake, Abner, tell me what I'm seeing."

"You're seeing what there is to see."

"That's bullshit, Abner. Bullshit! Who are these people?"

"Who *are* these people?" He was incredulous. "I'm surprised at you, Sam. These people are spooks. We live in a world of spooks." He put his hands hard on my shoulders as if to keep me where I was. He whispered harshly, "We live in a world of the dead. But the dead *live* in the walls, they live behind the doors and the windows, they live in the *air*, Sam, like the birds; and they fly, they do fly." His grip strengthened on my shoulders. He went on, his whisper changing to a high wheeze, "They fly like the birds do, and they come to rest on the tops of buildings, in attics, on statues, on the hoods of cars."

Beyond, far beyond the world I was seeing, the boy flying the Star Wars kite appeared at the top of a dune and charged down it, his kite fluttering behind him. "May the Force be with you," he yelled.

Abner said, behind me, "Did you see *Star Wars*, Sam? I saw it three times."

The kid stumbled on a rock and fell forward, so his elbows stuck into the dune. He pushed himself quickly to his feet and swiped frantically at his clothes as if trying to brush away a nest of spiders.

Because those people were all around him. He had fallen into their world.

They touched him, stroked him, a woman hugged him from behind. And he went on frantically brushing at his clothes until, at last, he panicked and began *pulling* at his clothes as if they'd gotten stuck to his skin and were burning him. "Mommy?!" he called. "Mommy?!" he called again. "Mommy?!" he pleaded. And then he started tugging at his kite string as if he could pull himself back to his own world with it.

Abner sighed. "He doesn't know what's happening to him. Poor kid. They'll pull him right down into the sand."

I looked around at Abner, open-mouthed. I could say nothing.

He repeated, "They'll pull him right down into the sand and tomorrow he'll be one of the missing."

And across the awful expanse that separated us I yelled to the boy, "Run! Goddammit, run!"

He looked at me, shook his head disbelievingly, and pushed at the people who were tugging at him and pulling him into the sand.

This is what separated me from that boy: the sand, the grass, the air. And the dead. As I watched, the boy's calves disappeared, then his knees, his thighs. "Mommy!?" he screamed, still tugging desperately at his kite string, pulling the kite closer. It shredded on a sharp rock—the same rock, I think, that he had tripped over. He continued pulling. "Mommy?! Mommy?!"

I started for him. I wrenched free of Abner's strong grip and, seconds later, found myself on my back on the kitchen floor, Abner standing stiffly above me. "Sam, you're a fool! There are no heroes here. Only fools!"

"But that boy—"

"You can't affect what these people do. You can only watch. And you watch, Sam—you watch because you *want* to watch, because something very deep inside you *wants* to *watch*. Otherwise, my friend, you wouldn't see a thing."

I scrambled to my feet, rushed to the door, and stopped. "My God!" I breathed.

The boy was gone.

Behind me, Abner said, "He can only feel them, Sam. He can feel their hands now, their mouths, their hair, probably. And he knows what's happening to him, I think he knows he's been sucked into the dune, but I doubt he knows why." He put his hand on my shoulders again. "And I wish to God that there was something you or I could have done for him, Sam. But there wasn't, you see. Not with these people. You might as well try to reason with a dinner napkin as try to reason with these people. They're not like the cop that stopped us; they're not like Al, or Phyllis. They're kind of like leftovers. Humanity's leftovers." He shook his head: "Madeline would shoot me if she heard me say that."

"You murdered that boy, goddammit!"

"No, Sam. He has merely become one of the missing. Thousands of people turn up missing every day. You know that. And some of them, like that boy, get pulled into sand dunes. Others get carried away, the way rabbits get carried away by owls. And others, a few others, get themselves stuck in the walls." He grinned slyly, as if keeping some dark secret from me. "They get put into the walls, Sam. And they *stay* there. With the dead! And no matter where they try to go—Good Lord, they could try to go into insanity, or into their pasts—the dead go after them and drag them back."

"Well, dammit," I said, "*I'm* going to go and look for that boy."

"Of course you are, Sam. I can't stop you. But I can tell you what you'll find. You'll find sand, and sand fleas, a few beer bottles. You'll find gum wrappers, maybe a rubber or two. But you won't find that boy. He's one of the missing. He'll always be one of the missing. Like Amelia Earhart and Judge Crater and Jimmy Hoffa. They all got grabbed."

SEVENTEEN

He was right. I found nothing. I looked for a good hour and a half. I dug furiously, and futilely—because no matter how fast I dug, the sand on the slope of the dune filled the hole up even faster. And finally, I lay at the bottom of the dune with my eyes on a gull circling gracefully in the tight blue sky. Abner appeared above me.

I asked him, "Where are they, Abner?"

"Where are those people?" he said, and nodded. "They're still here."

"Then why don't they take *me*, dammit?"

He shrugged. "Or *me*, for that matter? Or that old woman with the fat dog? She comes by every day. So does the man with the metal detector." He sat down next to me, elbows in the dune, and leveled a quizzical gaze at me. "I don't know, Sam," he said.

"Why do some people get stung by bees and others don't? I really don't know. Maybe someday we'll both get stung."

"That's comforting," I whispered.

He smiled. "This is temporary, Sam. This . . . *wild talent* you've got. It's temporary." He paused. "Maybe that's not the right word, maybe temporary's not the right word. Transient's better. This wild talent you've got is *transient*. It comes and goes. One day you've got it, the next day it's gone. Sort of like herpes."

I let out a grunt of disbelief.

He went on, grinning, "And *I* got it from a woman named Barbara W. Barber two years ago on the Amtrak out of Bangor. Good Lord, Sam, she gave me this *disease* on the Amtrak out of Bangor. And I guess she gave it to me because she didn't like me, because I offended her." He idly scratched his nose. "And I gave it to *you*, Sam, because you're my friend and friends help each other." He stood, extended his hand. I shook my head. "No, let me be."

"Sure," he said. "You know, Sam, I think it's like walking into a closet by mistake. You see that you're in a closet, you look around briefly, and you walk out. But the hell of it is, there are so many damned closets to walk into." After a moment he went on, "Touch the air, Sam."

"Huh?"

"Lift your hand and *touch* the air."

I sat up. "Why?" I said.

"Just do it, please."

I did it.

"Good," he said. "Now tell me what you feel."

"Nothing," I answered. "I don't feel a thing. I feel the air."

"Close your eyes."

I closed my eyes.

"Now what do you feel?"

I reached, groped in the air.

"Gently, Sam."

I touched the air gently.

"Tell me what you feel."

"Dammit, I don't know." I paused. "I feel the air." Another pause. "No. I feel someone's skin; it feels like water. It feels like cool water."

He said, "You see, Sam? They are still here, as I said. They're always here. Those poor, murderous slobs have always *been* here, in the air all around us, except now, for you, there's a difference. You can see them occasionally. And you can touch them, and you can—"

I pushed myself to my feet suddenly and grabbed him by the collar. He looked very surprised, which pleased me. "You're my *friend* so you did this to me, Abner?! Why do I find that so hard to believe? Tell me. What kind of friend would do this . . . this *thing*—"

"A desperate friend, Sam."

"You bastard!"

He nodded; his look of surprise was gone; it was replaced by grim resignation. "Sure, I'm a bastard. But I'm a stuck bastard. And I warned you. I did warn you, Sam, if you think back—"

"Where's that boy?"

"What boy?"

"Goddamn you!" My grip strengthened on his collar. "That boy with the kite. Where in the hell is he?"

Abner shrugged. "I don't know. Where would a pail of water be if you tossed it into the ocean? I don't know. Maybe he'll turn up in . . . in Schenectady, someday, or in Ottawa, or, Christ, right here. Chances are he won't turn up at all, Sam. And there's nothing you or I or anybody can do about it. He's fallen between the cracks. Lots and lots of people fall between the cracks."

I held my right hand up, palm open, near his chin. "Your keys, Abner."

"My car keys?"

"Yes."

"You're going to take my car?"

"Give me your keys, dammit!"

"I need my car." He fished in his pocket, found his key ring, which had a half-dozen keys on it, and let it dangle from his fingers so they were just touching my hand. "I always thought you were pretty bright, Sam. I guess I was wrong."

"Let go of the damned keys."

"*Think*, my friend. *Think!*" He let go of the keys. I let go of him and took a step back. He went on, "Think about what's happened here. Think about what's happened to me. Think hard about what could happen to you, Sam."

"Abner, you really are full of crap!"

He grinned. "I need my house key." He nodded at the key ring.

"You actually lock that place up?"

"Of course I lock it up. You think I want just anyone going in there? I've got . . . valuables in there, Sam. I've got things to protect."

I gave him the key ring; he took a key off it, gave it back to me, and said, "You've got to let her warm up a good three or four minutes, Sam. The choke advance needs work."

"Sure, Abner." I started for the side of the house. "At this point, I'm worried as hell about your damned choke advance."

Behind me, he called, "And don't leave her parked on some side street if you can help it. Don't leave the doors locked, either. It doesn't do any good. They'll just break a window or screw up the lock—" He said more, but I didn't catch it, because by then I was halfway around the house.

I parked the Malibu, doors locked, in an alleyway off Third Avenue near 10th Street. It was midafternoon. The clear blue sky had given way to a sultry overcast, and that alleyway looked like the inside of a cereal box.

The drive back had been an ordeal. Every inch of the way, I felt like I'd been drenched in gasoline and was being chased by a thousand people with torches.

Sort of like herpes, Abner had said. *It comes and goes. One day you have it, the next day it's gone.*

"You bastard, Abner," I whispered.

At the other end of the alleyway, a tall man dressed

in a dark suit and overcoat stood facing me. He held a cane in his right hand. I could see his features only indistinctly—a receding hairline, deep-set eyes, thin lips, a long straight nose.

"And what the hell do *you* want?" I yelled.

He pointed his cane at the Malibu. "If you park it there, young man, it will be vandalized. Are you new here, to New York?" He had a deep and resonant voice that dripped with authority and demanded respect, which I was in no mood to give. I growled at him, "What in the hell are you? My keeper? Take a hike."

He chuckled shortly, deep in his chest. "No. I'm not your keeper. I'm no one's keeper. Forgive me." And he turned to his left and was gone.

Torches, I thought. *Gasoline*.

I got back in the Malibu, put my head on the upper edge of the steering wheel and I wept.

EIGHTEEN

I parked the car in a parking garage near Fourth Avenue and 3rd Street, found a phone booth, and called Leslie's number.

Her father answered. I sighed. If there was anyone I didn't want to have to deal with then, it was Frank Wirth. I wasn't even 100 percent sure that I wanted to talk to Leslie, or at least that I *should* talk to her, because I was almost certain that an argument would start—that's the way things had been tending lately, ever since my ill-conceived remark that her father should be "where he can be taken better care of." But she was, after all, the person I loved most in this world; she was my reality, and I needed her.

"Hello, Mr. Wirth," I said. "Could I speak with Leslie, please."

"Who's this?"

"It's Sam Feary, Mr. Wirth. Is Leslie there?"

"I don't know no one named Sam Fury."

"Feary, Sam *Feary*, Mr. Wirth. I'm Leslie's . . . fiancé." It was half true. I'd asked; she hadn't given me an answer.

Silence.

"Mr. Wirth? Are you there?"

"You the one she's been seein'?"

"Yes, sir. Could I speak with her, please?"

"You the one ain't been around for a week?"

"Yes, sir. It's a private matter, sir. Could I please speak with her?"

"No," he said flatly.

"Why?" I asked.

" 'Cuz she ain't here."

"Could I ask where she is?"

"Sure you could. Go ahead and ask." I heard a grim little chuckle.

I sighed. "Okay, Mr. Wirth, I'm asking. Where is she?"

He answered, "She's somewheres else," and laughed. "She's somewheres else, Sam Fury." Another laugh.

"Mr. Wirth, please—" I stopped, waited for his laughter to subside. "Mr. Wirth, if you could please just tell me where she is."

"I'll give you a clue," he said.

"A clue?"

I sighed yet again; talking with Frank Wirth had always been an unpredictable experience. "Okay, Mr. Wirth," I said, "what's the clue?"

He chuckled. "The clue is, Sam Fury—what do people call women who got habits?"

I shook my head. "I give up, Mr. Wirth. Why don't you tell me."

He hung up.

I called back immediately. He answered, "Sam's Bait Shop, head worm speaking," cackled, and hung up.

I dialed a third time, listened to the phone ring once, and again, then I hung up. *Sisters*, I thought. *Women with habits are called sisters*. Leslie was at her sister's house. I smiled. "Gotcha, Frank Wirth!" I whispered. I stopped smiling. I'd been to her sister's house only once, when Leslie and I had met each other in the cab going to Queens. "Dammit!" I whispered, stepped back into the phone booth, looked up the name "Wirth" in the phone book, and found only "Wirth, Orlando A., D.D.S." I didn't know much about Leslie's sister, but I knew that she wasn't a D.D.S. and that her name wasn't Orlando.

I went back to the parking garage, got the Malibu, drove to the Jackson Heights section of Queens. And cruised around, lost, for two hours.

At last, I pulled up to a curb and called to a thin middle-aged woman walking her cat on a leash, "I'm lost. Could you help me?"

She came over to the car, looked through the passenger window, first at me, then cautiously into the back seat as if someone might be hiding there, then looked back at me. "So what are you looking for, then?" she asked. She turned her head quickly: "Don't do that, Britches"—I couldn't see what

Britches was doing—then looked at me again. "Not too much damage there," she said. "What'd you say you were looking for?"

I answered, "I don't know. A street. Something like this one." The street I was on was quiet and tree-lined, with neat two-story houses nestled close together. "But there's a church on one end. Maybe it's a synagogue."

"Russian Orthodox," she cut in.

I shook my head. "No, I don't think so—"

"Yes, it is. Russian Orthodox. Bolosco Street." She nodded to her right. "Three blocks up, two blocks over." She turned to Britches. "Stop that now," she said, and I said, smiling cordially, "What's he doing?"

"Spraying," she said, and added, "Three blocks up and two blocks over. That's where Bolosco Street is."

"Over where?"

She waved her hand in the air. "Over there, of course. You can't miss it." And, tugging the reluctant Britches along, she made her way slowly, one painful step at a time, back to the sidewalk.

I leaned over in the seat. "I mean . . . Ma'am? Ma'am?" I called.

She looked back at me. "Yes?"

"I mean, right or left? Three blocks up and two blocks right, or two blocks left?"

"Right. Two blocks right." She seemed agitated. "What'd you think I meant?"

"I wasn't sure. Thanks," I said, and pulled away from the curb.

* * *

Bolosco Street looked as if it could very well be the street that the cabbie had taken Leslie to several months earlier. The houses were all neatly maintained two-story houses in various shades of brown, green, and beige, each with a narrow driveway and a well-manicured hedge or two. And there was indeed a Russian Orthodox church at one end.

I pulled over at the center of the block, craned my head around to look behind me, then turned back. There were a few people on the sidewalks. At what I guessed was its north end, and coming my way, a young woman was carrying a bag of groceries in each arm and having a hard time of it; near me, an older man and woman were walking close together, so their arms touched. Every now and then the man stopped walking and pointed skyward—at a bird, I supposed—and the woman with him looked where he pointed and smiled a pleasant, grateful smile. They passed me as I sat in the Malibu and I heard the old man say, "There, Emma, didn't I tell you?" And Emma said, "Yes, Robert. *You* were right. Of course you were right. I'm very happy."

Four or five houses ahead, a woman who, I told myself, could easily be Leslie was standing on a porch as if waiting for someone. I pulled the car up, stopped in front of the house, glanced at the woman, saw that it indeed was Leslie, and called, "Hi. Remember me?"

"Sam?" she called. "What are you doing here?"

She was dressed in a dark unbuttoned knee-length coat; beneath it, she wore a snug-fitting purple dress.

I shrugged. "I got lost, I guess. I was taking this car back to the guy I borrowed it from—" I stopped, shook my head. "No, that's not true."

"Of course it isn't."

"I was looking for you."

"Were you? Why?"

"To talk."

"About what?" She paused only a second, not long enough to give me a chance to answer her question. "Who told you I was here? My father?"

"Kind of," I answered. I got out of the car and started up the walk to the house.

"I wish you hadn't come here, Sam," she said as I approached. "I'm still pretty upset with you."

I was halfway up the walk. I stopped, shook my head. "I can't imagine why, Leslie. That's the truth. So I said something you disagreed with. I take it back, okay?"

"No, it's not okay, Sam. I'm sorry. I can forgive you for saying it, but not for the . . . the mind-set that made you say it. You're like a million other people who want to shuffle their parents off to some dreary *home* as soon as trouble starts—"

"Wait a minute," I cut in. "Do you want to know how I found out where you were?"

"You said my father told you."

"Well, yes, he did. But not in so many words, Leslie; he made a *game* out of it—"

"Okay, okay, so he made a game out of it?! So what? He's playful. That's what I love about him;

that's what I've *always* loved about him—he thinks like a kid. That's wonderful! More people should be that way. But you . . . *you* see it as senility or something."

I took a deep breath, went to the bottom of the porch steps, and looked pleadingly up at her. "Listen," I said, "I've had a pretty rough couple of days and I came here because I want to be with you, because I want us to be together. Can't we just let this thing about your father . . . lie fallow for a while?"

"Lie fallow? What are you talking about?"

I shook my head. "I don't know, Leslie. I'm tired, and I'm confused, and I *need* you, honey—"

"Don't call me honey. I'm sorry, Sam, but I have a date."

My mouth fell open. "You have a what?"

"A date," she repeated. She paused, looked sheepishly at me. "Well, actually," she added, "it's with my brother—"

"I didn't know you had a brother."

"It's the same old story, then, isn't it, Sam? There are *lots* of things you don't know about me."

I nodded. "Sure there are, Leslie, but—" I stopped. Something was fluttering heavily in the air above the house. I glanced up. I saw what I supposed at first was a gull hovering close to the roof edge, so most of its body was hidden. I looked back at Leslie. "As I was saying, Leslie—"

"No, Sam," she cut in. "I don't want to talk anymore just now. I'm sorry, but as I told you, I'm still upset with you—I've got a lot of thinking to do . . . Sam, are you listening to me?"

"Yeah, sure," I managed, and it was the truth. But I was also listening to the fluttering in the air. It was behind me now. I turned my head, looked.

I saw a woman above me. She was hovering just at arm's length, her loose red blouse and pants fluttering on the breeze, her arms outstretched, her head to one side so it rested on her shoulder, her eyes closed, and her lips parted just enough that her bright pink tongue was visible.

She was a young woman. Her skin was smooth and very white. She was barefooted; her toenails were painted black. As I watched, she fluttered around me so she was between Leslie and me. I heard Leslie say, "Sam? What's wrong?" I started backing away, toward the Malibu. The woman's eyes popped open. Her head straightened. The thin, light pink line of her lips spread so that more of her tongue was visible.

I continued backing toward the Malibu.

"Sam?" Leslie called. "What are you doing?"

I shook my head. "Go away," I pleaded. "Go away, please go away!"

"What's *wrong* with you?" Leslie called.

I continued backing toward the Malibu.

"I love you," hissed the woman fluttering in the air above me. "Love me, please love me!"

"Go away!" I whispered.

"Sam, for God's sake—"

"Go away, go away!" I screamed, and I batted at the woman in the air above me as if she were some huge insect.

"Sam, you're scaring me!" Leslie called.

"Get out of here!" I screamed. And I backed hard into the Malibu, with my rear end first, then with the center of my spine—so it hit the roof edge—then, as I rolled to the right, I hit the roof edge with my jaw.

NINETEEN

From behind and above me, from the woman hovering there, her loose blouse and pants fluttering on the breeze like sheets hung out to dry, I heard, "Love me, love me, love me!" and from Leslie, who had run down the walk to me, I heard, "Sam, for God's sake . . ."

I felt hands on my back. I looked. It was Leslie.

"Love me!" screamed the woman in the air.

"Leslie," I managed, my jaw alive with pain, "do you hear that?"

"Sam? Are you all right?" She pulled me around to face her, and chuckled a clearly false chuckle, one intended to put me at ease. "God but you're clumsy!"

"Love me, love me, love me!" screeched the woman in the air.

"Do you *hear* that, goddammit!"

I looked at Leslie. She looked down the street, called, "I'll be there in a moment, Orrin," and turned back to me. "Are you okay, Sam? Do you think you're hurt?"

"Leslie," I said, "do you *see* her?"

A man came up to Leslie; he put his hand on her arm and glanced at me. He was tall, in his late thirties, strong-looking, casually dressed. "What's the problem here, Leslie?"

"Orrin, this is my friend Sam Feary. Sam, my brother, Orrin Wirth."

"Hi," Orrin said, and stuck his hand out. "Our girl here has mentioned you before, Sam. It's good to meet you." He let his hand hover near my belly for a moment, then withdrew it.

Leslie went on, as if in explanation of my rudeness, "I'm afraid Sam has hurt himself."

"Love me, love me!" screeched the woman in the air.

"For God's sake!" I looked at Leslie, at Orrin, at the woman hovering in the air. "For God's sake, don't you hear that?!"

The woman in the air screeched, "Love me, love me, love me!"

Leslie shook her head; a little frown appeared on her mouth. Orrin said, putting his hand on my wrist as if to steady me, "Are you drunk, Sam? Have you had a little too much to drink?"

Leslie said, "No, Orrin. I don't think Sam's drunk."

"Oh, Good Lord!" I whispered, and groped behind me for the car door handle, found it, pulled the door open, and scurried into the car, my eyes on the woman in red all the while.

Orrin said, "He shouldn't be driving if he's drunk."

"For God's sake, he's *not* drunk!" Leslie snapped. "He's hurt!"

"Love me, love me, love me!" screeched the woman fluttering in the air.

I closed the door, started the car, put it in gear, and floored the accelerator. In the moment before the car shot away from the curb, I glanced at Leslie. She still wore that little frown. She looked disappointed. "I'll—" she began, but the sound of the car's rear wheels screaming on the pavement drowned her out.

I was halfway down the block moments later.

I looked into the rearview mirror. I saw the woman in red at the back window; she was mouthing the words "Love me, love me, love me!" over and over again.

At the Queens Tunnel she drifted off into the gathering dusk and was gone.

I stayed in the apartment for the next three days. I didn't answer the phone, though it rang repeatedly. I didn't go near the bedroom. I left the curtains drawn on all the windows, and the doors locked, most of the lights on. I left the television on, too, and the volume turned up, though, at the end of the second day, after listening to the mindless, feel-good jabber of game show hosts, smarmy soap operas, and commercials that screamed *ad nauseam* about the "movers and shakers" and their coffee habit, I got to feeling awfully punk and surly, so I turned the TV down until it was just a soft, undulating, high-pitched hum, like a swarm of bees.

Abner's words came back to me a hundred times: *This . . . disease is transient. It comes and goes. One day you've got it, the next day it's gone. Sort of like herpes.*

I felt like an eight-year-old who's convinced there are trolls living under his bed. If he lets any fingers or toes dangle over the side of the bed, then he'll be minus those fingers and toes. The bed is his sanctuary as long as he stays centered on it.

Two giggling girls in pink taffeta lived in the wall in *my* bedroom. But the rest of the apartment was my sanctuary. If I left it, if I even opened the curtains, I'd lose something far more important than my fingers and toes. I'd lose my sanity.

But after three days of isolation, after a dozen peanut butter and jelly sandwiches and what was left of a box of stale Hi Ho crackers, after too much artificial light and not enough silence, even sanity can lose its appeal.

So when the phone rang for what could easily have been the hundredth time, I answered it.

It was Abner, and he was pissed. "Christ, Sam, when are you going to bring my damned car back? I had to walk a mile and a half just to buy a quart of milk and some cat food. I *need* my car, Sam."

I ignored him. "Abner," I said, "how do you cope?"

"Cope?"

"With this . . . thing, with this disease you've given me. How in the hell do you *live* with it?"

"What does that have to do with my car, Sam? I wouldn't borrow *your* car and forget to return it."

I took a deep breath to help me hold my temper. "I'll bring your damned car back. Just, please, for God's sake, tell me how you live with this thing, tell me how you drag yourself from moment to moment and from day to day? It's like walking in a minefield, Abner. It's like being blind and in a room that's filled with tiny bottles of nitroglycerin."

He chuckled. "It really is, isn't it? I mean, that's *exactly* the way it is."

I took another deep breath, felt my anger building. I lowered the receiver, cursed, raised the receiver. I said tightly, "I'll make a deal with you, Abner. You tell me how you live with it and I promise I won't come over there and break your head."

He said nothing.

"Did you hear what I said, Abner? Are you listening to me?"

"I'm listening, yes." His tone had changed; it had become deadly serious. "You bet I'm listening. And don't you think, Sam—" I heard *him* breathe deeply, as if to hold his temper. "Don't you think that what you're asking me is precisely what I wanted to ask that woman two years ago? The one I ran into on the Amtrak out of Bangor. How in the hell, how in God's name do you *cope*? Don't you think I wanted to find her and ask her that? Don't you think I wanted to beat the answer out of her if I had to? But there is no answer, Sam. I'm sorry, there is no answer. You cope with it the same way . . . the same way a quadriplegic copes with having no arms or legs. You accept it; you live with it. Or you simply give up."

I said nothing for a moment; then, "And which have you chosen, Abner?"

He answered, "I don't know. I live in my memory. I enjoy the present. I enjoy what is. I don't know *what* I've done, Sam. But understand this, please: *You* found *me*. I didn't find you. You sought me out. And I warned you. I warned you more than once. So whatever kind of shit you're in is not my fault. I have a world of problems all my own." He paused. "Now, are you going to bring my car back? I'm stuck here without it."

"Yes," I answered. "Soon." I paused, went on, "Abner? Is it you that's been calling here so much in the last couple of days?"

"I called two or three times, that's all, Sam. I didn't want to sound impatient. Now I don't care *how* I sound because I'm *stuck* here, and I don't like it at all—"

"For God's sake, Abner, I'll bring the damned car back. It's a piece of crap, anyway."

"Good. And make sure it's got a full tank of gas in it, please."

"Sure. A full tank," I said, and hung up.

A half hour later, the phone rang again. I answered it at once.

"Hi," I heard.

It was Leslie.

"Hi," I said. "I'm sorry I haven't been answering the phone, I—"

"I was going to give up on you after tonight. I was going to stop calling."

"I'm glad I answered, then, Leslie. I'm—"

She cut in, "Can we get together for dinner, Sam? There's an Italian place near here, on West 60th."

"Yes," I said, "I remember the place; we went there our second time out."

"No. That's on West 81st, Sam. This one's called Isadore's, and we've never been there." She paused.

"Leslie," I said, "is something wrong?"

"No," she answered. "Not really. I'd just like it very much if we could talk." A pause. "I've been thinking about a lot of things."

"Sounds ominous," I said.

"No. It isn't. Probably just the opposite—at least I hope so." She chuckled nervously. "So what do you say—Isadore's at seven?"

I wasn't about to be put off for two hours. "If it isn't ominous, Leslie, if it's just the opposite, what is it?"

"I'd rather we discussed it—"

"Is it a yes?

Nothing.

"Leslie? Is it?"

"It is," she said. "At least I think it is. But we've still got to talk."

"Sure," I said. "Sure we'll talk. Isadore's, seven o'clock. I'll be there with bells on."

Things had begun to take a very definite turn for the better.

I showered, I shaved, I put on a gray herringbone

tweed jacket, a pair of dark dress pants that I hadn't worn in years, ever since my cousin's wedding, and I whispered to myself again and again, "Jesus, things *are* getting better, things are really getting better."

Until it got to be six o'clock, time to leave the apartment and head for Isadore's, and I found that I could barely get myself close enough to the front door to touch it. And when I did touch it, when I reached out tentatively and turned the knob, it was like touching a coiled snake.

That's when I realized that I was still scared shitless. That the eight-year-old inside me had taken over and *he* was scared of the girls in pink taffeta who lived in the walls, scared of the woman in red who fluttered in the air, scared of the dead who pulled small boys flying Star Wars kites into the sand forever.

And that eight-year-old boy inside me wasn't about to leave the apartment. His sanctuary. He was stuck. And there was nothing at all that I could do about it.

After a good quarter of an hour, I backed away from the door and sat in a wooden rocking chair.

At eight, I heard the elevator doors open. I heard someone walk down the short hallway to my door. Then hesitate. And knock sharply.

I stayed quiet.

"Sam?" It was Leslie's voice.

I said nothing.

"Sam? Are you in there? Are you okay?"

My mouth opened. Closed. I clasped my hands, leaned forward in the chair, rocked slowly.

"Hey, we had a date, remember?"

I opened my mouth again. It stayed open. But still I said nothing.

"Sam? Are you okay? Are you in there?"

I made a noise that was supposed to have been *Yes. I'm in here. I'm okay,* but it came out only as a low, fear-ridden grunt.

Another knock. Sharper, more urgent. "Dammit, Sam—do you want me to get someone for you? Do you need help?"

"No," I managed.

"*I* think you do."

"Go away. Please." I was surprised that I was able to speak again. I pushed myself out of the chair, approached the door, got to within a couple feet of it. "Leslie," I called, "I'm okay. Maybe . . . maybe you could write me a note or something and slip it under the door. How does that sound? And tomorrow we could get together, we could talk—"

"It sounds stupid, Sam."

I smiled quickly, nervously. "Sure it does, sure it sounds stupid, but . . . but I have to be sure that you are who you say you are."

I heard faintly, as if she were talking to herself, "Good Lord, what is *wrong* here?"

"Nothing, really," I said, and moved closer to the door, reached out, put my hand on the knob, recoiled, put my hand on it again. "I'm just a little . . . nervous, very nervous, in fact—"

"Open the door, goddammit."

"Sure," I said. I turned the knob, hesitated, pulled on the door; it stopped against the chain lock. I closed it, released the chain, opened the door again.

She shook her head slowly, a small grin on her mouth, as if she were more amused than annoyed.

"Hi," I said. "I'm sorry."

She was dressed nicely, in a loose beige blouse and long earth-colored skirt; she had a gray tweed jacket thrown over her arm. It was the same outfit she'd worn when we first met. "Forget Isadore's," she said. "I guess McDonald's will have to suffice."

I smiled nervously. "No, we can do better than that." I opened the door wider, motioned toward the inside of the apartment. "Come in. Please."

She smiled back fetchingly, nodded, came in, and stopped just inside, with her back to me.

I suggested, my voice creaking and tentative, "We can eat here. I have some . . . I can send out for something from the deli on the corner."

The phone rang. I snapped my gaze toward it. She stayed still.

"That sounds fine," she said.

The phone rang again; I decided to ignore it. I closed the door.

"Let me have your jacket," I said.

She turned a little, handed me the jacket. The phone rang again. "Are you going to answer that, Sam?"

I shook my head. "No. It's a wrong number." I put her jacket in a closet near the door. Again the phone rang.

"Wrong number? How do you know it's a wrong number?" She stepped into the living room and nodded at the rocking chair I'd been sitting in. "That's very nice, Sam. Antique?"

"No. No, it came with the"—the phone rang again—"the apartment. You've seen it before. I doubt that it's an antique."

She sat, rocked a little, stood. She looked agitated. The phone continued to ring. "Do me a favor and answer that, Sam. I hate the sound of a phone ringing. It gets my adrenaline going, you know? A ringing phone is something that *begs* to be answered."

"Yes"—it rang again—"I know. But that's a wrong number." I gestured at the phone. "I know it's a wrong number because"—another ring—"he's been calling every hour on the hour"—another ring—"for the past week."

She looked confused. She sat in the rocking chair again, put her head back, started rocking. "Maybe it's someone giving money away, Sam. 'Dialing for Dollars,' or something." She chuckled. "Answer it and see. Maybe you're an instant millionaire." Her chuckle broadened, grew louder, stopped abruptly.

The phone continued to ring.

She went on, "Maybe a maiden aunt left you her entire estate—three cats and a philodendron." A chuckle; the phone rang again. "Maybe it's the phone company checking to make sure that *you're* who you say you are, Sam." A chuckle. Again the phone rang. "*Are* you who you say you are?" She continued to rock, slowly, steadily, her head back, hands on the arm of the rocking chair.

"It's a wrong number, just a wrong number," I said.

"Yes, Sam, I'm sure it is. But my adrenaline really is pumping now. It's making me lightheaded."

The phone rang, again, and again, and again. "And I'm just *dying* to find out if you've won something on 'Dialing for Dollars.' You could be a celebrity, Sam." She chuckled. "An instant celebrity, an instant thousand-dollar winner." Another chuckle; the phone continued to ring; she continued to rock steadily, as if in time with her heartbeat. "Answer the phone, Sam. Please answer the phone. I'm going to faint if you don't answer the fucking phone."

"Who are you?" I said.

She said nothing. She continued to rock.

I was standing five feet in front of her; the phone, still ringing, was just to my right. I reached out, picked it up, snapped, "Hello!"

"Sam?" I heard. "It's me, Leslie. What happened, Sam?"

The woman in the rocking chair started to change. It was a subtle change at first, and slow, like milk in its first stages of going sour.

But then, as quick as ice breaking, her chuckle became a coarse and brittle laugh. It ended in midnote.

Leslie said, "Sam? What's wrong? Sam? Are you there?"

The woman in the chair stiffened up. Her hands on the arms of the chair grew rigid and clawlike. Her mouth stuck open an inch; her eyes became round and white and dull, like the eyes of a puppet.

On the phone, Leslie demanded, "Answer me, Sam!"

Then, all at once, the room was bathed in the smell of rotten wood, like the smell of a damp cellar that's been closed for too long, and I put my hand to my mouth and nose and felt my stomach turn over.

The woman oozed between the slats on the back of the rocking chair like Jell-O.

I dropped the phone and backed away, toward the door. I heard the soft *plop, plop* of the woman's body as piece by soft piece it oozed between the slats of the rocking chair and hit the rug.

The smell of rotten wood grew overpowering.

I backed into the door, turned, released the chain lock, and ran from the apartment.

TWENTY

Abner said, "She thinks she's being funny, Sam. She thinks she's entertaining you. She's a comedian." I'd followed him into his kitchen and was sitting at the table. He was searching in his cupboards—which were quite well stocked, as if in anticipation of a hurricane—for something sweet to have with his coffee. "Kind of a habit I got into," he explained. "Would you like some coffee, Sam?"

"No, I don't want any coffee! What the hell are you talking about—'she's a comedian'? What is that supposed to mean, Abner? For God's sake, talk to me."

He rummaged in another cupboard, he glanced around at me and smiled a little. When he smiles, his deep-set eyes seem to go even deeper because his cheeks push up. He said, "You're really agitated aren't you, Sam?"

I shook my head in disbelief. "You drag me into *hell* with you, and you have the balls to ask if I'm agitated about it!"

He began rummaging in his cupboard again. "No. It's not hell. I don't think there is a hell. I could be wrong, of course." He glanced around, smiled playfully, added, "I thought I was wrong once, but I was mistaken."

"Good Lord," I whispered. "You were pulling that one in high school, Abner."

He looked confused. "Was I? I don't remember."

"Just tell me what you know about this woman."

He found a box of brownie mix in the cupboard, studied it a moment, put it back. He continued rummaging. "I don't know anything about her. I'm only guessing. But I'd guess she's the same one who was on the ferry with you—"

"She couldn't be."

He looked at me, surprised. "Why not?"

"Because they simply were not the same woman. One looked like Leslie, I told you that—she looked exactly like Leslie."

He found a box of Jell-O, studied it, put it back. "If she could look like Leslie, she could look like anyone. Hell, she could look like me." Another smile, broad and teasing.

"Don't make me nervous, Abner."

"I don't want to make you nervous, Sam. I just want to"—his eyes got very wide and round—"open your eyes." He laughed. "It's the only way to cope. It's the only way to go on . . . existing. By keeping your eyes open, by accepting nothing for what it seems to be, unless you *know* in here''—he thumped his chest—''that it's what it seems to be. And you'll find there's damned precious little that you *know* in here.'' Again he thumped his chest. ''She was a comedian, Sam. The world's full of comedians, living and dead, it doesn't matter much, except when they're dead the . . . special effects''—he grinned—''get a heck of a lot more interesting.'' A short pause. ''I remember going into this bar on East 79th Street—''

''And what if I don't want to cope,'' I cut in. ''What if I don't want to spend the rest of my life dodging shadows—''

''Oh, shit, Sam, you won't spend the rest of your life *dodging shadows*. This thing you've got is *temporary*, remember?! Temporary. That's what Madeline says, and whatever else can be said about Madeline, she does know her stuff.'' A pause; I started to ask who the hell Madeline was, because it wasn't the first time he'd mentioned her, of course, but he cut in, ''And Christ, they aren't *shadows*, Sam. They're a hell of a lot more substantial than that.''

''So,'' I suggested, ''what if I don't want to spend the rest of my life dodging *spooks*, then?'' I jumped to my feet, felt my pulse racing in my ears. I leaned over, suddenly dizzy, put my hands on the table. Abner came over, put a hand on my arm. ''Are you all right, Sam?''

I shook my head. ''And what if I don't want to cope? What if I want *out*? What if I want to see only what everyone else sees?'' I looked into his eyes. ''What then, Abner?''

He stepped back. He had a box of pudding mix in his hand; he put it on the table, tapped it with his forefinger, and shook his head slowly. "I've asked myself the same question a million times, Sam." He continued tapping on the box. "I don't think I ever really meant it. I mean, I've got kind of a special interest in what goes on in . . . that world, don't I? I'm in love, and that helps me to cope."

"Just answer my question, Abner. Later, if you want to talk to me about your love life, then we'll talk about your love life, but for now, just answer my question."

He picked up the box of pudding and took it back to the cupboard where he'd found it. He said, his back turned, "I've told you before, Sam. You see what you see because you want to see it. In a way, I guess you invite it. As I do. Maybe you're not aware of it. Maybe you'll deny it seven ways to Sunday. But that woman came into your house"—he glanced around at me—"because you wanted her to come in. It's the same reason those girls came into your bedroom."

"Horseshit! Why in the hell would I want two giggling girls in my bedroom in the middle of the night?"

He laughed shortly. "That's not for me to say, my friend. I guess it depends on how well you know yourself, doesn't it?"

I didn't answer him. I was still angry, my pulse was still racing in my ears, but I wasn't sure why I was angry, or at whom. I went to the back door. The shade was down. I lifted it and stared out at the hulking, dark shapes of the dunes. I could faintly hear the ocean; the sound was comforting. "And when I stop *wanting* to see?" I said. "What happens then?"

Abner answered immediately, "Like I told you, Sam, this *talent* you've got is temporary. I don't know when it will go away. Soon, I hope. Then your life will return to normal, and you'll see only what everyone else sees. That's what Madeline tells me."

The sound of the ocean grew steadily and slowly louder, as if a wind were building.

Abner said, "What's that noise, Sam?"

"The ocean," I answered.

He closed the cupboard door softly, came over to me by the back door. "Wind's picking up, huh?"

"Yeah," I said, "the wind's picking up."

"Maybe you should go now, Sam. I really think you should go." I looked quizzically at him. He went on, "You won't like it here in a storm. This is not a pleasant place to be in a storm."

"I wasn't aware that it was ever pleasant here, Abner."

He looked hurt. He took the shade I was holding, drew it up, leaned over, peered out. "It's going to be bad," he whispered. Then he straightened and looked earnestly at me. "I mean it, Sam. There's no reason for you to be here, so why don't you go? You can take my car again. Just please bring it back tomorrow, okay?"

Behind heavy white curtains, the windows to the left and right of the door began whining under the gathering wind. Abner drew the shade closed; he looked suddenly very agitated. He went to the sink and stood at it with his back to me, his hands gripping the sink hard, arms straight and stiff. Then he turned, got a backward grip on the sink, so his arms were still straight and stiff, and smiled a flat, false smile. "Please leave, Sam." His voice was tense and high-pitched. "Remember how I warned you before, about coming here?"

"Sure," I said.

"Well, I'm warning you again. This is not a pleasant place to be in a storm. It's very unpleasant, in fact. And I really . . ." He paused; his head fell forward, as if he were dizzy. He looked up. "For heaven's sake, get *out* of here, Sam! Get out of here, please!"

"No," I said.

The windows whined louder; the heavy curtains moved slightly. I said, "Where would I go? I can't go back to my apartment; I sure as hell can't go back there. Besides, like you told me before—you need a friend here." I shrugged. "So I'll stay."

He glanced nervously at the windows, then at me. "I've changed my mind, Sam. I don't need anyone here. Really. That's the truth. I want you to go—I'm telling you to go."

The house shook. The whining at the windows became constant and loud. "No," I said. "I like ocean storms; I've always liked ocean storms."

He was still at the sink, still had his hands on it. He closed his eyes, raised his head a little, and screamed at me, "You can't stay here, Sam—my God, you can't stay here!"

The whining at the windows grew erratic. Abner opened his eyes and looked about as if confused. The whining stopped, started, stopped. The wind died. A long sigh came from him. "Thank God," he said.

After we have been apart for a few days, Leslie and I approach each other with incredulity and caution. I'm not sure why. I said to her once, "It's as if we have to draw the curtains aside." She nodded. She agreed. "It's as if," I wrote to her, "we can't really believe what we have and so we sniff around it for a while to be sure it's real. And when we find out that it is, we touch and grin and hug in the way that we do," which means urgently, with fun and pleasure.

It's like meeting someone at an airport. Airports are full of good feeling—they are places where people take their masks off, however briefly, and let their love come out.

So it's as if we are always meeting each other at airports, always waiting for the arrival of the people we were the last time we were together.

TWENTY-ONE

In the real world—in what passes for the real world, at any rate—things are almost always what they seem to be. A mailman coming down the street with a bag under his arm is almost always just a man delivering mail. A window washer poised thirty stories up on a tether is only a window washer. A man wearing a dark suit and carrying a cane who tells us where we should and should not park the car is usually just someone who can't mind his own business. And a storm that comes up, makes some brief noise, and dies is usually just a fit of the weather.

That's very close to the way things are in the world that Abner drew me into. Most of the time, things are precisely what they seem to be. It is a world of sun, and sky, and earth, of streetlamps, telephone poles, garbage trucks, Dear John letters, and mistletoe. It's a world where people fall in and out of love, where people lie to each other and whisper to each other and shout at each other. A world of B-1 bombers and political parties, personal computers, and hayrides. A world where pets are buried, and trees fall, and spring slides into summer. But it is also a world whose rules can change from one moment to the next, a world where the mailman may evaporate or the mistletoe slither off across the ceiling, a world where the same tree may fall again and again and again.

I stayed at the beach house that night, despite Abner's halfhearted objections. He gave me a small square room down a short hallway from the kitchen. It faced the ocean, and was sparsely furnished—a black wrought-iron twin bed, a battered oval nightstand, a tarnished brass wall lamp, a small wood-framed picture above the bed. The room was painted a bright yellow. Abner said, "It's a pretty restful color with the light off, Sam. And you can hear the ocean. If you get to sleep right away, you should be all right." He paused. "Do you want anything?"

I sat on the bed. Its dull blue comforter had a slightly damp feel; the mattress beneath was soft and lumpy, as if it had seen a good many years of use. I looked up at Abner. He was standing near the door; he was obviously in a hurry to leave. "Anything?" I asked.

He shrugged. "Sure. To help you sleep. You know, sleeping pills. Do you want any?"

I shook my head, started to say *No, thanks*. He interrupted, "I'd recommend it, Sam. And I'd recommend something strong, too. Something that'll knock you out good."

Again I shook my head. I patted the bed. "This feels comfortable enough," I lied.

He smiled. "You think you're pretty tough, don't you, Sam?"

"No. I don't." It was the truth. "But I can sleep without help. I did it in Nam, I can do it here."

He shrugged again. "Whatever you say." He went to the door. "I'll see you in the morning."

"Sure," I said.

He left. The door stayed open.

His footsteps faded down the hall. I leaned back so I was supporting my weight on my elbows, put my feet up, and turned off the light over the bed.

"Abner?" I heard. The sound seemed to come from the other end of the hallway he had just gone down. "Abner?" It was a woman's voice, and there was a strong whisper of urgency in it.

I got up, went to the door, and looked to the right, toward the kitchen.

"Abner?" I heard again. I saw his shadow cast obliquely across the stove and sink, and I guessed that he was near the door that led to the beach.

"Abner?" I heard again.

His shadow grew fatter.

"Abner?"

He appeared. He was standing sideways to me, facing the kitchen wall. He had his hands raised to waist level, as if he were preparing to hug someone, and a little smile was on his lips—a smile, I guessed, of thanks, and disbelief.

He said, hardly above a whisper, "Phyllis?" and took a step closer to the wall, raised his hands higher. "Phyllis?" he said again.

An arm appeared from that wall—first the hand, then the wrist, the forearm. The hand clawed desperately in the air and Abner grabbed it and held tight to it. Then he tugged hard, as if he were fishing and pulling an eel in, and the opposite shoulder appeared, then the arm, the hand, which he also grabbed and tugged on, murmuring, "Phyllis, Phyllis!" all the while.

A woman's naked torso came out of the wall. Then her legs, her feet.

The head was last. It came out of the wall at a hard backward angle, as if something inside the wall were holding the long dark hair and it was an awful struggle for her to free it.

I heard a long, low groan that was clearly a mixture of great pain and pleasure. I didn't know whom it had come from. It could have come from them both.

They embraced. It was a hard and wonderfully close thing, the kind of embrace that is so much more than two bodies merely touching. The kind of embrace that is the happy mingling of two souls.

"Oh, my God, Phyllis, Phyllis!" Abner whispered.

"Abner, my love!" she murmured into his shoulder.

There was silence then. They continued embracing.

She had her face turned my way; her eyes were closed. She opened them, leveled her gaze on me. She mouthed the word "Please" at me. Then, "Leave us alone."

And I backed quietly into the bedroom and closed the door gently behind me.

She was a tall black woman, nearly as tall as Abner. Her eyes were large, her face an exquisite oval, and her body perfect.

I slept very little that night. I lay on my back on that soft and lumpy bed, with the light off, and I let the hours slide by. Now and again, a sound of pleasure drifted down the hall to me from the kitchen. Once, toward the end of the night, I said, "I'm happy for you, Abner," then I turned over and shivered at what I had witnessed.

When the beginnings of daylight were filtering through the window, I was awakened by a scream. I pushed myself up on my elbows. "Abner?" I whispered.

"No!" I heard.

"Abner?" I said aloud.

Nothing.

"Abner?" I called.

He appeared in the doorway. His face was red and puffy, as if from weeping. "Go back to sleep," he said, voice trembling. "Everything's all right."

"Are you sure, buddy? I heard a scream."

He nodded. "Yes," he said. "I'm sorry if I woke you."

"You're sorry you woke me? Don't be dumb. Just convince me you're all right so I can go back to sleep."

He nodded. "I'm all right, Sam." And he disappeared down the hallway.

TWENTY-TWO

I slept through the morning and into the afternoon. The soft and lumpy mattress had proved to be comfortable enough after nearly three days without sleep, and it was at about one in the afternoon that Abner woke me.

He said, standing over me while I struggled out of sleep, "She was here, Sam. Phyllis was here."

I swung my feet to the floor, put my elbows on my knees and my head down. I felt a headache starting. "Yes," I whispered. "I know. I saw her."

He sat on the bed and glanced at me. Out of the corner of my eye, I guessed that he was grinning. He looked away. "What do you think?" he asked, his voice low, as if he were embarrassed. He looked back and repeated, his voice louder, "What do you think?"

"Think of what?"

"Of her. Of Phyllis." He chuckled self-consciously. "Isn't she something?"

"Abner, I'm not awake yet."

"I've never loved anyone the way I love her. I know how corny that sounds—"

"My God, Abner." I looked him squarely in the eye. "The woman is dead! Phyllis is *dead*!"

He gripped my knee hard. "Sam, we're *all* dead in one way or another. If we're not physically dead, if our blood still pumps and our sweat still flows, if we can scarf down a Big Mac, is that supposed to mean that we're *alive*? Shouldn't *alive* mean something else, something deeper and more spiritual?" His grip on my knee strengthened. He nodded at it. "You can feel that, right?"

I sighed. "Abner, I'm sorry, but this is bullshit! If that hurts you—" I shook my head. "If it hurts you, then I'm sorry." My headache was getting worse by the second.

He smiled a little. "No," he said, "it doesn't hurt me, because I know you're wrong." He nodded again at his hand gripping my knee. "You're probably convinced, like everyone else, that because you can feel that, because, if I squeezed hard enough, you'd feel *pain*, that that means you're *alive*." His grip loosened. "*Phyllis* feels pain. She feels it every second of the day. You might say that every moment for her here, in this house, she's *alive* with pain." His smile broadened as if he had suddenly stumbled upon some great truth.

I glanced at him. "Do you remember Susan Burdorf, Abner? She went to high school with us, in Bangor."

He clasped his hands in front of his knees, lowered his head. "You simply can't understand how I feel, can you, Sam? You refuse—"

I cut in, "Do you remember you had the hots for her? Do you remember you used to write her this really awful love poetry? *I* remember, because you were just about impossible to be around that entire school year; you had your damned tongue hanging out all the time, and a hard-on the size of a baseball bat."

He stood abruptly, whirled around, and said tightly, his temper on a very short fuse, "That wasn't love, goddammit! That was biology! Don't try to cheapen what Phyllis and I have, Sam, because we have something very, very special—"

I looked up at him and let out a long, weary sigh. "I need some aspirin. I feel like shit."

"You think this relationship Phyllis and I have is . . . perverse, don't you, Sam? Admit it."

I looked down at the floor. I whispered, half to myself, "Well, for God's sake, it's not *going* anywhere, is it?"

He laughed quickly, mockingly. I looked at him, surprised. He shook his head: "It doesn't have to *go* anywhere, Sam. Why the hell do relationships have to *go* anywhere? That's a trap. That's a stupid, lousy trap. A relationship *is*; it's like ice cream—you have it, you enjoy it, but it doesn't have to *go* anywhere."

I stood again, fought back the expected wave of dizziness and nausea and pushed past Abner to the doorway. I stopped there, supported myself with my hands on either side of the door frame and my back to Abner. "Just tell me where the damned aspirin is, would you?"

"Sam, I love her. I love her more than I thought I could love any woman."

"Yeah. I'm happy for you," I said. "Invite me to the wedding," and I stumbled down the short hallway to the kitchen.

We had a picnic behind the beach house that day. It was a pretty ludicrous affair. Abner was dressed—for effect, he said—in gray knee-length shorts, ankle-high sneakers, a pink long-sleeved shirt, and a ragged red plaid sports coat. He had gathered up some driftwood and started a little fire with clumps of newspaper. We used the grating from a rusted hibachi we found on the beach to cook chicken hot dogs and reheat leftover artichokes in a pan of water. He'd also driven to a deli several miles away and bought a six-pack of Michelob.

We ate seated cross-legged, facing each other on the sand halfway between the house and the ocean. My headache from an hour before was still lingering around the back edges of my brain, but as I ate, the food—awful as it was—eventually overcame what was left of it.

"That little kid's down there, right, Abner?" I said through a mouthful of chicken hot dog. I nodded toward the sand and took a long swig of the Michelob. "That little kid flying the kite?"

Abner was busy with an artichoke. He stuck a leaf into his mouth, scraped the meat off, looked satisfied. "I try not to think about it," he said.

The day was on the uncomfortable side of cool. I was wearing the dress pants and the tweed sports jacket, but a brisk wind was making me shiver. I took another swig of the beer; Abner hadn't put it in the refrigerator, so it was warm. "What do you mean, you don't think about it?" I drained the bottle, stuck it neck-first into the sand beside me, gobbled down half the hot dog, put some Gulden's Spicy Brown Mustard on the rest of it, gobbled that down, then got another bottle of beer. "You *have* to think about it. He was someone's little boy. I'm surprised" —another swig of beer; I realized I was trying to get drunk—"I'm surprised his mother hasn't come looking for him." I eyed Abner suspiciously. "She hasn't, has she?"

He shook his head while he gnawed at another artichoke leaf. "No. No one's come looking."

I nodded at what was left of the six-pack of Michelob in the sand between us. "Aren't you going to have a beer, Abner?"

"Don't drink," he said, and worked at another artichoke leaf. "You know, Sam, there are a lot of injustices in this world. What happened to that little boy is an injustice, for instance—an obscene injustice. But sometimes, justice does get done. It really does. If we just . . . help it along a little." He smiled secretively.

I said, "If you're trying to tell me something, Abner, why don't you just spit it out."

He shrugged. "I don't know," he said, and his tone became casual, that secretive smile reappeared. "Take murder, for instance." Another shrug; he was trying very hard now to look casual. "I don't mean the murder that's done on the spur of the moment, out of passion—something like that is really kind of an accident of emotion, don't you think? And we're all capable of it. I mean the other kind of murder. The one that's done by a murderous *soul*. Do you have any idea what I'm talking about, Sam?"

"I'm not sure," I said.

"Of course you understand. You were in Viet Nam; you probably saw lots of people who got a kick out of murdering other people."

I shook my head. "Not 'lots' of people, Abner. Some. A few. They usually got theirs in the end, though."

His smile broadened. "Yes, I'm sure they did." He took another bite of artichoke leaf, murmured, "This is very good, don't you think?" paused and continued, "Phyllis was murdered, Sam. I'm sure I've told you that."

"No," I said. "You haven't."

He nodded, his mouth set in a grimace. "Yes. She was murdered. She got beaten up and she died." He scraped some more of the artichoke leaf into his mouth. "Our friend Art DeGraff did it, Sam."

"Good Lord."

"No," Abner said, "not so good to let something like that happen."

Halfway through the picnic, Abner said, "I thought you were dead. I thought you got killed in Viet Nam."

"Yes," I said, "you told me that."

"Did I?" He shrugged. "Sorry, I guess it gets annoying to be told repeatedly that you were . . . presumed dead." Another pause. He added, pointing dramatically at the sky, " 'The reports of my death have been greatly exaggerated.' "

I took another swig of the warm beer, grimaced, and asked, "How do you live, Abner?"

"How do I live?" Again he looked confused.

"How do you get money to pay for your food, your heat, your electricity, et cetera, et cetera?"

He shrugged. "I've got some money." He dug with his spoon at the spikes of his artichoke heart.

"From where?" I asked.

He shrugged again, popped the artichoke heart into his mouth, chewed it with obvious delight for a few moments, swallowed. "From that book I told you about. The one I was going to do on Manhattan. The book of photographs."

"They paid you for that? I thought they canceled it."

"They did." A pause. "But they paid me anyway. The full amount of the contract, too. I guess they felt guilty."

"You're lying, aren't you, Abner?"

He looked offended. "I don't lie. I got paid for it. The full amount."

"And you're still living on what they paid you? Why do I find that hard to believe?"

He took a handful of sand and sprinkled it in a narrow stream on the fire. "You find it hard to believe, Sam, because not only do you think I'm lying, you think my whole life here, at this house, is a lie. Isn't that so?''

I chugged half the bottle of Michelob. "Of course that's what I think, Abner." I was beginning to feel giddy.

He shook his head quickly. "But it isn't a lie. I have a purpose here. I'm . . . taking care of someone. Someone who's got a very large debt to pay." He grinned a flat and self-satisfied grin that had a trace of secret and delicious guilt in it.

"Who?" I asked.

"Who?"

"Who are you taking care of here? I want a name."

He looked confused. "I can't give you a name. That would be foolish—"

I held my hand up; he stopped talking. "Listen, Abner, are you talking about another one of these people who live in the walls? Is that what you're talking about?"

He nodded. "Yes. Kind of."

"Oh." I smiled. "I'm getting drunk, Abner."

"Good for you, Sam." He smiled back. "I may be leaving here before long."

"To where?"

"It depends," he answered, "on . . . a number of things. What goes right, I guess. And what doesn't. I can't tell you where I'm going, exactly. I don't want you coming after me." A pause. "There's this man, Sam. His name's Whelan—I shouldn't be telling you any of this. My God, I've passed enough crap along to you as it is."

"Agreed," I said. "Agreed, agreed." I took a long pull of the Michelob.

"But I read somewhere once, Sam, that you live longer if you share what's troubling you. It takes a load off your heart, I guess. And anyway, this man, this guy Whelan is after me. He's a cop—well, he *was* a cop, and I guess he's trying to pin something on me; I can't tell you what. I want to, I do want to. But I really don't know you very well, do I? Actually, how well can you know *any*one?

"Good question," I said, and burped. I realized that I was enjoying myself despite the cold breeze and the awful chicken hot dogs. "Is it Al? Is it that woman I saw the other day?"

"Is it Al what, Sam?"

"Is she the one you say you're taking care of here?" I was slurring my words. "Have you—" I giggled. "Have you got her . . . stashed in a wall somewhere with all the other spooks?" I giggled again.

"Oh," he said. "We're back on that subject, are we?" He shook his head. Let's drop it, okay, Sam? I shouldn't have brought it up."

I took another swig of Michelob. I nodded. "Sure we can drop it, pal. But only because I'm getting drunk."

"Good for you," he said.

"Good for me," I said.

He stood abruptly, turned away so he was facing the ocean, and put his hands in the pockets of his red plaid sports jacket. A gull flew over, squawked several times, then flew off. "Al never lived here, anyway, Sam. She stayed here a couple of days during . . ." The wind carried his words away.

"I can't hear you, Abner."

He turned his head, looked at me. "I said she stayed here a couple of days. During her transition."

"Transition? What's that?"

He smiled and turned away again.

"Abner!" I shouted. "What are you talking about?"

"Have another beer," he shouted back. He looked around at me, nodded at what was left of the six-pack, said again, his voice lower in volume, "Have another beer, Sam. Get drunk."

"Sure," I said.

TWENTY-THREE

When I got back to the apartment, I was still wearing the herringbone tweed sports jacket and dress pants I'd put on to meet Leslie at Isadore's two days earlier. They were a mess. The coat smelled of sweat underlaid by the strong odor of damp wood that permeated the beach house; the pants had a small, ragged rip in the knee, I had no idea why, and a big mustard stain on the breast pocket.

Minutes after I got back, the phone rang. I screwed up some courage and answered it. It was Leslie. "Sam," she said, and I could tell that she was trying hard to control her temper, "what the hell is going on?"

"Hi, Leslie. Listen, I'm sorry about missing you the other night—"

"You've got exactly one minute to explain yourself, Sam. Starting now."

"One minute? Gee, I don't know, there's really quite a lot to sort out—"

"Eight, nine, ten—"

"Don't count, Leslie. If you want to count, count to yourself, okay?"

"You're not very reliable, are you, Sam?"

"Reliable? I don't know. I always thought I was."

She sighed. "Can we get together? We really do have to talk."

"About getting married, Leslie? Is that what you want to talk about?"

"My God, Sam, you make it sound like a day at the amusement park."

I cleared my throat. I was very nervous. "Yes, I do, don't I? I don't mean to. It's more than a day at the amusement park, I realize that. It's a very, very important . . . step in our lives—"

"Stop babbling, Sam."

"Yes. I am babbling, aren't I? I don't mean to babble—"

"Isadore's, Sam. No, wait. Not Isadore's. They're closed until five. Let's try Jerry's instead. In an hour, okay? It's at 65th and Broadway. Promise me you'll be there, Sam. Because if you're not there, I'm sorry, but—"

"I promise."

"Uh-huh," she said. "And the check's in the mail." A pause. "Okay, Sam. In an hour. At Jerry's, 65th and Broadway. Have you got all that?"

"Yes." I repeated it. "Thanks, Leslie. I'll be there with bells on."

"I've heard that one before, Sam. I don't need bells. I just need you."

Jerry's was an Italian deli that smelled strongly of cheese and meat. There were whole bologna sausages and salamis hanging everywhere, rounds of provolone on display on top of the counter, and four or five dark-haired thirtyish men in white shirts, white pants, and stained white aprons barking orders not only to each other but also to the dozens and dozens of customers who piled in.

I found Leslie at the rear of the place sitting at one of six round, glass-topped tables. There was a fake rose in a tiny cream-colored vase at the center of the table, and a demitasse cup filled with very dark coffee in front of her—espresso, I guessed. When she saw me, she smiled stiffly and motioned me to sit down. I leaned over, kissed her—which she at first tried to avoid—then I sat across from her. The table was small enough that my knees touched hers. I said, leering, "I have fingers in my knees."

"Yes, and rocks in your head."

I stopped leering. "I'm sorry, Leslie."

"Sorry for what?"

"For . . . standing you up."

She leaned closer to be heard above the noise in the deli. "No, Sam. We were going to talk about getting married. Maybe you don't think that's important."

"I think it's important, Leslie. I think it's the most important thing in the world. Believe me. It's just that, in the past couple of days . . ." I stopped.

"Yes?" she coaxed.

"I have a friend . . ." I paused. "I have an old friend from high school, his name's Abner and . . ." Another pause. "He lives on Long Island, in this . . . house—" I gave her a quick, nervous grin.

"And?" she said.

"And I guess you could say he's in trouble. He's in a lot of . . . *trouble*."

"And you've been trying to help him, is that it?"

I thought a moment. "Well, 'help him' probably isn't the right phrase. I think what I've been trying to do is *be there* for him."

"What kind of trouble is he in, Sam?" She looked genuinely concerned; it was one of the things I loved about her—her ability to be truly concerned about people she didn't know.

I answered, "Emotional trouble, Leslie. Deep emotional trouble. I think he may be . . . suicidal. I'm sorry if that sounds melodramatic."

"Has he said as much, Sam? Has he actually said, 'I'm going to kill myself'?"

"Not in so many words, but the feeling's there, and I guess that's why I've been kind of . . . out of touch in the past few days."

One of the thirtyish men in white appeared beside the table, order pad in hand. He mouthed some words that were completely lost in the noise; I shouted at him, "We're all set, thanks," and he shrugged and went away. I turned back to Leslie. She was looking earnestly at me. She said, "This friend of yours really is in trouble, isn't he, Sam? And you're really concerned about him, aren't you? I can see it in your eyes."

I nodded. "Yes. But there's more . . . lots more that I can't tell you now—"

She cut in, putting her hand on mine, "You're a very good person, Sam." She took her hand away. "And when you've got this thing . . . resolved, we'll talk." She stood.

Another nervous smile flitted across my mouth. "Leslie—"

She shook her head. "I misjudged you. I'm sorry, but I misjudged you." A small happy smile appeared on her face. She said, "I love you very much, Sam."

"Well, my God," I said, "I love you, too, Leslie."

"I know you do," she said, then she turned and quickly left the deli.

I stood. One of the waiters cornered me for the bill. I fumbled in my pockets for my wallet, paid the bill, and went after Leslie. I ran out onto the sidewalk. She was quite a few paces off. "Leslie!" I called.

She turned her head and mouthed the words "Call me," then hailed a taxi, got in, and was gone.

"I will," I whispered, as the taxi turned on Broadway.

Then I went back to my apartment.

I've learned one thing at least: The dead don't look forward. They don't plan for the future. They don't put money away for their kid's education. They don't take pictures, or decorate their houses, or read horoscopes, or fill calendars up with events. They don't brush their teeth or check their clothes for signs of wear. They don't write letters, or bad checks, or poems (unless they were letters, or bad checks, or poems that they had written when they were alive). They don't paint, they don't dust, and they don't wax their cars. They live only in the present and in the past. The past is their present.

It's one way to tell the dead from the living, you see.

Because the dead don't look where they're going. They look only where they've been.

Back at the apartment, I got a phone call from Abner: "Sam? It's me," he said, his voice warbling on a high note as if he were imitating some strange, nervous bird. "It's Abner." He paused only a moment, not long enough for me to say anything, then hurried on, "Something's wrong, Sam. Something's awfully wrong, terribly wrong." He paused.

"Yes," I said, "continue."

"Continue?" he said.

"Go on. Continue. Tell me what's wrong."

"Yes," he said. "Wrong." Another pause. "It's Art."

"Art DeGraff?"

"Yes, Art DeGraff." His voice was surer now, less singsong, as if he'd settled on what exactly was troubling him. He repeated, "Art DeGraff," hesitated, then added, "He's gone."

"I don't understand that, Abner."

"Art was here." A short, odd chuckle came from

him. "He was here at the house. He was in the walls. He was my prisoner, Sam."

"Abner, I don't understand that."

"Art was my prisoner. He was *our* prisoner! Phyllis and mine. He was here. Alive! In the walls! And now he's gone, he's gone, Sam. Someone . . . got him out. Someone sprung him."

"You realize that you're making absolutely no sense?!"

He chuckled grimly. "Of course I realize that. But it's the truth, Sam. He was here and now he's gone. And my guess is that he's awfully damned mad."

"Of course he's mad."

"Sorry?" Abner said.

"It was a joke, Abner."

He ignored that. "Art's after me, Sam. And there's only one place for me to run to, only one safe place—"

"Abner, let me come over there; I'm coming over there now—"

"My place is with Phyllis. I wanted to tell you that. I wanted to say good-bye. I wanted to thank you for being a friend."

I took a breath. I thought he might be challenging me, asking for help. I said, "Your place, Abner, is with the *living*!"

He said, "Of course it is, Sam. And so is yours." Then he hung up.

TWENTY-FOUR

When I got to the beach house several hours later, it was empty. I found a big, ragged hole in the hallway wall and a note on the kitchen table. The note read:

Friend Sam,

We grab what happiness we can, when we can, where we can. In this case I have no choice, thank God, but to go for the gusto, to wrap myself in Phyllis, and she in me.

Old Art is pretty damned mad, and for good reason—if I'd been locked up in someone's wall for a year I'd be mad, too. So I can't blame him if he wants to get even. But that doesn't mean I have to stick around for it.

Please don't come after me. You'll just get yourself in a hell of a mess, and there's really nothing at all you can do for me now—even if I wanted you to.

You can use the Malibu. Phyllis and I have transportation to where we're going. The key's under the mat. Remember—let the engine idle fast a good three or four minutes in cold weather.

Maybe I'll be back, Sam. Maybe I won't.

If I have a moment, I'll give you a call.

Abner.

"Dammit!" I whispered, and stuffed the note in my pants pocket.

The hole in the hallway wall was man-size. There were ragged edges of furring strips beneath the plaster, and when I stuck my head into the hole, I could dimly see that there was indeed room for a man to stand or sleep inside. But not room enough for anything else. Above, a hole the size of a fist let air in from the upstairs; I assumed that poor Art was fed through that hole.

I pulled my head back after a few seconds because the smell inside that wall was overpowering.

"Are you looking for Abner?" a female voice said.

A quick screech of surprise escaped me; I started to hyperventilate, forced myself to breathe slowly, deeply. I turned my head. A woman stood just behind me. She was short, brunette, and appealing in an innocently vivacious way. She was dressed in jeans and a green halter top, and there was an overwhelming air of sadness and confusion about her. She went on, her voice a kind of high-pitched purring sound with a vague southern drawl to it. ''Abner's not here. Abner''—it sounded like ''Abnah''—''had to go away. I don't know where. I wish I knew where. He's done left us all alone.''

''Us?'' I asked.

She smiled pleadingly up at me like a small child. ''He's done left us all alone,'' she said again, and her smile faded. ''Who are you?''

''I'm Abner's friend,'' I said.

''Are you gonna''—*gawna*—''leave us alone, too?''

''Us?'' I repeated. ''Who's 'us'?''

She was several feet away from me but I could feel cold air coming from her, as if from an open refrigerator. ''All of us,'' she said. ''I'm Myrna. This is Stephanie, this is Jodie, this is Max,'' and they appeared one by one, like lost children, behind her as she spoke their names. Stephanie looked to be Myrna's age, but was very tall, and very thin, as if she were anorectic, and Jodie was midway in height between Myrna and Stephanie, her face flat and round, like the face of a pig, the dark eyes small, close-set, squinting; Max was gargantuan, and vaguely malevolent-looking, like a bouncer at a nightclub where everyone usually behaves themselves.

''I can't help you,'' I said, ''I'm sorry.''

''We don't want no help,'' Myrna drawled. ''We just don't wanna be left alone.'' I saw then that she was still and stiff, that when she spoke, only her lips moved.

''I can't help you,'' I said again. My voice sounded peaky from fear.

"We don't want no help, we just don't wanna be left alone, don't't"—*doan*—"leave us alone."

Max picked it up. "Doan leave us alone," he growled. Then Stephanie followed: "Doan leave us alone," and Jodie, who looked like a pig, but whose voice was sweet and high-pitched: "Doan leave us alone," all of them still and stiff, so only their mouths moved.

It became a chorus, a refrain, "Doan leave us alone." Their voices blended into something sweet and sour, something that was at once pleading and cajoling and demanding and futile: "Doan leave us alone. Doan leave us alone."

"But you *are* alone!" I screamed. And as soon as the words left me I wanted desperately to snatch them back. "I'm sorry," I whispered. Their mouths stuck open; their gazes were wide, accusing, and hurt. Then, like raindrops hitting parched earth, they dissipated and were gone.

I went and sat shakily at the kitchen table. "Maybe I'll go back to Bangor," I whispered. "It's nice in Bangor. People are simple and happy there." Sure, I thought. Leslie and I could get married and we could go to Bangor together. We could have a little house, a few kids, some cats and dogs, a garden, a sump pump, an ant problem, menus made up a week in advance (meat loaf on Monday, spaghetti on Tuesday, Welsh rarebit on Wednesday). We'd have each other. And Bangor was where it would all happen, because Bangor was what I knew. It fit me. It was like an old sweater. But I walked very lightly on these possibilities because, like expanses of spring ice, they were insubstantial and could crack and expose the dark water beneath, where Abner was. Soon, I realized, he would push himself panic-stricken from one thin patch to another—where the sunlight shone through—in a desperate search for air and life.

And that's where I had to come in for his sake. I had to punch a hole in the ice and jump in and pull him out of the water. Or drown in it, too.

I poked my head back into the man-size hole in the hallway wall where Art DeGraff had been held prisoner. I stepped into the hole and stood inside the wall, trying, I think, to call up the same awful feelings of claustrophobia and aloneness that Art had to have felt. But that was impossible. The wall was open for me; it had been closed for him. I stepped out of the wall, ran my hand along the jagged furring strips surrounding the hole, and wondered if Art himself had somehow smashed out of the wall—like Superman—or if someone else had gotten him out. Which is when I remembered what Abner had told me on the telephone. "Someone got him out. Someone sprung him."

I whispered, trying for a smile, "I'm going to take my balls and go home," but my smile trembled, and my head whirled. Then I began to methodically search the beach house for something that might tell me where Abner had gone.

I began in the small, sparsely furnished damp room I'd slept in a week earlier. There was a wrought-iron twin bed in that room, a small wood-framed picture—

some anonymous countryside scene, faded and pinkish green—above the bed, a battered oval nightstand alongside the bed. I opened the one drawer of the nightstand; it looked empty, but it also looked to be too shallow by half for the depth of the nightstand. I felt around inside. My fingers hit what I guessed was a picture frame keeping the drawer from opening all the way. I pulled the frame down, opened the drawer, took the frame out. It had a five by seven black-and-white photograph in it of Art DeGraff—I recognized his mannequinlike handsomeness—and a stunning black woman dressed in a very brief light-colored bikini. They were standing together on the bow of a cabin cruiser. The woman was Phyllis. I took the photograph from the frame and studied the back of it. Alongside the Eastman Kodak Company logo was a date that indicated the photo had been taken two and a half years earlier. I turned the picture around again and studied it more closely. Because there was a curtain over the room's only window, the light was not good, so I pulled the curtain open and held the photograph up to the daylight. My gaze lingered on Phyllis, on the breasts that promised to come spilling wonderfully out of that skimpy top, on the marvelous flat belly, the smooth dark thighs, the hint of a pubic shadow beneath the equally skimpy bikini bottoms. And when I looked at Art's face, I saw a kind of *Look what I've got here!* grin on it.

But as I held the photograph closer to the window, I saw that that *Look what I've got here!* grin was not a grin, but a grimace of fear, and I said to myself, *Well, of course, this photograph never did show him grinning,* although I knew it had, and then I said to myself, *It's the way the light's falling on the picture; it makes him look frightened,* but I knew that that was wrong, too.

I put the photograph back in the frame, and the frame back in the drawer of the nightstand. Then I noticed for the first time what I supposed was a closet door in the wall opposite the bed. I went to the door and tried it; it was locked. I took my wallet out, got a VISA card, and tried to slip it between the door and the frame to spring the bolt. It didn't work. I stuffed the card in my shirt pocket. I tried the knob again. Nothing. I decided to take the hinges off the door. For that I'd need a screwdriver, or something like a screwdriver. I searched my pockets and found a couple of dimes, a quarter, five pennies. I shoved one of the dimes beneath the flange of the pin on the top hinge. The pin wouldn't budge. "Dammit," I whispered. I stared at the door for a good half minute. At last I decided that instead of taking the hinges off the door it probably would matter to no one if I bashed it in. I liked that idea. I needed to engage in a bit of mayhem at that house—I needed to exercise some *control* over it.

I stepped back from the door and gave it a hard kick. Nothing. I felt a sudden sharp pain in my big toe and I supposed sickeningly that I'd broken it. "Damn it all!" I whispered. I turned angrily to the bed, tore the mattress and box spring off, and found beneath it a half-dozen sturdy wooden slats. I grabbed one, turned again. And saw that the closet door was standing open a good three inches.

I stepped forward, put my hand on the knob, hesitated, and yanked the door open. I peered in.

It was a large walk-in closet, and except for some dust mice on the floor, and one yellowing, crackly page from the Leisure section of the *New York Times* on one of the five floor-to-eye-level shelves, it was empty.

My search of the house had just begun, and yet, somehow, I felt as if the rest of my search, through all fourteen rooms, was going to be as futile and as frustrating as my search of this room had been. But that, I quickly realized, was only a kind of wearying combination of laziness and fear—it was a *big* place, after all, and whatever I might find in it would probably much rather be left alone—like the black widow spiders that hung out under people's porches, or rattlesnakes that sunned themselves on rocky hillsides—"Don't bother them," my dad used to say, "and they won't bother you."

I left the small bedroom and headed for the narrow enclosed stairs that led to the second floor. Abner had pointed toward those stairs the day before, after our picnic; "Nothing up there, Sam," he told me. "Just smelly and cold up there," and I thought I could tell from the casual, offhand way he'd said it that it was true. Abner was never much of a liar. In Bangor, he tried gamely, but it was usually clear from the flickering of his eyelids and the way he shuffled his feet that he was lying. I like people like that—people who can't lie; I think it's a sign of character. It was, in fact, one of the things that kept

Abner and me together in Bangor—the fact that he had character.

Now I realized that people can learn to lie.

So I started up the narrow enclosed stairway.

Improbably, it smelled of spaghetti sauce. I found that its dirty-with-age beige walls had names written on them variously in pen, pencil, crayon, even what looked like some kind of dark liquid (not blood; it was the wrong shade for blood). There was a "Tammy," a "Fred the Frog," a "Minerva G.," the initials, scrawled childishly in that dark liquid, "S.T.M," a "Victor Darling" (and I spent a moment or two trying to decide if that was actually the man's name or if, perhaps, his lover had written it there). "S.T.M." was lower on the wall. "Victor Darling," "Minerva G.," and some of the others were higher up.

I'd left the door open at the bottom of the stairway. The light switch didn't work, so the only light was what filtered up from the first floor. In that light, a kind of dim yellowish-green light, I thought I could see other names, much fainter than Victor Darling's and Minerva G.'s, et cetera. Names so faint, in fact, that I would not have seen them had I not stopped to look. I could read some of them—"Ransom" something-or-other, "Lord Ali," which made me think, of course, of Muhammad Ali, a "Rebecca," a "Thomas Pillson." I guessed that there were two hundred or more names in that hallway and I supposed that they were the names of people who had lived in the house, that someone had long ago started a kind of tradition of signing the hallway if they lived in the house. So I stopped. searched my pockets, came up with my house keys, and used one to scratch my name halfway up the wall, next to the name ''Eli Wallberger,'' which had been done in fine, black block lettering that had faded nearly to invisibility.

It pleased me to see my name there, on that wall. Maybe it was the same kind of pleasure I'd gotten from trying to kick the closet door in—see *this*, feel *this*?!—*I'm* in control here!

And when I was done scratching my name into the plaster, I went up to the second floor.

TWENTY-FIVE

What struck me first about the second floor of the beach house were the colors. Someone had gone crazy with high-gloss lacquers—red, pink, green, yellow, purple; I could see no black, no white, no cream or beige, nothing neutral.

I stood at the top of the stairs, at the beginning of a very long hallway that had high ceilings and a number of tall, narrow, apparently unpainted doors. The colors were arranged in a hippieish pattern—"psychedelic" is the word—as if gallons of various bright-colored paints had been thrown willy-nilly into a very strong wind, frozen, then transferred to those walls. In the middle sixties a cousin who had painted her room like that had explained that it was "life art."

"Huh?" I'd said.

"Life art," she repeated, adjusting the hem of her

granny dress. "You look at it and you say to yourself, 'The person who did this is *alive.*' You know? This is the art of the living."

It was cold in that hallway, as Abner said it would be. And there was a vague, indefinable smell wafting about. Every now and then my nose caught it briefly and I said to myself, *Yes, that's the smell of* . . . but I could never finish the thought because by then the smell would be gone. The phrase *mown grass* comes to mind now.

I counted seven doors in that hallway: three on the left and five on the right. They looked as if they might have been oak, but it was not until I screwed up some courage and looked closely at one that I realized it was covered with an oak-print Contact paper that was bubbly and torn in spots and peeling at the edges. As tacky as it was, it merely carried on with the tacky theme that the psychedelic walls had begun.

It was very quiet. I hadn't expected that. I'd expected . . . devils, I think. I'd expected that some gateway to the Other Side was being hidden up there and when I looked too closely I'd find it and unleash a whole crowd of drooling, gelatinous monsters.

I was *hoping* for monsters. Because with monsters, at least it's clear right from the start who your enemies are.

I knocked on the door I'd looked closely at; I got no answer. I knocked again. Then I tried the knob. It turned. I let it rotate back. I hadn't expected the room to be unlocked.

"Hello," I called again.

I heard from within the room, "Who's there?" It was a woman's voice, and it surprised the hell out of me because it was so human, so annoyed-sounding. "If you're selling something, I'm not buying."

"No," I managed.

"What?"

I stepped closer to the door. "No, I'm not selling anything." My voice sounded pathetic, gurgling. I cleared my throat. "I'm not selling anything. I'm looking for someone."

I heard her curse. I heard what sounded like a chair being pushed back on a hardwood floor, then the sound of footfalls. Moments later the door was pulled open and a tall, handsome middle-aged woman dressed in a long green satin robe appeared. She pursed her lips. "And *who* are you?" she said.

"Sam Feary," I answered.

She nodded once, casually. "Yes. Abner's friend. I was wondering when you'd show up." Her annoyance seemed to have changed to resignation. She had a square face and shoulder-length salt-and-pepper hair which she wore full around her head. Her hazel eyes were large, and expressive of much living—they were the eyes, I thought, of someone who has seen quite a lot and knows with grim certainty that she will see much more. She had a habit of pursing her lips often. At first I thought it was the result of her annoyance; later I grew to realize that it was a sort of nervous habit. "I suppose you have to come in, don't you?" she went on, and gestured vaguely toward the room.

"Do you live here?" I asked.

She smiled wearily. "I live where I have to," and she turned and went into the room. I followed.

She sat in a very large white Queen Anne armchair. She looked aristocratic in it, especially in that long green satin robe. It seemed to please her to sit, as if she were tired from her little walk to the door and back. She nodded to indicate a love seat to my left, near the door. The love seat was covered in a worn flower-print-on-white fabric and had dark stains at the arms. I sat in it, and glanced quickly around the room; there were several hundred books in a tall dark oak bookcase between two windows, some knick-knacks in a white plastic étagère near the love seat, and on a tall thin mahogany end table next to her chair, a battered, dirt-smeared softball.

"My name is Madeline," the woman said pointedly, as if the fact of her name were something that hinged not only on the rest of our conversation but also on everything that concerned me at the house.

"Madeline," I said, and added, "Yes, I've heard of you."

She pursed her lips. "Through Abner, I assume."

"Yes. Through Abner."

She nodded. "I'm no one." I could tell from her tone that she meant it. "I'm only a middle-aged former housewife whose son has . . ."—a small, quivering grin came and went quickly on her mouth—". . . has passed on. We'll be reunited someday. I know that. I have no doubt of it. It's as clear and true to me as gravity. But, until then, what I have chosen to do . . ." She stopped, thought a moment. "No, that's incorrect: What I have been *forced* to do, Mr. Feary, is to sit here in this . . . this *throne*—it *is* something like a throne, isn't it? And it isn't very comfortable either; it puts my backside to sleep, so when I get up and try to walk around, Lord—I look like a goddamn drunken sailor." She stopped, apparently having lost her train of thought. She went on after a moment, pursing her lips again, "What I have been forced to do, Mr. Feary, is to try and dissuade people like you from doing the abominably stupid things that people like you invariably end up doing." Another quick, quivering grin. "So humor me, won't you?"

She looked and sounded like Maude from the old sitcom of the same name, the kind of woman who is very easy to talk to, but hard as hell to contradict, the kind of woman who makes no bones of the fact that she is the bearer of wisdom and that those around her are merely the bearers of sweet ignorance. There was no overt manifestation of ego in this. Only truth, as she saw it.

I started to say something about the house, about the cold and the smells and the bizarre things that happened in it, and she held her hand up to stop me: "I have a little speech, Mr. Feary. When I have delivered it, and you have absorbed it, as I am *certain* you will"—her voice was dripping with sarcasm—"then you can say whatever it is you have to say, and we can both go about our business as if we never met.'' She stopped, apparently as a cue for me to settle down and listen; so I did.

''Good,'' she said. ''Thank you. You're much easier to talk to than your friend.'' She crossed her legs and leaned forward in the chair with her hands on her knees. ''This is my speech, Mr. Feary. Listen closely:

''Mind your own *p*'s and *q*'s.'' She smiled thinly.

After several moments of silence, I said, ''Yes. Continue.''

She said, ''I'll bet you can't tell me where that comes from? That phrase. 'Mind your own *p*'s and *q*'s.' ''

''Sorry,'' I said.

''Printers used it,'' she said. ''It has something to do, you know, with the fact that the *p*'s and the *q*'s are the same, only reversed, and I guess it was easy to put a *p* into a *q* box by mistake.''

''That's your speech?'' I asked.

Again she shrugged. ''Who likes speeches? I do have another one prepared, if you want to hear a speech. It's a speech about *them* and about *us* and how we're really all the same but actually quite different, about—now get this: This is a quote—about how 'Death changes nothing but a person's biology,' and 'You are now what you will always be.' That sort of thing. But I've retired it, you know. Too long-winded. And, anyway, what it all boiled down to was simply that—'Mind your own *p*'s and *q*'s.' '' Another thin smile. ''You can go now.''

''I don't want to go,'' I said. It was true. I didn't want to leave her. I liked what she represented. She was solid. She was real. Those nonexistent devils and zombies and gelatinous monsters could suddenly burst into the room, all of them hell-bent on gobbling me up, and she would know precisely how to deal with them. She would wave her hand in the air and say with regal exasperation, "Oh, get *out* of here!" And they'd leave, each of them muttering an apology.

She shrugged. "So stay," she said.

"You don't understand," I said.

She smiled thinly once more. "Of course I do, Mr. Feary. You know very well that I do." She reached out suddenly, grabbed the battered, dirt-smeared softball on the end table near her chair, and threw it to me. I reacted none too soon; as it was I had to juggle the ball for a few seconds to keep it in hand. "What's this?" I asked.

"It's a softball."

"I can *see* that it's a softball, what I mean is—"

"Gerald's in it. Gerald's my son."

"Huh?" I got an image of her boring a hole in the skin of the softball, injecting the ashes of her dead son into it, meticulously mending the hole, then covering its edges with dirt. "You mean his ashes are in it?" I asked.

She shook her head. "No. *He's* in it. *Gerald's* in it." She held both hands up. "Throw it back, would you?" I got the uncomfortable idea that we were going to play catch. I gave the ball a stiff but accurate underhand toss. She caught it and put it back with a thump on the end table. She must have seen my look of surprise because she said, "You're thinking that if Gerald's really in this ball then why am I being so careless with it?''

''No,'' I lied, ''not at all.''

She smiled, pleased. ''I like you, Mr. Feary. You're polite. Abner wasn't polite.'' She grabbed the softball again and began tossing it back and forth between her hands. She said as she tossed it, ''When Gerald was a baby, of course, I had to be careful with him. I could tickle him, throw him a few inches into the air. But if I dropped him, he'd hurt, he'd have pain. And then, as he grew, I had to watch out for various diseases. He had chicken pox once. It devastated me because I hated to see him so sick.'' She stopped tossing the ball, held it tight in her left hand. ''But he's dead now, Mr. Feary, so I don't have to be careful anymore. Just like the mother of a college kid can stop worrying whether he's turned out okay, because by then whatever he's turned into is going to stick, and whatever she tries to do to change him isn't going to mean doodly squat.'' She set the softball down again, a bit more gently. ''In other words, Mr. Feary, what's done is, in point of fact, done.''

I had no real idea what she was talking about. I asked, feeling like a child, ''Do I *have* to go?''

She nodded slowly, apologetically. ''At some time or other you do, yes. I mean, I can't feed you, and the toilet facilities are downstairs, of course, such as they are.'' She cocked her head to one side and pursed her lips. ''You've sort of latched on to me, haven't you, Mr. Feary?''

That got me flustered, as if she'd caught me stealing. I stammered, "No, no, of course not, it's just that . . . it's just that—" I could think of nothing to say.

She smiled broadly, as if pleased. "You may stay for as long as you wish, Mr. Feary. But you should know that your friend isn't here. In this room I mean."

This jolted me back to reality, to the reason I was at the beach house in the first place. "Well, yes," I said, "I *know* that, I can *see* that."

She smiled thinly yet again, as if at an old and tired joke. "You're not quite as . . . intuitive as your friend. You're more courteous, it's true. But you're not as intuitive. You don't *see* Gerald, do you? And yet, he is here"—she nodded—"in that softball."

"I'd have to accept that on faith, wouldn't I, Madeline?"

Another thin, weary smile. "What you accept and why you accept it really is of little consequence, least of all to me, Mr. Feary." This was not said unkindly, as a put-down, but merely as a statement of fact. "I'd say you've probably seen more than enough in these past few days to put your . . . how do the writers say it?—your 'willing suspension of disbelief' on a pretty low level, isn't that right?"

"I haven't become a gullible fool, if that's what you're saying."

"You're losing your patience, Mr. Feary. Remember—*courtesy*; where would we be without courtesy? The Japanese are the most successful people on the planet because of their courtesy. My God, they're even courteous about killing themselves.''

''Okay, then,'' I said—I sensed that she was toying with me—''where is he? Where is Abner?''

''Mr. Feary,'' she began, ''you know as well as I that he's with Phyllis. That's what he told you, I think. Isn't that what he told you?''

''Yes.''

''Then that's where he is. Of course, you do have the task of finding Phyllis, and if you're not going to mind your *p*'s and *q*'s, as I've asked, if you're not going to leave the whole thing alone, then for the sake of us all, Mr. Feary, so you won't go charging around like a wild animal and destroy the very delicate balance that exists between their world and ours—even now I shudder to think what you did to those poor sanitation workers, and I gasp when I think of that woman in red who certainly fell head over heels for you—then I suppose that I should tell you exactly where Phyllis is, shouldn't I?''

I was stunned. ''How did you know . . . I mean—''

She had been leaning forward, elbows on her knees, hands clasped. Now she leaned back, put her hands flat on the arms of the chair, and assumed a regal air. ''I have my sources, Mr. Feary,'' she said. ''I'm afraid there have been quite a few people trespassing where they oughtn't in the past few decades. I don't know why; maybe the world's getting overcrowded—by both the dead and the living, I mean.'' She waved the observation away. ''Whatever the reason, there are other people . . . like myself, hundreds of them, I'm sure, who have taken on the task of monitoring the comings and goings of . . ." She seemed stymied. She continued, "Of *everyone*. No! Not everyone. Not yet." She seemed suddenly very agitated. She pursed her lips repeatedly and her ample bosom rose and fell in time with her deep sighing. "I'm sorry, Mr. Feary; I'm confusing you, aren't I?"

"No, honestly," I answered. "I understand." It was another lie, of course.

"You're so po*lite*," she said again, but now as if it was beginning to wear on her. "I don't often give advice, Mr. Feary. I make pronouncements, I dispense wisdom"—she grinned—"and sometimes I act pretty damned pompous, I'm sure. But I never give advice. Now I'm going to give advice. I'm going to advise you to get together with that woman, what's-her-name?"

"Leslie?"

"Yes." She nodded. "Leslie. And marry her, or do whatever it is you want to do with her—I'm certainly not going to make judgments about how people choose to live. Buy a house, rent an apartment, live in a tent. I don't care. Just *be happy*, Mr. Feary. *Live!* You'll see—in no time at all, a few months, a year, tops, these *visions* of yours will stop and you can go back to being Sam Feary, Gentleman. That's my advice. Now take it and get out."

TWENTY-SIX

It was good advice, all of it, and I ached to take it, but I couldn't, of course. She knew I couldn't. So, sighing yet again, she lowered her head and apologized for what she called her "inexcusable outburst."

"Sure," I said, "it's okay."

And she said, "You'll find Abner and Phyllis in Vermont, in a little house near Burlington. Do you know where that is? Burlington, I mean."

"I'm sorry?" I said.

"Burlington. In Vermont. Oh, for heaven's sake, go get a map."

I shook my head. "Are you telling me that Phyllis and Abner are . . . cohabiting—"

She smiled a slight, amused smile. "Yes," she said almost wistfully, almost dreamily, her voice a high, breathy whisper, "cohabiting."

And, though I should have known better, and, in fact, I did know better, I said, "But, my God, Phyllis is dead, the woman is dead, how the hell can she and Abner *live* together in a little house in Vermont if she's dead? The whole thing is stupid . . . the whole thing is . . ." I cast about for the right word.

Madeline pursed her lips, in annoyance now. "Mr. Feary—*people* do not die. *Bodies* die."

"And what is that?" I burst out. "Pop philosophy? Let's put it on a bumper sticker, for God's sake—"

She broke in, her tone brusque, "I am not here to fence with you, Mr. Feary. The name of the town is Brookfield. They have a little house there and they are living in it, *cohabiting* in it, to use your phrase. And since you are obviously not going to take my advice, my suggestion would be to go to Brookfield, assess the situation carefully, very carefully, Mr. Feary, and then bring that asshole friend of yours back here. Alone!" She waved agitatedly at the door. "Now please go."

I stood at once, turned to the door, put my hand on the knob.

Madeline called, "One more thing, Mr. Feary."

I glanced around at her.

She said, a small note of apology in her voice, "I thought at first that I could deal with Mr. DeGraff myself."

"Art?" I said.

"Yes. But I can't deal with him. He has . . . how can I best say this? He has gone beyond my sphere of influence, I'm afraid.'' A wry smile flitted across her mouth. ''It happens.''

''And?''

She shrugged. ''And I guess you'll have to keep an eye out for him.''

''What's he got against *me*? Sure, I never liked him, but—''

''I doubt that he has anything against you, Mr. Feary. But what he does have, in amazing abundance, is anger. I really believe that were it not for his anger, he would quite literally fall apart.'' She allowed a second or two for that to sink in. It didn't. At the time, I thought of it only as a turn of phrase. Then she said in a tone of clear finality, ''Now you may go.''

And I did.

Leslie *whoops* at the Philharmonic. When the concert is over and she is pleased with the way it's been done, she whoops and cheers almost as if she's at a hockey game. Some people turn around and look. At first they're taken aback and the impression they want to make, apparently, is that they do not want their evening at the Philharmonic upset by someone who loves being there so much that she *whoops* about it. But then they see her. And she sees them. And it's all right. I like to think that some of them, the next time they are at the Philharmonic and they have been bowled over by what they've heard, that they too will *whoop*, and cheer. But I don't think they will. They are who they are, and she is who she is.

She brings life to them for a moment or two.

* * *

Her hands are small and thin. They are very artistic-looking, though she denies that she is creative or artistic. I think she's wrong. I think she hasn't given herself a chance.

I often find myself looking at her hands, especially when our hands are together, hers over mine so my palm is up and hers is down. I think how fragile her hand looks in mine, and it awakens some protective sense in me, although she is not at all fragile and doesn't need to be protected by anyone. When I squeeze her hand tightly—which I do when we're listening to music—and also when I become aware, all at once, of how happy I am with her, she squeezes back and I know how physically strong she is. But still, in those moments when I'm studying her hand, or when she is tilting her head toward me and closing her eyes, I feel protective of her; I feel tender toward her.

I didn't drive straight to Brookfield from Abner's beach house. I went back to my apartment. I showered, I shaved. At one point, while I was walking from the bathroom to the living room with only a towel wrapped around me, I heard giggling from the bedroom. I didn't turn to look. I was trying to cultivate an *ignore them and they'll go away* attitude. It seemed to work then. After a few seconds the giggling stopped abruptly, as if a door had been slammed shut on it.

I called Leslie.

Her father answered. "Mr. Wirth?" I said.

"Yes," he said, "this is Frank Wirth." He sounded very formal, very stiff, not at all what I was used to.

"Hi," I said. "This is Sam Feary. Is Leslie there, please?"

"Yes, hold on."

Moments later, Leslie came on the line. "Hi, Sam. I didn't expect to hear from you so soon."

"Leslie, I'm going away for a few days—" I hesitated. "Is your father all right? He sounded a little . . . he didn't sound like himself."

"Daddy's ill, Sam."

"Oh. I'm sorry. Is it serious?" I felt foolish asking that.

"Yes. It's very serious." She paused; when she went on, her tone was stiffly casual. "You say you're going away for a few days?"

I was suddenly nervous. I got the clear impression that she didn't want to talk and I wasn't sure why—whether it was because she was concerned about her father or because she merely didn't want to talk to me. "Well, like I said, I'm going away, I'm going to a place called Brookfield—"

She cut in, "Yes, that's nice. I hope you have a good trip, Sam."

"Thanks. Actually, what I called about, what I was wondering was—"

"No, Sam," she interrupted. "I can't come with you. I'm sorry. My father is very sick, as I said, and I'm afraid that . . ." She stopped suddenly. I thought I heard her sniffle.

I said, "Are you okay, Leslie?" Nothing. "Leslie, are you still there?"

"Yes, Sam. I'm sorry. A touch of asthma. It happens now and again." A short pause. "Sam, I'd like to come with you—" Another pause. "I really would like to come with you. But I can't leave Daddy. You understand."

"Of course I understand. I hope he's going to be all right. I like him; I mean, he's odd, sure, but—"

"Thank you, Sam. I'll see you when you get back, okay?" I heard her sniffle once more. Then she hung up.

That's when the giggling started again—louder, closer—and when, without thinking, I looked at the open bedroom door, I saw the two young teenage girls in pink taffeta standing very stiffly there, giggling like babies. And, remembering Madeline, I waved toward them with my right hand and I barked, "Oh, get *out* of here!"

It didn't work.

They moved closer, in little shuffling steps, as if in stiff imitation of an Oriental walk, the volume of their giggles rising with each step.

I still had the towel wrapped around me, of course. I was desperately holding it in place with my left hand.

"Get out of here!" I tried again, but it sounded strained and anemic and I suppose that's the way it sounded to them, too, because their giggling suddenly grew much louder, the pace of their small mincing steps quickened, and I got what I hoped was a wildly improbable picture of myself being eaten alive by these two teenage girls in pink taffeta.

"Get *out* of here!" I tried once more, but they continued to advance on me, their giggling now more like the raucous screeching of a flock of blue jays.

I heard a hard knock at my apartment door, followed quickly by, "Hey, keep it *down* in there!" It was my neighbor, Steve Gresham, from across the hall.

I thought happily, *He can hear them, too. Steve can hear them, too.*

"Keep it *down* in there, for Chrissakes!"

The girls in pink taffeta were very close now, a couple of arm's lengths away, shuffling toward me.

"Get *out* of here!"

"I'm gonna call the cops, Feary, I'm gonna call the cops!"

"Get the hell out of here!"

"Okay, pal, that's it!"

The girls in pink taffeta were within arm's reach now. Their giggling was not giggling at all; it was a kind of strange, off-key, shrieking cry.

I wanted to plead with them, "Please, leave me alone!"

But I realized that for several moments I had been screaming, much the way, I think, that a man falling screams—a scream of fear and desperation, and, above all, a scream of awful resignation: *I am going to hit the ground and there is nothing at all I can do about it!*

Fear starts crazy fires inside us all, you see. It can create a sort of cohesion that keeps us from flying apart.

They reached out for me then. I felt their cold fingers on me.

"No!" I screamed.

Their fingers pressed hard into my stomach, my chest, my jaw. One hard, cold finger pushed into my ear.

And the high, keening sound of their giggles continued.

I closed my eyes. I saw a big white farmhouse, and a man and woman in their thirties in front of it, pruning some hedges, and a boy of seven or eight running happily about nearby, a pair of cap-powered six-guns blazing harmlessly away at anything that moved.

That boy was me.

He vanished as quickly as he'd appeared. So did the man and woman pruning hedges. And the big white farmhouse.

"Hey, buddy!" I heard. "Hey, buddy!" I was standing. I felt a sharp pain in my cheek.

"Jesus, Feary, what the hell were you doin' in here?" It was Steve Gresham's voice.

I felt another sharp pain in my cheek. "C'mon, buddy, snap outa it now!" The voice was heavy with a tired, bored authority, and I knew even before I opened my eyes that it was the voice of a cop.

I opened my eyes. The cop was as tall as I, dark-haired, thin-faced; his nametag said "Sgt. A. Luciano." Steve Gresham stood just behind him. Steve is short, rotund, swarthy-complexioned. He and I shared a few beers once and found that we had little in common.

Sergeant Luciano said, grinning ever so slightly, "Hey, you better put some clothes on there, huh?" I realized that the towel was around my ankles and that I was stark naked.

I took a deep breath to steady myself. I wanted to believe that I was beyond simple embarrassment. But I wasn't. I bent over, picked the towel up, wrapped it around myself again. I apologized; "Sorry for all the noise," I said.

The cop said, "Whatcha got, some kinda epilepsy or somethin'?" He was concerned; it touched me a little.

I shook my head. "No. I don't think so."

Steve Gresham said again, "What the hell were you doin' in here, Feary?"

I shook my head again, then let myself enjoy the luxury of a long, weary sigh. "Nothing, Steve." I could speak just barely above a harsh whisper. "I didn't mean to disturb you."

The cop said, "You want I should call for an ambulance?"

"No, please," I answered, "I don't need an ambulance." I was starting to get my voice back. "I'm okay. I've just got to get some rest, I think. I'm going away for a few days. A vacation—"

Eventually I persuaded Steve Gresham and Sergeant Luciano that I was indeed okay, that they could leave me alone.

When they were gone, I climbed into a pair of jeans and a warm shirt, packed a suitcase, and left the apartment. I went to an auto teller, withdrew most of my savings—about $240—and was out of Manhattan and on my way to Brookfield, Vermont, in Abner's beat-up Malibu a half hour later.

PART TWO

A Drive in the Country

TWENTY-SEVEN

It's odd, but many of us, even under perfectly normal circumstances, can convince ourselves that we're being followed—either because we're paranoid or simply because we like to play games. We glance in the rearview mirror and we see a car behind us that looks like it's following a little too steadily, a car that stays the same distance behind, its driver's adjustments in speed, to compensate for our own, a bit too precise. Maybe that car has only been there for a minute or so. Maybe it's only made one or two of the same turns we've made, but still we wonder, mock seriously, *Is he following me?* Of course, 999 times out of a thousand, it's only Joe Schmo out for a drive and eventually he turns off, because practically none of us is ever actually followed by anyone. It's just a game we play.

It was a game that I played on my way to Brookfield that early April afternoon. It was a wonderful, blue-sky, warm afternoon, and I was enjoying a cautious sense of relief and freedom, as if, as long as I was driving, as long as the landscape was moving past at a good clip, nothing could touch me. I'd rolled the driver's window down, had put my elbow up on the rim of the door, and I was listening to a Manhattan AM station playing rock and roll hits of the sixties. I was looking forward to my long drive in the country.

I'd stopped at a Texaco station just inside Connecticut for gasoline and a map and had found that the best route to Brookfield would take me through a dozen or more small towns. Some of them close to New York were the original "bedroom communities" —Glenville, Norwalk, Riversville, South Wilton, Cannondale—all of them comfortable Connecticut towns and villages whose primary reason for existence is that their inhabitants can work in New York but don't have to live there.

It was as I was driving north out of Riversville, Connecticut, where the narrow two-lane road, Highway 15, was straight and smooth and bordered by an on-again, off-again succession of fields and pine trees that crowded the shoulders, that I saw a dark blue Ford behind me. There were other cars on the road, of course; I remember, particularly, some crazy man in a silver Chevette Scooter who had stayed only inches from my bumper for a mile or so and then had catapulted past me around a curve, sending a station wagon careening onto the shoulder. "Shit for brains!"

I breathed at him. It was a couple of minutes later that the Ford appeared, hung a precise couple of hundred feet back, and I said to myself, "Is he following me?"

When I got on the four-lane Merrit Parkway, which would lead me north of Norwalk, Connecticut, to U.S. Route 7—which would take me, eventually, to Brookfield, Vermont—I lost the Ford in what seemed like a crowd of 10 million midafternoon commuters. But when I got past Norwalk, and was on Route 7 heading north toward South Wilton, I saw the Ford again, still a precise couple of hundred feet back, dogging me.

I whispered into the rearview mirror, at the Ford's reflection, "So you want to play games, huh?" and took the first right-hand turn that came up, about a half mile later.

The Ford stayed on Route 7.

I was a little disappointed. I was up for a bit of harmless fun. I drove a mile or two down the road I'd turned onto, found a small shopping center where I could safely turn around, and headed back toward Route 7.

The Ford, going like a bat out of hell in the other direction, passed me on the way.

"Jesus Christ!" I squawked when he passed, because his air turbulence had flung the road dust into my face like tiny shotgun pellets.

I glanced in the rearview mirror, fully expecting that he'd screech to a halt and turn around. But he kept going. He was crazy, I decided. Just like the man in the silver Chevette was crazy. At that moment, on that marvelous spring day, I did not want to deal with crazy people.

I didn't see the Ford again until I was past the tiny village of Kent Furnace, Connecticut. The Ford was only four or five car lengths back so I could easily read "LTD" in tall chrome block letters on the front of what looked like ten acres of dark blue hood. And I could see the suggestion of a driver, too—someone who was hunched over slightly, someone above average height, because even hunched over, the top of his head intersected the top of the windshield.

In South Canaan, ten miles or so from the Massachusetts line, on Route 7, I lost sight of the Ford. It was about 5:00 P.M.

And that was when I made my second stop, in South Canaan, at a quaint and tidy restaurant called the Tea Kettle.

When I went in, I was stared at by two men in red plaid hunting jackets and baseball caps who were seated in a booth at the back of the restaurant. There were three booths with dark wood seats that looked like church pews; and there were a half-dozen small round wooden tables, *sans* tablecloths, three ladder-back pine chairs at each of these tables, and a dark wood counter with five or six revolving stools with wicker seats. The whole effect was, I guessed, what some mid-sixties entrepreneur thought "Connecticut Country" should be.

I sat at the counter. The place was empty except for the two men in hunting jackets. A chunky, red-faced waitress whose tight reddish-blond curls were mashed into a hairnet and whose small, round, light green eyes twinkled with affability came over.

"What can I do ya for?" she asked.

I smiled; that was a phrase I hadn't heard since I was a kid in Bangor. "I'd like to see a menu," I said.

She shook her head; her eyes twinkled. "No menu as such," she said, and nodded to indicate a chalkboard behind her, above an ice-cream freezer. "Got real New England style clam chowder on special today, though. Whyn'ch I bring you some?"

I glanced at the chalkboard. It read, in bold green letters on black, "REAL NEW ENGLAND CLAM CHOWDER—FRESH!—$1.50/cup—$2.50/bowl."

"I like the red clam chowder," I said.

She got her order pad from beneath the counter and stood with her pen poised on it. "Whyn'ch I bring you some real New England style clam chowder? You don't like it, you don't pay for it. That's fair, ah?"

I heard from behind me, "Go ahead. Florence made it fresh this mawnin'."

I turned in the seat. One of the hunters was smiling toothlessly at me. I smiled back, made what I hoped was a friendly noise (though I'm not sure how it came out; casual friendliness was something I had grown to mistrust in my months in New York), and turned back to Florence. I nodded. "Sure, thanks," I said, and she jotted in her order pad.

"Coffee, too?" she asked.

"Milk," I answered.

"Milk," she said, eyes twinkling mightily. "Large or small?"

"Large, please."

"Milk's fresh this mawnin', too," called the same hunter, and I turned halfway on the stool and gave him another smile, because he was again smiling at me, and now so was his friend, who looked a hell of a lot like him, enough, in fact, that I turned to Florence and said, "Twins?"

She nodded happily, as if eager to share big news. "The Haislip boys," she said, eyes twinkling, pen poised over her order pad. "Trippe and Ryan," she went on, voice lowered, "so named 'cuz their ma had a crush on two state troopers by the name of Officer Trippe and Officer Ryan, and she weren't sure who the father was, you know, and she didn't want the troopers gettin' mad. You gawna have somethin' with that chowder? A sandwich, mebbe?"

I nodded, said, "Grilled cheese on whole wheat," and added, "That's an interesting story."

Her eyes twinkled a thank-you. "I don't tell nothin' but interesting stories." She looked over at Ryan and Trippe Haislip. "Ain't that right, boys?"

And, as if they'd been listening in, they answered in unison, "That's right, Florence."

She shook her head. "Ain't got whole wheat, though. We got white and rye and pumpernickel."

"Pumpernickel. Thanks."

Her eyes twinkled. "Right polite young man, you are," she said, and disappeared into the kitchen.

From behind me, one of the Haislip boys called, "Thatchore Malibu parked out there?" I looked at him, then looked where he was nodding, at Abner's Malibu parked in front of the restaurant. "Yes," I said.

"Well," he said, "I'd go an' check it if I was you 'cuz there was a man lookin' at it jus' now."

"A man?"

"Big man," he answered, and his brother nodded and agreed, "Ver'a big man."

"Fat man," said the other brother.

I thought, *Damn, it's the man driving the Ford.* I went to the front door and peered out. A few cars were moving slowly down the narrow main street of South Canaan. An old couple, hand in hand, was going into the South Canaan Hardware Store across from the restaurant, a young woman carrying a baby in a backpack and a bag of groceries in her arms was coming out of an IGA store next to the hardware store. But there was no fat man looking at the Malibu, and no dark blue LTD.

I stepped outside, keeping the door open with my arm. I looked right, then left. Still nothing. I heard just behind me, as if from a short distance, "And that little girl, she put those cats in that Igloo cooler, Ryan, she locked 'em up in there—musta' been a hundred degrees that day—and she plumb forgot about 'em, an' you know"—the distance shortened— "when her ma found those cats she said they looked godawful. I guess that'd be kinda like bein' buried alive, don'tcha think, Ryan? Kinda like bein' buried alive. And it'd be kinda sad, too, I guess, if it wasn't so damned funny."

I turned my head; the Haislip brothers were standing just behind me, they were apparently waiting for me to get out of the way. I stepped aside.

One of them said, "Nice cars, those old Malibus," as they both stepped past me.

"Sure," I said.

And they said in unison, "You have yourself a good day now."

I went back into the restaurant and ate my clam chowder and grilled cheese sandwich.

I was in Massachusetts a half hour later, on U.S. Route 7, heading toward the town of Ashley Falls. I'd developed a little tickle in my throat, and every time I coughed I tasted Florence's Real New England Style Clam Chowder all over again, which was less than pleasant. (It seemed to have been seasoned right, the sauce wasn't too heavy, the potatoes and clam bits were cooked well, and I wished, even as I forced it down, that I could enjoy it, if only for Florence's sake, who looked on expectantly, hoping for a compliment. But I couldn't. It smelled the way Abner's beach house did—of wet wood. After a while I said, "It's good, Florence; really good!" She looked pleased, said "Thanks," and went back into the kitchen.)

The road to Ashley Falls from South Canaan was smooth enough, but it was narrow and as twisted as a Slinky. It had so many twists and turns, in fact, that the Massachusetts Department of Transportation had, I guessed, given up trying to erect enough hazard signs on it. Eventually, there were no signs at all, and I was left to guess what the road was going to do within the next five hundred or a thousand feet. And that meant, of course, that I had to slow down from fifty-five to about forty.

I had just come out of a severe left-hand turn—and had noticed happily that the road was straight for another half mile or so—when I looked in the rearview mirror and saw the blue LTD a good five car lengths back, its speed precisely matching mine.

The glare of the late afternoon sun put a glaze of light on its windshield, but when we passed a line of tall trees that blocked the sun, I saw that there were several people in it—two in front and two in back.

Then we were past the line of trees, and the glaze of sunlight hid them.

TWENTY-EIGHT

That's when the Malibu started acting up, when I was past that line of trees, five miles south of Ashley Falls. I heard a ticking noise from the engine first, and though I know precious little about how cars work, the word "tapits" came to mind. I didn't know what "tapits" were; maybe there was no such thing; maybe it was simply a word that men used when they wanted to sound knowledgeable about cars.

The ticking noise soon became a knocking noise and the Malibu started bucking and coughing. Then the knocking noise became a thumping noise, and the engine powered down all by itself, so the Malibu slowed to thirty, then twenty, then fifteen. It stuck there, and no matter what I did with the accelerator, that's where it stayed. I cursed, glanced in the rearview mirror at the LTD, and saw that it was still a precise five car lengths behind me.

I pulled over to the shoulder and shut the car off. What else could I do?

The LTD shot past, engine roaring, as if the driver were happy to have such a slowpoke as me off the road.

I couldn't help it. When the LTD was a hundred yards or so down the road, I flipped the bird at it: "Assholes!" I yelled, and I got a quick mental picture of the LTD and the silver Chevette Scooter colliding head-on. "Shit for brains!" I yelled. It made me feel good, even if the effort started up that tickle in my throat again, which made me cough repeatedly, which brought back the taste of Florence's clam chowder, which quickly got me grimacing and spitting, over and over again in an effort to get that taste out of my mouth.

"It'll stick with ya," Florence had said, pushing the bowl of clam chowder at me across the counter. "You'll be back for more, gar-un-teed."

I opened the Malibu's hood, and in the failing, early evening light I mentally cataloged the items beneath—fan belt, generator, carburetor, radiator, little black tubular doodad sticking out of the engine block that I assumed was the PCV valve (and I prided myself on knowing what PCV stood for; I used to think it meant "pollution control valve." It doesn't. It means "positive crankcase ventilation"). I had shut the engine off; now I decided that it would be smarter to have the engine running while I tried to figure out what was wrong, so I got back into the car, started it, and went back to listen under the hood. A hard thumping sound came from the front of the engine block, and I said to myself, "Hell, it's a rod. I've thrown a rod," although I didn't know precisely what a rod was, either.

And from behind me I heard, "Ain't a rod. It's your torque converter." I whirled, heart thumping. A tall, thin, middle-aged man was standing behind me. He was wearing oil-stained bib overalls and a cream-colored long-sleeved shirt. He grinned, his blue eyes twinkled; he nodded at the engine. "Torque converter," he said again.

"Torque converter," I said. "What's that?"

"Helps your car go," he answered. "If you got a busted torque converter your car won't go."

"Oh," I said, and noticed an old Dodge Power Wagon behind him, on the shoulder. "Is it hard to fix?"

"Ain't hard to fix, no." He rubbed his bewhiskered chin as if in thought. "But it's expensive."

"Oh? How expensive?"

"Well, I guess that's gawna depend on how bad you want your car to go, ain't it?" He stuck his hand out. "Name's Anton Kenney," he said, pronouncing it "An-*twawn*," and I thought it a very unlikely name for him.

"Sam Feary," I said, and shook his hand. "I don't have much money, Mr. Kenney."

"Anton," he said. "You just let me take care of it, Sam, and I gar-un-tee you'll have a happy car come mawnin'."

I believed him. What choice did I have? ''Thanks,'' I said, and he went back to his Dodge Power Wagon, which I noticed then had a tow bar on it, hooked the Malibu to it, and ten minutes later—during which he greeted my attempts at conversation with either a grunt or a disinterested ''Uh-huh''—we were in Ashley Falls.

It was much like South Canaan. There was a hardware store—the Ashley Falls Hardware Store—an IGA near it, a beauty parlor, a hotel—the Ashley Falls Hotel, housed in a huge white Victorian house—and a small, quaint-looking restaurant called the Coffee Cup.

Anton drove through the village, made a left onto what appeared to be Ashley Falls' only side street—the street sign appeared to read ''Haywire Street,'' and I told myself that I hadn't read it correctly—to a white cement block building a couple of hundred yards up the street that had the words ''Anton's Garage'' painted in black over the entrance. He parked the Power Wagon in front of the garage, got out, opened the garage door, got back in, pulled back onto the street, and turned around. Then he backed the Malibu into the garage, all the while softly whistling ''Swing Low, Sweet Chariot.''

''Sounds nice, Anton,'' I told him.

''An-*twawn*,'' he corrected. ''Just like you were gawna say 'Antoinette,' you know, but you stop halfway.''

''An-*twawn*,'' I said.

"Good," he said, smiling, and we both got out of the truck.

He unhooked the Malibu, closed the garage door, and led me to his boxy two-story house next to the garage. The house's white clapboard exterior was much in need of paint.

We went in a side door through a tiny mudroom, where he took off his mud-encased boots, then into the kitchen, where a woman was peeling potatoes under running water at the chipped, white enamel sink. "This is Mrs. Kenney, my wife," Anton said. The woman could have been his twin, I thought. She, too, was tall, thin, blue-eyed, dark-haired.

"Hello, Mrs. Kenney," I said.

She nodded and said "Hello" in a tiny, apologetic voice, as if to tell me her presence in the kitchen, as irksome as it was, was required, so please pay her no mind.

"Sam here has got trouble with his Malibu," Anton said.

"Trouble with his Malibu," Mrs. Kenney said.

Anton nodded at a square white wooden table with three chairs at it in the middle of the kitchen. "Have a seat there, Sam; take the load off."

I sat. Anton sat. Mrs. Kenney continued peeling potatoes under running water at the sink. I began, "I saw a hotel in town—"

Anton, waving the observation away, cut in, "You're gawna stay right here tonight, Sam. Wouldn't have it no other way."

Mrs. Kenney echoed him, "No other way."

"Thanks, An-*twawn*," I began. "Like I said, I

don't have much money, but if it's all the same to you—"

"Who has money, Sam? Who?" He spoke with a hearty chuckle in his voice. "Besides, money don't mean much to us. Can't say, Sam, that money's ever done us much *good*."

"Oh?" I said.

"Money bought me a wedding dress once," Mrs. Kenney chimed in. "I know that, An*twawn*."

Besides the wooden table and the not very sturdy wooden chairs around it, the kitchen was empty. To either side of and above the sink where Mrs. Kenney peeled potatoes, there was a row of three white wooden cupboards with black iron latches. Like the house, these cupboards needed painting badly; there were areas the size of dollar bills where the light green primer beneath was visible, and a hundred other spots where it looked like someone had been throwing darts. Beneath the countertop—which looked disconcertingly as if it had the same kind of oak-print Contact paper on it that I'd found on the doors at Abner's beach house—there was another row of equally rough cabinet doors, also with black iron latches.

The floor was covered with a beige linoleum that had specks of green, blue, and red splattered through it.

"Distressed," said Anton.

I looked confusedly at him. "Distressed?" I asked.

"The cupboards," he explained, and seemed to swell with pride suddenly. "They's distressed."

I misinterpreted what he was telling me. I began, "Well, yes, but—"

He cut in, "I did it myself. Used nails and paint thinner."

I looked around at the cupboards again. "Nails and paint thinner," I said while I looked. "Yes. I see." I paused. "It looks very nice, An*twawn*."

Mrs. Kenney offered, "Makes 'em look antique, Sam. This ain't an old house, you know." She looked questioningly at her husband, her hands still working skillfully at the potatoes, the water still running. "Isn't that so, An*twawn*?"

I looked at him. He nodded once. "That's so."

And I said again, "I see."

I looked at her. She was grinning at me over her shoulder while the water ran onto her hands peeling potatoes. She said, "You're stayin' for supper, right. We're gawna have real New England style potatoes." I found that as she talked it was hard to concentrate on anything but her mouth. It was wide, full-lipped, and her bright reddish-orange lipstick reflected the light of the fluorescent lamp overhead.

"Thanks," I began uncertainly, "I'd like to."

"We make you nervous?" Anton said, chuckling.

"No," I lied. "You don't make me nervous."

He chuckled again. "Well, that's strange, Sam, 'cuz we make ever-buddy else nervous. Heck, we even make ourselves nervous—can you imagine that?" He glanced at his wife. "Don't we make ourselves nervous, Mother?"

"Cabbage, too," said Mrs. Kenney, and plopped a peeled potato into the colander beside the sink. "Ham, too," she added, and looked questioningly at her husband. "We got us some ham, ain't that right, An*twawn*?"

He nodded heavily. "Slaughtered it myself, I did. Just last week." He grinned hugely. I noticed then that he, like the Haislip brothers, was all but toothless. "Slaughtered it myself," he repeated. "Name-a Lucille. That was her name. Lucille. Lucille the pig. Had her . . ." He looked questioningly over at his wife. "Mother, how long'd we have Lucille? Musta been twenty years, isn't that so?"

She grinned almost as toothlessly as her husband had. Her white gums looked pathetic beneath that reddish-orange lipstick. "Heaven's sake, An*twawn*, she were *your* pig. How'm I s'pose to keep tracka *your* pig?" She turned back to her potato peeling. "Land-a-goshen," she whispered.

"Lucille," I said, smiling nervously. "Nice name for a pig."

"Nice pig," he said.

"And she'll make some real good eatin'," Mrs. Kenney said.

"Can't thinka nothin' I'd rather eat," Anton said, staring wistfully at the ceiling. " 'Ceptin', of course—"

"Enougha that, An*twawn*," his wife broke in with mock severity.

I thought that Anton had been making a little sex joke. But I was wrong.

Anton stood suddenly. "Well, c'mon, then, Sam, and help me with this pig."

"Help you with the pig?" I said.

"Sure," he said, "you wanta eat, you gotta help with the pig, that's my motto."

"That's so," Mrs. Kenney said. "That's been his motto a long time, Sam." She looked questioningly at her husband. "How long's that been your motto, An*twawn*?"

"Long time," he said.

"Long time," she said.

"What are you going to do with the pig?" I asked.

Anton grinned in expectation, "Well, we gotta slaughter it, you know."

I heard one of Mrs. Kenney's potatoes go *plop!* into the colander. I said hopefully, "But I thought you'd already slaughtered it."

He looked confused. His big right hand rubbed his bewhiskered chin as if in thought. At last he said, "Well, I did say that, didn't I? You are right, Sam."

I smiled uneasily, "Then that means you don't have to slaughter it?"

He shook his head slowly, a little forgiving smile playing on his lips, as if I had committed a *faux pas* and he was about to give me the benefit of some country wisdom. "Well, now," he said, "these pigs are a lot like chickens sometimes. You know, you cut a chicken's head off and nine times out of ten it'll keep on runnin' 'round. Pig's the same way, Sam. You cut the damned thing's head off and before ya know it she's up on her feet and rooting around like nothin' happened, 'cept she ain't got no head, of course."

"*Awful* thing to see," Mrs. Kenney chimed in, and another potato plopped into the colander.

I said, "You're joking, right?"

Anton shook his head slowly. ''I never joke, Sam. I used to, but I don't no more.''

I heard, distantly, a low, continuous snorting sound from outside. It quickly grew louder, and closer, and suddenly Anton jumped to his feet, ran stiffly to a closet door, and threw it open to reveal a long-handled axe standing inside. He said, his smile an orgy of expectation, ''There's old Lucille now, Sam. By God, I think we're gonna have us some real fun!''

TWENTY-NINE

I looked at him with an asinine quivering smile on my mouth and I said again, "You're joking, right?"

He lifted that mammoth long-handled axe out of the closet, hefted it over his shoulder like a lumberjack, and gave me a big, happy grin. "Joking, Sam?"

"He never jokes," Mrs. Kenney said, looking very serious, her full, bright lips set in a straight and serious line.

"I never joke," said Anton.

The snorting noises were much closer now, as if they were coming from just outside the door to the mudroom. Then I heard something banging against that door, hard, and I whispered, "Oh, Jesus!"

Anton said, "But I'm joking now."

"Huh?" I said.

He called toward the banging and snorting noises, ''Okay, Matthew, he's on to us.''

The noises continued.

''Matthew,'' he called louder, starting for the door, axe still on his shoulder, ''I said he's on to us.''

The banging noises continued. The snorting noises continued. Anton looked miffed. ''God Almighty,'' he whispered.

''God Almighty,'' whispered Mrs. Kenney, and plopped another potato into the colander by the sink.

''Oh, Jesus!'' I whispered.

''Matthew, you can stop that now,'' Anton called. ''Matthew, you can stop that now.'' He disappeared into the mudroom. Another of his wife's potatoes went *plop!* into the colander. ''Matthew, stop it!'' I heard above the racket of crashing and snorting. ''Stop it, Matthew. Stop it, goddammit.''

Then silence.

Plop! went another potato into the colander by the sink. ''That's a dozen,'' said Mrs. Kenney. ''You like potatoes, Sam?''

''Huh?'' I whispered, feeling once again the hard knot of fear starting inside me.

Another potato went into the colander. ''That's thirteen,'' she said.

''*Surprise!*'' I heard, and lurched in the chair, found myself toppling backward to the floor, grabbed for the edge of the table, caught it, and straightened myself up. I looked toward the doorway to the mudroom. Three faces were sticking around the edge of the doorway, one on top of the other. There was Anton's grinning, bewhiskered face at the bottom, and above it another male face, also thin, dark, blue-eyed, but with the stub of a chewed cigar sticking out between thin white lips, and, on top, the huge, squinty-eyed, dark pink face of a pig.

"Jesus Christ!" I breathed.

The pig face vanished into the mudroom. Seconds later, it reappeared in the hands of a middle-aged woman dressed in bib overalls and a cream-colored shirt. She stepped out into the kitchen a few feet and I saw that she looked much like Anton and his wife and the man with the cigar—thin, dark-haired, blue-eyed.

Anton and the man with the cigar straightened and stood next to the woman as if they were responding to a curtain call. "Did we scare ya?" Anton asked enthusiastically.

I said, a warble of fear in my voice, "I think I should leave, I really think I should leave."

And Anton said, sounding hurt, "Jus' havin' a little fun, Sam. You oughtn't leave becaus'a that."

Plop! went another potato into the colander. "That's a hundred," said Mrs. Kenney.

I noticed then that Anton was still carrying the huge, long-handled axe. I noticed, too, that his big hand was rhythmically gripping it hard, loosening, gripping it, loosening, gripping.

Plot! I heard. "That's a million billion," Mrs. Kenney said.

And I said, that little warble of fear now clearly a tremor of panic, "Who *are* you people?"

"We's country people," said Anton, and his wife and the man with the cigar and the woman carrying the pig's head echoed him—the voice of each overlapping the voice of the other, so it sounded as if they were singing a round, like *Row, row, row your boat* . . . only it was, "We's country people" . . . " 's country people". . . "untry people."

My chair scraped shrilly against the linoleum as I pushed it back from the table and stood unsteadily. "I'd better leave," I said. "Really, I'd better leave."

"Can't leave," said Anton.

Plop! went another potato.

" 'Cuz your car's broke," Anton explained.

"I'll walk," I said. "I don't mind walking, I've done a lot of walking."

"You scare't, boy?" said the man with the cigar, with the same kind of hopeful enthusiasm I'd heard from Anton.

I answered, "No, of course not, why would I be scared?" and I backed toward an open doorway a half-dozen feet behind the table. The doorway led, I guessed, into the living room.

Anton said, "Aw, don't go in there, Sam. You don't wanta go in there." He sounded annoyed.

But I did go in there. Into a room that was straight out of a 1945 issue of *Better Homes and Gardens*—here an overstuffed blue velvet armchair, there another, but smaller, for "the lady of the house," there a floor-standing Victrola, there an overstuffed red couch with white doilies on the arms.

And from the kitchen doorway a trio of human shadows was cast long and lean on the living room floor by the blue-green glow of the kitchen's overhead fluorescent light, and I could hear Anton whistling "Swing Low, Sweet Chariot" as he had in his truck, except now it was ragged and dissonant, as if he were trying to whistle through a fistful of mud clogging his mouth.

The other man called, "We make you nervous, boy? You scare't, boy?"

Plop! I heard. "That's a hundred billion trillion zillion."

The blue-green fluorescent glow died. The shadows vanished.

And the room I was in changed. It aged. The chairs sagged and grew soiled as if through decades of use. The couch collapsed at its center. The musty smell of decay and abandonment grew heavy in the air.

And I laughed. Loudly, shrilly, hysterically. I'd laughed like that only once before, in Nam, after I'd gotten separated from my squad on a jungle patrol and had to spend three hours finding my way back. And when I did get back, I laughed shrilly, hysterically, with relief. But when I was done laughing, you see, I knew where I was. I knew I could reach out and touch things that were real and familiar—my bunk, my little stash of *Playboys*, my cigar box filled with letters from home, my buddies—Stan, Frank, Herbie, several others—who were watching me laugh and knew why I was laughing, that I was no more a fruitcake than anyone else who'd spent time in Nam. But, in the village of Ashley Falls, Massachusetts, in Anton Kenney's boxy white clapboard house, in his vintage 1945 living room, I knew that when I stopped laughing there'd be nothing familiar for me to reach out and touch. No stash of *Playboys*. No cigar box with letters from home. Only someone else's smelly overstuffed couch and chairs and someone else's walls. And someone else's life gone by.

And when I stopped laughing it was only because my throat hurt and my sides ached and I had begun to feel dizzy. Then I sat on that big overstuffed couch, right in the middle of it, where the broken frame rested on the floor—so my knees jutted high above my stomach—and I let my head fall back and my arms rest on my thighs. It was a comfortable position. It felt good. And after a few moments I began to make quick, weary sighing noises, the kind of noises a sleeping dog makes when, we say, it's having bad dreams. I whispered, "Oh, Jesus, Jesus," again and again. And I thought that being there, in that house, in what passed for Ashley Falls, Massachusetts, was like being in a closet filled with hornets. The only thing to do was sit tight. Move slowly. If they attacked, you ran for the exit. If there was an exit.

Plop! I heard. I didn't jump up and run for the exit. I waited. I was being rational.

Plop! I heard again. *Plop! . . . Plop!*

"That's just water dripping," I told myself.

Plop! . . . Plop!

"That's just water dripping," I said.

Plop!

"Only water dripping."

Plop! . . .

"Dammit!"

Plop! Plop! Plop!

I bolted from the couch, across the living room to the front door, hesitated only an instant, and pulled the door open.

Dusk had fallen. A line of flat, wispy clouds—cirrostratus is the correct name for them, I think—painted the sky a bright red-orange. At the house directly across the street, a house much like the one I was in, a boy of five or six was climbing up and down the porch steps; with each step he sang a part of the alphabet: "*A-B-C-D-*" . . . he was at the top of the steps. "*E-F-G-H-*" . . . he was at the bottom. I watched him do this for a minute or so, until he'd gotten through the alphabet once and had started it again. Now and then he glanced at me and smiled. He was a good-looking boy, with a mop of dark curls and what looked, from across the street at dusk, like huge dark eyes in a round, cherubic face.

I saw, too, that in a few of the other houses lights were burning. From one of the houses I could hear some kind of classical violin music (and since I don't know Mozart from mozzarella, I can't say what composer it was). From one of the other houses, I heard two voices raised in anger, each trying to subdue the other with sheer volume.

I said to myself, "This is no hornet's nest. This is only a side street in a tiny village in southern Massachusetts."

And there was one really great moment, a moment that came and went as quickly as a heartbeat, like the moment when something really tasty first passes over the tongue, that I actually believed it.

THIRTY

Then the boy changed, you see.

First his knees buckled, and he fell. Hard. Face forward down the bottom two porch steps. And I said to myself, "Well, kids fall all the time. And they bounce back. Kids are tough." But when that boy fell, he banged his chin very hard on the cement walkway, and a quick, loud "Uhh!" of pain and surprise escaped him. Then he lay still. And silent.

Until he hitched backward on his belly, with his arms straight out in front of him and his spread legs pointing toward the house, his bones crunching and snapping audibly as his body conformed to the shape of the porch steps, as if he were some sort of huge, misshapen, jellylike crab dressed in corduroys and a red plaid shirt.

And while this was happening, he relentlessly recited his ABCs: "*A*"—hitch—"*B*"—hitch—"*C*"—hitch, until he had hitched backward all the way to the top of the porch steps. And there, very slowly, one vertebra at a time, like someone doing a weird kind of aerobic exercise, he straightened. And as he straightened, his body made a sound like paper being crumpled, and I realized that his bones were snapping back into place.

Then he began climbing up and down the steps all over again, just like a real boy, reciting his ABCs and glancing over at me occasionally and smiling. *He's enjoying himself now,* I thought. *He's being a kid.*

And there was no way in hell I was going to wait around for him to fall again, no way in hell I wanted to hear again that small grunt of pain and surprise. What I was going to do was get into the Malibu, fire it up, and drive out of this bizarre little village that was masquerading as Ashley Falls, Massachusetts. Even if the Malibu wouldn't top fifteen miles an hour, it was still faster than walking. And besides, I'd grown strangely attached to it—it was mechanical, it was predictable, it was ordinary; it was *real*, for God's sake.

I ran down the front porch steps, turned right, rounded the edge of Anton's house. And found that there was no white cement block building called "Anton's Garage." There was an old Dodge Power Wagon half rusted to oblivion, beside it Abner's Malibu, and around them a quarter acre of mud where Anton's Garage should have been.

I fished in my pockets for the keys to the Malibu. I

came up with my wallet, a Philharmonic ticket, a couple of quarters. But no keys. I went around to the driver's door, bent over, peered in. The keys were in the ignition. I tried the door. It was locked. "Shit!" I breathed. I glanced about. The dusk had turned rapidly to early evening darkness. Across the street, in the row of white clapboard houses, I could see half a dozen lighted windows; I could see the boy in corduroy hitching backward up his porch steps, "*A-B-C-D*"; I could hear the classical music; I could hear the argument intensifying, curses shrieked, doors slammed. And as I took it all in, I saw a human form appear at one of the lighted windows. It was a good sixty or seventy-five yards off, and it was backlit, but it was clearly the form of a young woman, and its head appeared to turn in my direction. "Shit!" I breathed again. Another human form appeared, at another window, in another house. The form of a child. And it, too, turned its head in my direction.

I peered frantically through the Malibu's driver's window at the passenger door. It, too, was locked. I tried the driver's door again. Nothing. I pulled hard. "Shit, goddammit!" I shrieked.

Across the way, the loud argument stopped abruptly. I looked up from the Malibu. The boy in corduroy—"*D-E-F*"—was at the top of the porch steps. He straightened, glanced my way, smiled. Continued smiling.

At another lighted window, another form appeared, and its head turned in my direction.

I thought, *This is perfect! Here I am in this town made up of the dead and I want to leave and my car's stuck in the mud and they're all looking at me!*

Just as the sanitation workers had, and the woman in red, and the girls in pink taffeta.

"Mind your own *p*'s and *q*'s," Madeline had told me. I was beginning to understand what she was talking about.

The mud around the Malibu was studded with rocks. Most of them were small and flat, like small pancakes, but there were a few as large as fists. I bent over, picked up one of the fist-size rocks, muttered, "Sorry, Malibu," and smashed the driver's window with it. I unlocked the door, opened it, brushed away the broken glass, and climbed into the driver's seat.

The scenario I expected then—following in the old Hammer Films tradition—was that I'd first have trouble starting the car. And while I was trying to start it, I'd glance up and see the dead all around, coming my way, arms outstretched, mouths wide open. Then, when they were within twenty feet or so of the car, I'd get it started, breathe a sigh of relief, put it in gear, hit the accelerator, and listen to the sickening, soul-deadening sound of the tires spinning in the mud.

That was the scenario I expected. That, in its predictability, would have been satisfying, even comforting.

This, however, is what happened:

The car started easily enough. I listened to it idle a few moments, thought it was idling slow and rough. Then, before turning the headlights on, I looked again at the houses across the street. I saw that there were people at all the lighted windows now, their heads turned in my direction. I turned the headlights on, bent over, and looked to the left at the side door of Anton's house, the door that led into the mudroom. That door had a window in it and I could see that a light was on in the kitchen. I could also see a number of people there, in the doorway beyond the mudroom.

I put the car in gear and hit the accelerator.

The engine died.

"Shit!" I whispered, put the car in park, and turned the ignition to "on" again. The engine roared to life. I put the car in gear again, my foot on the brake, hesitated, looked once more at Anton's side door. The kitchen light was off now, but I could see a group of people clumped darkly together behind the door. I straightened, took my foot off the brake. Again the car stalled. I hit the dashboard. "Dammit!" I barked, and turned the ignition key again. The car roared to life. I floored the accelerator, listened to the engine thump, looked at the side door again. The clump of people was outside the door. I looked straight ahead. Like strange, tall hedges that had sprung up between the front of the car and the houses across the street, clumps of people appeared at the perimeter of the headlights.

I frantically put the car in gear and floored the accelerator. The Malibu shot forward a few feet. And the engine died.

"It's your torque converter," I heard.

I shrieked, reached desperately for the key, banged my knuckles against the steering column, found the key, turned it. Nothing. "Dammit, goddammit!" I breathed.

"It's your torque converter, Sam. It's your torque converter."

I tried the key again. Again nothing. "Dammit!" I realized that the car was in drive. I put it in park, tried the key; the engine roared to life.

"I can fix it, Sam."

"No, you can't," I whispered, as if to myself.

"I can fix anything now."

Plop!

"I got my own garage now, Sam."

"No, you don't," I whispered.

Plop!

"I got my own garage now, Sam."

"You scare't, boy?"

Plop!

I whispered to the Malibu, "Go, please. Go!" And I floored it, it shot forward a few feet. And the engine died.

"You scare't, boy?"

"Shit, yes," I whispered, turned the engine on again, put it in gear, and pulled very slowly out onto the street.

Again the engine died. I hit the steering wheel furiously, the horn blared, my heart began to race. I fumbled for the ignition, turned the key. Nothing. I tried it again. Still nothing. I took a breath. "Calm down, Sam," I whispered. "Calm down!"

I heard, to my left, outside the broken window, "You gotta put it in park, Sam. Put it in park."

I put it in park. "Thanks," I said.

"Ain't nothin'," he chuckled.

I glanced at him. He had the long-handled axe raised high over his head.

THIRTY-ONE

"What are you *do*ing?!" I squawked.

"What's he doing?" a woman said.

"What's he doing?" a man said.

Anton's axe crashed through the Malibu's roof and ended up only a couple of inches from my head.

"Gotta eat!" Anton shrieked. "We all of us gotta eat; *this* is what I eat!" And he pulled the axe out of the roof. "This is what I eat, Sam! Even zombies gotta eat, Sam! This is what *zombies* eat!"

"Zombies?" someone said.

"Jesus," I muttered. I crouched low in the seat and groped desperately for the key in the ignition.

Again Anton's axe crashed through the roof, above the back seat now. I found the key, turned it. The engine fired up.

"Zombies!" Anton shrieked. "Zombies gotta eat, too."

"Zombies?" someone said.

I was still crouched very low, my torso on the passenger's side of the seat. Again the axe came crashing through the Malibu's roof. I groped for the gearshift, just an inch or so up from where I could safely reach it.

"Zombies got to eat, too!" Anton shrieked.

"Zombies?" a woman asked. I heard a strange kind of sad confusion in her voice.

"Zombies eat *people*!" Anton shrieked.

I straightened a little, grabbed the gearshift lever, pulled it to reverse, and found that because I was still prone in the seat, I had almost no control over the accelerator pedal; I was able to touch it only lightly, so the car moved slowly and erratically across the street.

Again the axe head smashed through the Malibu's roof, near the top of the windshield; the windshield cracked in a crazy zigzag pattern.

Anton shrieked, "I'm gawna *eat* you, Sam! I'm gawna *eat* you, Sam!"

"Zombies?" said the same woman, with the same kind of strange, sad confusion in her voice.

"Zombies?" said another woman.

The car thudded into the curb and stopped. The engine again threatened to shut off. Either I took a chance or Anton was going to split me in two with that long-handled axe. I sat up quickly in the seat, grabbed the wheel, turned it hard left, and touched the accelerator. The car lurched forward, the engine again threatened to shut off. I touched the accelerator.

"Zombies?" I heard. A half-dozen or more voices

were saying it at once now, the voices of the women and the men and the children who had come out of their houses to watch the trespasser make his getaway. And each voice had that same sad confusion in it, so their voices together were a loud lament, a wail—*Zombies?* they were saying. *We aren't zombies! We're human beings!*

And, at last, the Malibu sprang to life and I found myself pulling away from Anton and his long-handled axe at twenty miles per hour, then thirty, then forty, and I realized that I couldn't see anything, only the vague flat plane of the road and the dark clumps of weeds and grasses to the side of the road, and I whispered to myself, "Oh my God, I'm going blind!"

Then I grimaced at my stupidity, flicked the headlights on, and I wasn't blind anymore.

At the beginning of Haywire Street I stopped quickly, looked right, then left—"Courtesy will prevail, Sam," I thought Madeline would say—and turned left, rocketed past the Ashley Falls Hotel, where a human form, head turning as I sped past, stood at each of the windows. And I passed the Ashley Falls Hardware Store, doing fifty or fifty-five now (smiling to myself in thanks to the Malibu for its miraculous resurrection), where all the lights also were burning, and where there were a dozen or more people standing, watching, then past the Coffee Cup, where a man dressed in bib overalls stood just inside the door with a bowl in his hand and a spoon held halfway to his mouth, and then out of Ashley Falls and onto that narrow winding stretch of road where Anton had found me a million years ago.

* * *

I had figured it out. All of it. The whole thing. At some fork in the road I had made a wrong turn. Somewhere on my way from Manhattan to Brookfield I had missed a turnoff and so had ended up on a road that led to . . . Ashley Falls. And South Canaan. And God knew where else. But they weren't *real* villages—they were places where the dead hung out and pretended to be alive and tried to do the things that the living do.

I smiled to myself on that lonely, narrow, twisting stretch of road which, I figured, would take me soon enough into what masqueraded as South Canaan, Connecticut. I smiled. I'd figured it out. There were no secrets anymore. No one was going to pull the wool over my eyes again. I had my car—I was beginning to feel very proprietary toward it—and my life, and a purpose, and I knew precisely what this world that Abner had gotten himself into was all about.

A route sign slid past, caught briefly in the glare of the high beams. *U.S. Route 7*, it read. "Sure, sure," I whispered. When I glanced in my rearview mirror I could see nothing and I imagined that as I passed over the road, it disintegrated behind me, it got swallowed up. If I were to turn around and go back toward Ashley Falls, the same thing would happen only in reverse. As I sped forward, a kind of reality—a *masquerade* of reality—would build itself up in front of me and then disintegrate in back of me.

But then I looked into the rearview mirror and saw

headlights. I thought they were a pickup truck's headlights, because pickup trucks' lights are set higher up, so they look brighter than normal headlights.

I thought, *Well, that's someone else who's gotten himself caught on this road,* and I pictured the road disintegrating behind him, instead of me. And then I thought, as the headlights gained on me, *No, you idiot, that's Anton Kenney and he's going to split you in two with that long-handled axe.*

So I mashed the accelerator pedal to the floor and felt the Malibu gain speed with aching slowness, from 60 to 63 to 65 to 68 to 72. And that's where it stuck. At 72. With the headlights of what I assumed was a pickup truck just a car length behind.

"No way you're going to catch me, Anton," I whispered. That's when the flashing red light appeared, the siren wailed, and I realized that it was not a pickup truck behind me but one of those mammoth old Plymouth Furys the cops used to use.

I was not about to be fooled. "Cop, sure!" I whispered. "Tell me all about it." And, to coax a few more miles per hour out of the Malibu, I breathed at it, "C'mon, baby, c'mon!" In response the Malibu's engine started thumping loudly, and it slowed from 72 to 50 to 25 to 15 in a matter of a few seconds.

What could I do? I pulled over. And the Fury pulled over. Its siren went off, its pulsating red light stayed on. And I waited. And waited. And waited. All the while in a sort of fit of resignation; *Yes,* I told myself, *they are going to pull the wool over your eyes, Sam. Because you're a fool.*

"Got a license, boy?"

A small burp/grunt of surprise escaped me; I turned my head and looked at the man standing beside the car. He was wearing what looked, in the glow of the Fury's headlights, like a regulation deputy sheriff's uniform—black leather jacket with chromed badge, gray shirt, gray pants, black, highly polished shoes, gun belt and gun—a very big gun, a .45. His face was a regulation deputy sheriff's face—white and nondescript. His hair was neatly combed, short, and black.

"Sure I've got a license," I said, feeling grimly playful. "I wouldn't drive without one."

" 'Sthatso?" the deputy said, and he produced a flashlight from his gun belt, bent over, and shone it around the interior of the car. "You got a hell of a car here, don'tcha?"

"It gets me around," I said, and wished that my voice were steadier.

"Does it, now?" he said, and continued to shine the flashlight around the interior of the car. Finally he said, "You got contraband in here, boy?"

I guffawed. I couldn't help it. "Sure," I said, "I've got STP in here, and mescaline, and eight kilos of hash, and a half ton of coke, and eighteen bushels of horseshit."

"Do ya, now?" he said. He was clearly a man of few words.

"I never lie," I said. I was certain that this rural cop was what Anton was, and Anton's wife was, and all the others in Ashley Falls were. And that's why I was feeling so grimly playful. I was thinking, *Hell, at least I can have a little fun before I die.*

He shone the flashlight into my eyes. ''You're a damn troublemaker's what you are, boy!'' he said.

I looked away from the glare of the flashlight. ''I give it my best shot,'' I said.

''And I'll tell ya, boy, we're real tireda troublemakers 'round here. We're real tired of people tearin' about like they's already dead and don't give a damn!''

''I'll bet you are,'' I said.

''So what I'm gonna have to do with you, boy, is take you back into town—''

''Into Ashley Falls?'' I said.

''That's right. Into Ashley Falls. And we're gawna put you up for the night, boy.''

''Uh-huh. Sure you are,'' I said, and I put the Malibu in gear, said, ''Bye-bye,'' pressed the accelerator. And went nowhere. The engine died. ''Shit,'' I whispered, and that old familiar knot of panic started in my stomach.

''Yeah,'' the cop said, ''real nice car you got there, boy.'' He put his flashlight back in its place on his gun belt. He unholstered that cannon of his, and he pointed it directly at my head, Dirty Harry style.

''Oh, for God's sake,'' I muttered.

''You get on outa there now, boy, or so help me God—I don't give a good goddamn what the Su*preme* Court says—I'll blow your brains from here to kingdom come!''

''This can't be happening!'' I whispered, as much to myself as to him.

''Now, boy!''

I put my hand on the door handle. I heard the low growl of an engine being revved at a distance. I hesitated.

"*Now!*" the cop said again, and cocked the .45.

The low growl grew rapidly louder. I glanced in the rearview mirror, saw only the glare of the Fury's lights there.

"I will!" the cop snarled. "Don't you fuckin' test me, boy!"

The low growl became a high whine. I saw another set of lights in the rearview mirror, but just briefly. I glanced at the cop. His face was bathed in the glare of two sets of headlights now—his own and the headlights of the car careening toward him. His snarl drooped. His jaw fell open. His head turned stiffly, resignedly toward the vehicle bearing inexorably down on him.

Then he was gone.

And through the cracked windshield of the Malibu, in the light from the Plymouth Fury, I saw the back end of the LTD lose itself in the gathering night.

I didn't want all that to happen. Not when I realized what that cop was exactly—that he was a real cop with a real gun and a real purpose—to get the maniacs off his roads. And how was he to know that some of those maniacs were precisely what he'd called them—"People tearing about like they's already dead and don't give a damn!"

At that moment, just before the night swallowed him up, I would have willingly gone anywhere with him, because he was a link to reality. He *was* reality.

But then the LTD took him from me.

And left me alone. On U.S. Route 7 a couple of miles south of Ashley Falls.

Alone. With no place to go and no way to get there.

Except Brookfield, Vermont. In that huge Plymouth Fury that still had its gumball machine twirling.

And, because fear really does start crazy fires in us all, I got out of the Malibu, thanked it for being as good a car as it could be, right up to the end, got my suitcase from the back seat, went over to the Fury, climbed in, turned it around on the narrow road, and headed north.

Leslie used to say, in our first couple of weeks together, that I brooded. She's right. I do, and did, though much less so after we met than before. She's entirely the reason I don't brood very much anymore. And I don't think I brooded *because* of anything, because I was unhappy about foreign affairs or the plight of the whales (no one *broods* about things like that; they *think* about things like that).

I brooded so much because I wasn't happy. I wasn't *unhappy*. Someone who's been standing in a cold rain all his life isn't unhappy about it; he doesn't give it a thought—that's the way things are. Life consists of standing in a cold rain and scowling, because a cold rain doesn't make anyone whoop with joy.

She does. Alone in the Chevy Nova, I used to whoop. I've danced, too—alone in my apartment. And I've sung out loud. And hopped straight up into the air—which she told me looked "fruity," though I knew she enjoyed it, because I enjoyed it.

A memory: We're in Ithaca, New York, a college

town. We're there for the day. We're in love, and it's obvious to anyone with eyes or ears. We go into a little clothing shop that specializes in voluminous skirts and white cotton blouses; the place could have been called "The Organic Clothing Store." She wants to look around. Fine, I say, we'll look around.

There's some music playing—elevator music, but that's okay. It gets my feet going. And suddenly I hop straight up into the air. It must be quite a sight, because I'm over six feet tall and weigh 230 pounds. Her mouth falls open. She closes it. A little half-embarrassed, half-gleeful smile appears on it.

She pleads, reading my mind in that instant, because I, too, have a little smile on my face, "No, don't do that again." Her smile becomes imploring.

I hop.

She giggles.

I mince over, in time with the elevator music, to a clothing rack that has long-sleeved blouses hanging on it. I do a small, quick two-step. Again her mouth falls open. A young woman walks by and grins at me.

"That woman's looking at you."

I smile. I hop again.

"They'll kick us out."

"No, they won't. We're in love."

And of course they don't kick us out. We dance out, arm in arm, a few minutes later, smiling to ourselves.

THIRTY-TWO

As I headed toward Ashley Falls in the big Plymouth, I realized that I hadn't taken a wrong turnoff, I hadn't zigged left when I should have zagged right, at a fork in the road veered east instead of west. I really was traveling north on U.S. Route 7 toward Ashley Falls, Massachusetts, which would lead me to Burlington and then to Brookfield, Vermont.

It was all simply a matter of *perception*. My perception was different. Like when the Malibu broke down that first time and I got out and stuck my head under the hood and pretended to understand what I was looking at. Lots of people find themselves in similar situations, and I think lots of people get told things like ''It's your torque converter'' by people like Anton Kenney—people whose chances for being helpful have all gone by, because life is behind them.

But they still hang in there, they still try to do their job, they still try to be helpful. And so they say, "It's your torque converter," or, "It's your internal rotator," or, "It's your headlight fluid." And 999,999 times out of a million they're ignored. No one hears them. And they shrug and wait for someone else to come along. Why not? The popular mythology says that they've got lots of time and no place to go. And they believe it. Why shouldn't they?

Or maybe they're door-to-door salesmen with vacuum cleaners under their arms or they're teachers or mailmen or waitresses. Whatever they are, they try like hell to carry on. Habits die hard, I guess. *People* die before their habits do. And who, after all, really wants to leave behind what's familiar and comfortable so they can dive head first into *The Great Unknown*? Who really wants—excuse me, I've just got to say it—who really wants to give up the ghost?

But eventually some poor slob like me comes along and actually hears what they've got to say, actually sees them and responds to them. And it's like a shot in the arm, it nurtures them, picks them up, helps renew their sagging self-image.

And for a while they're as real again as the rocks and the grass and the trees.

Real enough to bury the head of an axe in the roof of an old Malibu.

These were the things that I figured out on the road to Ashley Falls. It didn't please me to figure these things out. They were things that I should have figured out long ago.

* * *

I didn't plan to go back through Ashley Falls, I planned to take a road that would lead me around it. But when I stopped and checked my interstate map I could find no such road, and a quick check of the Plymouth's glove box turned up an area map that was yellow with age, coffee-stained, doodled on, and illegible. Perhaps, I thought, I could simply turn onto a likely-looking road, and hope my usually reliable sense of direction would keep heading me north. It was an idea I clung to as I approached Ashley Falls. I passed two dirt roads, a dead-end road, and, at last, a two-lane paved road. I turned down that road. A couple of miles later, I realized that I was heading south. I turned around and went back to Route 7. A minute later, I saw a sign that I hadn't seen from the passenger's seat of Anton's Power Wagon: The sign read, "VILLAGE OF ASHLEY FALLS—WELCOME!"

I slowed from sixty to the posted speed limit of thirty. I passed a couple dozen big clapboard houses of indeterminate vintage, and when I got to the business district I slowed to twenty.

It was not the village I had been through a million years before. I knew that. (Abner had told me once, "You'll know in here, Sam"—and he thumped his chest—"what's real and what isn't." This was one of those times.) It occupied the same space, but it was not the same village.

The buildings in this village's business district were pretty much the same as that other village's, except the hotel was not called the Ashley Falls Hotel, it was called the Haskins Hotel, and the restaurant was not called the Coffee Cup, it was called Mary's

Coffee Cup. That other village, the one I'd been through with Anton Kenney, was like a tracing of this village, an approximation of it. A clever imitation.

I'm not sure why I turned onto Haywire Street. A combination of curiosity and stupidity, perhaps.

It wasn't called Haywire Street. It was called Drumlin View Row. And there were no big white clapboard houses on it. All the houses were cedar contemporaries with too many right angles, too few windows, and flat, well-manicured, brightly lit lawns. (If there had been any drumlins to view on Drumlin View Row, they'd all been bulldozed into oblivion.)

I pulled into the driveway of a house under construction, put my foot on the brake, and looked about. *They're all dead*, I thought. *They're dead, their children are dead. Even their houses have been demolished to make way for the new.* "It's a pity," I whispered. And in the glare of the headlights I saw Anton rising up out of the blacktop, that long-handled axe poised high above his head.

I stiffened, panic-stricken. Then I slammed the Plymouth into reverse; I felt the tires spinning on the blacktop.

"Damn you!" Anton shrieked. "Damn you! Damn you! Damn you!"

"Good Lord!" I hissed.

"Damn you!" Anton shrieked, and he rose out of the blacktop like someone rising from dark water.

I let off slightly on the accelerator. The Plymouth's tires caught; the car squealed out of the driveway and onto Drumlin View Row. I stopped, slammed it into drive, hesitated. I saw Anton sinking back into the blacktop like a man drowning. I floored the accelerator and moments later had turned right off Drumlin View Row and was heading north out of Ashley Falls.

I hadn't counted on that. I hadn't counted on anger from the dead. And for twenty miles north on U.S. Route 7, I found myself shivering as if from cold.

The Plymouth was fast and comfortable and handled beautifully. I'd shut the two-way radio off because every five minutes or so a woman's voice came over it and said, "Rick? Come in, Rick," until, finally, she said to someone else, "I think something's happened to Rick." I knew that Rick had probably radioed in the license number of the Malibu, but the Malibu was out of commission now. Eventually an alert would be broadcast for the Plymouth. That would happen by morning, I guessed, which gave me the night to use it. And that, I figured, would be more than enough time to get to Brookfield, Vermont. Especially since I planned to make no more stops.

It was about 8:00 P.M. when I was thinking this. My calculations told me I'd be in Brookfield by 2:00 A.M., maybe, with luck, a little earlier.

But, at around 8:30 on a long straight stretch of road a couple miles south of Pontonosuc Gardens, Massachusetts, a pair of headlights appeared in the rearview mirror, advanced on me at a good twenty or thirty miles an hour faster than my own sixty, then paced me five car lengths back.

It was the LTD. I knew it.

And I told myself that, at last, I knew who was driving it. And why.

I told myself that Art DeGraff was driving it. And he was following me because he knew I'd lead him to Abner.

So I pulled over.

The LTD pulled over.

I shut my lights off.

The LTD's lights went off.

Then, taking a very deep breath and wishing to God that I wasn't *enjoying* this so much, I put the Plymouth in gear and mashed the accelerator. It didn't disappoint me. That huge engine fishtailed the Plymouth away from the shoulder and catapulted it down the road a good quarter mile before the LTD had its lights on again.

I kept my lights off. I negotiated a long, easy curve at eighty or so, braked hard and fishtailed onto a gravel side road, then pulled over and stopped, so the curve of the side road hid me. Smiling, proud of myself, I decided then and there that all those hours I'd spent watching TV as a kid hadn't been wasted after all.

I sat tight. Five minutes. Ten minutes. I grew more and more certain that my devilishly clever ploy had worked.

I hadn't, however, taken one very simple fact into account. Dust spits up from gravel roads and hangs in the air for a very long time. The Plymouth had kicked up a lot of dust; it had surely been like a road sign pointing to where I was. And I think that dust was also why I hadn't seen the LTD sitting just behind me with its lights off, its five acres of hood gleaming dully in the light of the half moon.

I whispered tightly, "God*damn* you!" threw the door open, and stepped out of the Plymouth.

The LTD's lights went on. High.

"God*damn* you!" I bellowed, and threw my arm up in front of my eyes. "Who *are* you, who the hell *are* you?!"

Silence.

The LTD's engine was off. If I stood there long enough in the glare of its high beams, its battery would wear down and that would be that.

The LTD's engine fired up. It sounded very powerful, very fast. I bellowed again, "God*damn* you!"

Then I realized that cops carried shotguns in their cars.

I leaned back into the Plymouth's interior and groped frantically around the front seat. Nothing. I turned toward the back seat, hit the top of my head on the wire screen separating the seats, cursed under my breath, backed out of the car, tried the rear door. It was locked.

I heard the LTD change gears. I looked. It was backing slowly away, off the shoulder and onto the road. It did a quick, skillful turn, then sped toward U.S. Route 7.

"Nuts!" I whispered.

THIRTY-THREE

The shotgun was in the Plymouth's trunk, along with a pair of emergency flashers, a spare tire, a black rubber raincoat, a big metal tackle box with lures and bobbers and spools of nylon line inside, and a blue lunch pail. The lunch pail held a peanut butter and grape jelly sandwich on rye, a pickle, two Oreo cookies, and a pint-size silver thermos filled with apple juice. I was going to eat all that, but I got to thinking that poor Rick had been meant to eat it, and never would, so I closed the lunch pail and put it back where I'd found it.

I was going to keep the shotgun on the front seat with me, too, just in case I had another encounter with the LTD. I had planned on doing something very daring with it, like shooting out the LTD's lights or blowing up its radiator. But the hard truth is that I have never liked guns. Even in Nam, when your weapon was almost literally your best friend, I hated it. It made me feel unclean to hold it.

So I left the shotgun in the trunk. Stupid, you'd say, and you'd be right.

I closed the trunk and got back into the driver's seat. I had come to a decision. I was going to drive to within three or four miles of Brookfield, ditch the Plymouth and then hike cross-country into Brookfield. That way I'd lose Art DeGraff and his friends in the LTD, because I was sure they'd fall in behind me as soon as I hit Route 7 again.

And once in Brookfield, I'd find Abner. I hoped that wouldn't be the most difficult part of my trek. Because it was not until I crossed into Vermont—at about ten o'clock, with the LTD a precise five car lengths behind me (it had, as I'd expected, picked me up just a few minutes after I'd gotten back on Route 7)—that I realized I didn't know where in Brookfield Abner and Phyllis were staying. "They have a little house in Brookfield, Vermont," Madeline had told me. And I guess at the time I pictured some sleepy, twelve-house hamlet and I assumed that the house where Abner and Phyllis were staying would be easy enough to find. I would, in fact, be able to make a beeline to it. That was, as career Marines, say, "P.P.P.P."—*piss-poor prior planning*. Actually, it amounted to no prior planning at all. Just wishful thinking.

I don't know when it first struck me that Abner had once mentioned the house in Brookfield. The problem was, try as I might, I couldn't remember what he'd said, whether he'd said the house was green or white or yellow, or whether it had a porch or a rose trellis or whatever. Perhaps he'd mentioned it during our drunken picnic, but there, in the Plymouth, on U.S. Route 7, I couldn't remember his words exactly. I chalked it up to the fact that I'd been concentrating on getting smashed at the time.

I resigned myself to having the LTD on my tail all the way to wherever I ditched the Plymouth. I counted on it. It was how I was going to make my getaway in the night. I was going to stop on some side road, get my map out of the glove compartment, figure out where I was and in which direction I had to walk to get to Brookfield. Then I was going to get out, casually wipe my fingerprints off the door handles and everything else I'd touched, get back in, and unscrew the interior light so it wouldn't go on when the door opened. Then I was going to sneak out the passenger door and into whatever convenient woods lay nearby. It seemed to be a very good plan. And, on a day when most of my plans had turned into cow manure, I decided that fate owed me something, anyway, so it was a plan that would probably work.

I'd been through the Green Mountain National Forest in Vermont once before, when I was twelve or thirteen and my parents had driven to Rhode Island to visit friends. U.S. Route 7 doesn't go through the Green Mountain National Forest, though. It skirts it to the east. That was too bad, I thought, because I had liked the high hills there; they were somehow greener than the hills around Bangor. Greener and more luxuriant, as if they were the homes of knights and dragons. I believed in knights and dragons then, when I was twelve or thirteen. I did not believe in them at night on U.S. Route 7. They were the stuff of fairy tales. I believed in other things.

I believed in love and friendship. They were, after all, the forces that had driven Abner from the beach house and me through three states to find him. To save him. I clung to that belief. It seemed necessary that I cling to it, especially with that hellish Ford on my tail and God-only-knew-what ahead of me.

Love and friendship. They make things happen, I told myself.

At just before eleven that night I stopped in the village of Shaftsbury Center, ten miles north of Bennington, Vermont, and about seventy miles south of Brookfield. I stopped to use the men's room at a Chevron station, and I calculated that the LTD would simply wait till I was done.

I parked the Plymouth in darkness to the side of the Chevron station. If someone had, improbably, found poor Rick's body already and an alert had been put out for the Plymouth, then leaving it under the arc lights would be stupid.

I went over to the men's room door, tried it. It was locked. I took a breath, hoped for the best, and went into the station to ask for the keys.

The man inside the station was short, old, and very wrinkled. He wore a red baseball cap and a pair of white overalls that had the name *Lou* sewn in blue over the breast pocket. He gave me a once-over and stared hard at my mouth while I asked him if the rest rooms were in working order. He grunted an affirmative.

"Good," I said. "Do you have the keys?"

He grunted again, turned and got the keys, which were hooked to a big, highly polished wooden likeness of a grizzly bear. Lou, I thought, was a man of few words.

As I made my way to the rest room with that cumbersome wooden grizzly bear in hand, I told myself that everything at this Chevron station was as it should be. There were no Antons here, and no girls in pink taffeta. There was only an odd old man who liked to keep his rest rooms clean.

I put the key in the rest room door, turned it, then glanced around behind me. The LTD was on the shoulder of the road a hundred feet south of the Chevron station, with its headlights off.

I smiled at it, nodded, waved a little. Then I went into the rest room, found that it was indeed spotlessly clean, which pleased me more, somehow, than the cleanliness of a rest room had ever pleased me before. And after I'd used the toilet I stood in front of the mirror and said, "You cocky son of a bitch." I waved at myself in the mirror; "Hello, Art, you asshole! Why don't you come over here; we'll *talk* this out." I quite often talk to myself in mirrors. It's good therapy.

I washed my hands, patted them dry with a continuous roll of immaculate cloth towel near the sink, then turned to go.

I heard a very heavy rap at the rest room door.

I froze.

My knees actually began to knock; my throat grew dry; I got vivid mental pictures of what might be on the other side of the door. Art DeGraff, perhaps, grinning and murderously angry: I imagined him telling me that he wouldn't kill me until later if I showed him where Abner was.

Or maybe Anton, his long-handled axe held high and his hunger mounting with each passing second.

Or the local police, with a warrant for my arrest on charges of car theft and murder.

I muttered a little curse of frustration and disbelief. Then I heard another heavy knock at the door, heavier than the first; it even set up a short-lived, whining, sympathetic vibration in the mirror over the sink.

"God Almighty," I whispered. "God Almighty, God Almighty!"

Another knock. Then another. Then two more in rapid succession.

"Yes?" I croaked.

There was no answer. Only another series of knocks—very frantic now and loud.

I backed away from the door until my rear end hit the wall. I felt the wall—it was cold, made of polished stone blocks. I hit it with my fist repeatedly.

Another series of loud, suddenly frantic knocks.

"Yes?" I croaked again. "Yes?" I said louder.

Then there was silence.

"Yes?" I said, finding sudden courage in the silence. "Yes, who's there, please?"

Silence.

"This room is occupied," I said, and stepped forward to the door. I put my hand on the knob, turned it.

Another knock. Very hard, and very loud. Followed by, "Hey, you okay in there, mister?" It was a young man's voice.

"Huh?" I said.

"Mister, are you okay in there?"

"Yes," I managed.

I took a deep breath and opened the door. A chunky young man of twenty or so, dressed in the same kind of overalls that Lou was wearing, stood in front of the door. Lou stood beside him. According to the pocket of the young man's overalls, his name was Tim. His brow furrowed, his full, bow-shaped lips went into a nervous pout. "What'sa matter with you, mister? You can't hear?"

I nodded. "Yes, I can hear. I'm sorry."

Tim nodded at Lou. " 'Cuz Lou, he don't hear so good—he don't hear at all, ak-chooly."

"Yes," I said. "I'm sorry."

He shrugged. "No need to be sorry. He been deaf all his life. It's just that when you didn't answer the door—"

"Well," I stammered, "you know, I was . . . occupied—"

Tim grinned. "Sure you were. But like I say, when you didn't answer the door, Lou figured you had a heart attack or somethin'—it happens; it happened not more than a year ago in this very toilet—so he come and got me an' here I am. All he wanted to know was you want any gas?''

''Gas?'' I said.

Tim nodded. ''Sure. Gas. It makes your car go.''

I glanced at the LTD, still parked a hundred feet south of the station, then at the Plymouth, in the shadows to the right of the station. I didn't know if it needed gas. I thought it probably did, considering its size and the distance it had traveled.

I let out a long sigh of relief. ''Sure,'' I said. ''Fill it up.''

Tim looked at the Plymouth. ''Sheriff, huh?'' he said. ''You undercover or somethin'?'' He looked impressed. I decided to play along.

''Yes,'' I said, and cleared my throat, which had gone dry. ''Undercover.''

Lou, who'd been studying our lips as we spoke, shook his head.

''Drugs?'' Tim asked.

''Can't say,'' I answered, and cleared my throat again, nervousness clutching at my stomach once more.

''Yeah,'' Tim agreed, ''I know. My brother-in-law, he's a sheriff, kind of. You know, a rent-a-cop.''

''Yes,'' I said. ''A rent-a-cop.''

All the while we were talking, Lou was shaking his head furiously and grunting and staring hard at me. He reminded me of a huge, wrinkled, olive-skinned, bald rat. I looked at him; ''She-riff!'' I said, shaping the word in an exaggerated way.

He continued shaking his head.

Tim asked, ''What kind you take? No lead?''

"I don't know," I answered.

"You don't know?" He sounded skeptical and it took me only a moment to realize why; if the car were indeed mine, I'd certainly know if it took leaded or unleaded gasoline. "Regular," I said, guessing.

Lou continued shaking his head furiously. Tim appeared not to notice. "New car?" he said.

"New car?" I said. I was confused.

"Yeah," Tim said, grinning, apparently pleased to be chatting with an undercover cop, "did—you know—did the department just release it to ya?"

I nodded. Lou continued shaking his head furiously. "Yes," I said, trying for a casual tone, and missing it by a hair. "Yes," I repeated, "I had a Malibu, one of those old Malibus. Nice car. Very fast. But I . . . I wrecked it. Bad torque converter—"

"Bad torque converter?" Tim said, again looking skeptical.

I nodded. I realized sinkingly that I was talking myself into a corner. "Among other things," I added. "So we had to junk it." Lou looked very angry now; Tim still didn't seem to notice.

"Too bad," he said, and nodded at the Plymouth. "Takes regular, huh?"

"Yes," I said, "regular. I'll pull it over to the pumps."

"Sure," Tim said.

And Lou said, "Fawrk!"

Tim looked confusedly at him.

I tried to smile, as if Lou had just told us both some weird one-word joke.

"Fawrk!" Lou said again, and pointed very stiffly at me.

Tim said, "That's a new one on me. He don't talk so good, you know, on account of he's deaf and he ain't never heard no one talk, and I thought I had his whole vo*cab*ulary figured out. But I ain't never heard that one before. Sounds like he's sayin' 'fuck,' don't it?"

I tried to smile again; I was sure it looked asinine. "Yes," I said. I knew what Lou was saying. He was saying, "Fake!" I added, my throat dry, "I'll pull the car up. I won't be a moment."

And I went over to the Plymouth, started it, backed out of the shadows, and roared off, through Shaftsbury Center, toward Arlington, Vermont, the LTD five car lengths behind.

A couple miles south of Arlington, the Plymouth ran out of gas.

THIRTY-FOUR

I actually said to myself, "This is a comedy of errors," although there was nothing funny about it, and I wasn't laughing. Behind me, the LTD pulled up and parked a few car lengths back. I glanced at it in the rearview mirror, then quickly looked away. "Fuck you," I whispered at it.

I sat in the Plymouth for a good long time. After ten minutes or so I shut the lights off when a car coming my way flashed its high beams at me. The light of the half moon showed me rolling countryside to either side of the road. At the horizon, there was a soft bluish glow that might have been Arlington.

Fate, I decided, had chosen to dump on me yet again. It was fair. Anyone who wasn't bright enough to check his gas gauge now and again deserved to get dumped on.

I did something very stupid then. I picked up the mike, I turned the radio on, and I said into the mike, "Hello? Is anybody there?" I waited. There was no answer. I adjusted the squelch and tried again. "Hello? Is anybody there?" This time, a man answered, "Yes. This is the Arlington substation of the Vermont State Police," he said, "you are on an illegal frequency—"

"I know," I cut in. "It's just that I'd like to report a murder." And I went on at length about what had happened south of Ashley Falls, about why I had taken the Plymouth, that it had run out of gas, and that I was abandoning it somewhere south of Arlington. The cop asked my name. I told him that he didn't need to know my name because I was only someone who had done what was necessary to save a friend. Then, at last, feeling a great sense of release at having shared the events of the past hours with another human being, I grabbed my suitcase, got out of the Plymouth, and began walking. It was, I guessed, about forty miles to Brookfield.

I wasn't stupid enough to use U.S. Route 7. Before I got out of the car I checked my map and saw that a railway line of couple of miles east paralleled Route 7 through Vermont and into Maine.

So, not wanting to discard my previous plans altogether—it was a matter of pride—I shut off the overhead light, reached up, unscrewed it, found a napkin under the seat, wiped my fingerprints off all the smooth surfaces in the front of the car, then I wriggled across to the passenger door, hesitated, and peered cautiously over the seat at the car behind me. Its lights were off. Good. I pushed the passenger door open a little, wriggled out, keeping low, then crawled off the road, onto the shoulder—pushing the suitcase ahead of me—down a slight incline, stood, wincing because I'd scraped my knees and palms on the gravel at the shoulder of the road, and started across a field of quack grass toward a stand of piney woods.

Behind me, I heard someone else moving through the weeds. I stopped. A man's voice called breathlessly, as if the effort of following me through the weeds was gargantuan, "Please stop. I don't have the strength to come after you."

"Dammit!" I whispered. "No!" I called, but instead of sounding angry, or determined, as I'd meant it to sound, it sounded petulant, like a little boy refusing to put his toy trucks away and go to bed.

"Oh, give me a break!" the man called.

I stopped. *Give me a break?* I knew that the man behind me (when I turned my head I could see him only as a massive swelling in the darkness) was not Art DeGraff. Art was my age, and his voice, at least when we'd gone to high school together twenty years before, had been like a high-pitched whine. This man's voice was middle-aged and it had a deep and weary kind of authority to it. It was, I realized deadeningly, a cop's voice. I called back to him as I continued on through the field of quack grass, "I haven't done *any*thing. Leave me alone, dammit!"

I heard the man cough; I heard him wheeze heavily. I stopped. "Are you okay?" I called.

He continued to wheeze heavily.

"Dammit," I called again, "are you okay?"

The wheezing lightened up. Eventually, the man called back—his voice clearly the voice of someone struggling for air—"Asthma. It's all right."

"Who are you?" I called.

"No one." He cleared his throat noisily. "I'm a friend of Abner's. Sort of. I'm a cop." Another pause; he wheezed a few times. "My name's Whelan."

"Jesus," I breathed. I remembered what Abner had said about Whelan: *There's someone after me. A detective; his name's Whelan. He's trying to pin something on me.* I called, "You're no friend of Abner's. He's *told* me about you."

Whelan chuckled gurglingly.

I repeated, "You're no friend of Abner's."

He'd been moving closer to me through the tall weeds and now was only about a dozen feet away. He stopped there, as if afraid he'd spook me.

I could see him more clearly. He was a big man, stout, and tall, and his breathing came in small, quick gasps.

I asked, "Do you have any medicine for that?"

"Sure," he answered. "I've got an inhaler."

"Don't you think you should use it? You sound awful."

Again he chuckled. "Yeah, I know." A quick breath. "I did use it."

I paused, then I said, "I can't help you, Mr. Whelan."

He chanced a step forward, then another. He stopped. "Well," he wheezed, "maybe you can, and maybe"—a quick breath—"you can't."

In the light of the half moon I could see his face now. It was square, the nose large, the eyes small and close-set, the cheeks puffy. It was a face which once might have been bearishly handsome. Now it had a kind of weary strength. He was wearing a ridiculous, private-eye kind of hat, a dark fedora, and he had the stub of an unlit cigar in his mouth, which he rolled back and forth theatrically between his lips as he spoke. "Maybe," he repeated, catching his breath at last, "you can help me, Mr. Feary. And maybe you can't."

I was going to ask him the predictable *How did you know my name?* but decided it would have surprised me if he *hadn't* known my name. I said, instead, "You have no jurisdiction here, Mr. Whelan."

He rolled the stubby cigar back and forth between his lips as if in thought. He was wearing a light-colored overcoat, open, and what I supposed was a brown suit.

He shoved his hands into his pants pockets.

"Well, Mr. Feary," he said, again finding that weary, low-pitched kind of authority he had had five minutes earlier, "I don't have any jurisdiction anywhere. I'm retired. And I'm glad of it, too. I put in forty long years and I deserve a rest. I got myself a little house down in Florida. You know, practically all my life I swore I'd never move to Florida. Too hot, I said. Too buggy. And you've got to put up with the Floridians, you know. But then I got old; I'm sixty-seven, Mr. Feary. *Sixty-seven years old!* Jesus, there are *trees* that aren't that old." He paused. I smiled at his little joke. He took a quick breath, continued, "And I got to feeling the chill of these god-awful winters in my bones, and I got this fuckin' asthma. So I went down to Florida and bought my little house, and I found out that the Floridians aren't half bad, if you give them a chance. So I'm going to give them a chance. As soon as I catch up with Art DeGraff. And that'll happen as soon as you find your friend, Abner Cray."

I said, "That's quite a speech, Mr. Whelan."

He shrugged. "I've had a few hours to practice it." He rolled the cigar back and forth. "You're a hard man to keep track of, Mr. Feary. Where'd you learn your little disappearing acts? Jesus, it's easier to keep track of a cockroach."

I sighed. "Yes," I said, "I imagine it is." I paused. "I'm sorry, Mr. Whelan, but I still can't help you."

He took a few more steps forward and gently took hold of my arm, as if he needed my support. "Then maybe I can help you, Mr. Feary." His breath smelled of asthma inhaler and chewed cigars.

I looked at it this way: He was a lot older than I, he was out of shape and overweight, and when he'd been standing there with his coat open I had seen no evidence of a gun. Hell, if necessary, I could always clobber him with my suitcase. So I shrugged and said, "Why not?" and with him wheezing and panting up the short slope to the shoulder of the road—I tugged on him once, to help him up—we went back to his car.

It was the silver Chevette Scooter.

I got in. He climbed into the driver's seat and

started the car. The interior also smelled of cigars and asthma inhaler.

I said, "You drive this thing like a maniac, you know?!"

He turned the headlights on and started the engine. "No, Mr. Feary," he said, and pulled onto the road, "you're the maniac. You and that friend of yours in the Ford. I couldn't be a maniac in this thing if I *wanted* to."

I smiled, grimly amused at the revelation I was about to make. "That 'friend' of mine in the Ford is Art DeGraff, Mr. Whelan." I expected a gasp of surprise. I expected he'd slam on the brakes, grab me by the collar, and swear in frustration and anger and disbelief. But he didn't do any of that. He said matter-of-factly, "No it isn't. It's some other asshole."

I continued smiling. I still thought my revelation was sneaking up on him. "Oh, but you're mistaken, Mr. Whelan," I said.

"No, I'm not. I've seen the guy driving that Ford, and it isn't Art. It's some old fart in a gray suit."

I said nothing.

Whelan said, "I went after him when he ran down that cop. I got this piece of shit all the way up to eighty-five before it started rattling. So I turned around and went after you."

"Christ," I breathed.

"Don't be upset." He tuned his radio to a classical station; harp music ebbed and flowed on waves of static. "We all make mistakes." He glanced in his rearview mirror, then at me. "There he is now, Mr. Feary."

I craned my head around. I saw the headlights of the LTD five car lengths back. I turned back. I said, my gaze straight ahead, "Do you have a gun, Mr. Whelan?"

Out of the corner of my eye I saw him shake his head. "Nope. I gave them up. I gave up booze, too. And cigars—well, I don't light 'em, anyway."

"Great," I said.

"And so," he asked with mock cheerfulness, "where are we going?"

"Brookfield," I answered.

THIRTY-FIVE

I don't know when, precisely, I became aware of the woman in red. I'd dozed off (which normally would not be an easy thing for me to do in the bucket seat of a Chevette Scooter, but I'd had a long and tiring day), my head to the side, so I was facing Whelan, and as I came around I noticed, out of the corner of my eye, someone sitting stiffly in the cramped back seat. I lurched in surprise.

"What's the matter," Whelan asked, "you got a pain or something?"

I didn't answer at once. I stared hard at the woman in red sitting so very stiffly in the back seat. The only light in the car was from the dashboard and some reflection from the high beams, but I could see well enough. She looked seedier than when I'd first seen her, as if she were a vegetable that had been left out on a table for a day or two.

She was wearing a kind of wretched smile. Not the I've-just-swallowed-a-canary smile of the Mona Lisa, but a smile that said, *I'm going to do something murderous; you wait and see.*

I said to Whelan, "I think you'd better stop the car."

"Why?" he asked.

"For your own good, you'd better stop the car, Mr. Whelan."

"That's not a threat, is it? I don't like threats; they give me asthma."

I shook my head. "No, it's not a threat. It's just that there's someone—" Out of the corner of my eye I saw movement in the back seat; I looked. The woman in red had raised her hands and was moving her upper body with aching, stiff slowness toward Whelan. "Jesus," I screamed at her, "no, for God's sake!" She continued moving her upper body forward, arms outstretched, fingers spread wide, that wretched, murderous smile stuck on her mouth.

Whelan said, "What in the fuck is *wrong* with you?"

"You'll kill us both!" I screamed at the woman in red.

"No, I won't!" Whelan protested.

"He's driving!" I screamed. "He'll go off the damned road!"

The woman hesitated. Her murderous smile altered, as if she was thinking about what I'd just said. She cocked her head toward me, then, with equal slowness, settled back and let her hands fall to her lap. Her murderous, expectant smile returned.

"You're a crazy man," Whelan snapped. He'd lost the classical station and had found a station that was playing big band music.

I said, "Yes, I know. I'm sorry. It's just that I . . . see things." I looked quickly at the woman in red, saw her hands rise again. I said stiffly to her, "You'll kill *both* of us, dammit!" Her hands lowered.

Whelan said, "We all see things, Mr. Feary. I hope that the things you see are pleasant." This sounded strangely philosophical, I thought, for a man who was trying hard to cultivate a hard-boiled-former-detective persona.

"Not all the time," I said, and added, "We'd better drive straight through to Brookfield, Mr. Whelan."

"No problem," he said, "it's only twenty-five miles."

I glanced again at the woman in red. She was sitting very stiff and still, that awful smile stuck on her mouth. I looked out the back window at the LTD; it was still a precise five car lengths behind the Chevette. I looked at Whelan. I said, "I'd give anything to be somewhere else right now."

"Yeah," he said gloomily. "Florida."

"Bangor," I said. "1962."

We had to stop eventually, I realized. But he did it so quickly that I had precious little time to react.

"Nature calls," he said, and pulled the Chevette onto the the shoulder of the narrow road. A white sign with black letters a hundred feet ahead read "TOWNSHIP OF BROOKFIELD."

Behind us, the LTD stopped five car lengths back.

In the rear seat of the Chevette the woman in red moved her upper body inexorably forward, arms outstretched, fingers wide. Her murderous grin was now a leer. Whelan opened his door.

My arm shot across the seat, over Whelan's lap. I grabbed the door handle and slammed the door shut. It didn't close; I'd shut some of his overcoat in it. He looked at me, frightened. He began to wheeze.

The woman in red had the collar of his coat in her hand now. I said to him, nodding at her fingers, my words slow and measured, "Do you *see* that, Mr. Whelan?"

He said nothing. He continued wheezing.

I took a deep breath. "Mr. Whelan," I said, "please listen to me." The hands of the woman crept forward spiderlike over his collar and found the sides of his neck. "You *must* continue driving. Please continue driving!"

He said nothing. His wheezing was very bad now.

I asked, "Where's your inhaler, Mr. Whelan?"

He thumped his right-hand coat pocket with his open hand. I reached in, found his inhaler, held it up to his mouth. The fingers of the woman in red were at the front of his throat now. I squeezed the inhaler once, then again, and again. He waved frantically in the air. I pulled the inhaler away. His wheezing stopped. He started choking, as if he had a piece of meat caught in his throat. "Drive!" I screamed. He continued choking. I reached out, grabbed the arm of the woman in red. It was like grabbing a steel pipe. I let go. Whelan continued to choke. He tumbled forward; his head hit the steering wheel, the horn sounded. The woman in red came forward with him, so the back of the bucket seat cut into her stomach and her head pushed into the area just above the windshield. "Stop it!" I screamed. "For God's sake, stop it!"

Whelan's choking grew quieter; he was beginning to gurgle.

"Oh, shit, shit, goddammit!" I breathed. I aimed the inhaler at the woman in red and squeezed.

The scream that came from her was pitiful, like the scream a rabbit makes when it dies. She folded backward, like an accordion, into the back seat. Her body began to liquefy—just as it had in my apartment a billion years ago—and at last there was only a small dark pool on the seat. The pool evaporated quickly.

And I realized all at once what had happened. I had shown her that her murderous love for me was unrequited. So she went away.

Whelan came around by and by, and after clearing his throat for several minutes, and a couple of applications of the asthma inhaler, he said, "Peed my pants, anyway," and pulled back onto the road, the LTD dogging us.

"Do you have any idea what was happening to you back there?" I asked.

"Yeah," he answered, "I had a fucking asthma attack, a fucking doozie of an asthma attack."

"No," I whispered.

"I didn't hear you, Mr. Feary."

"Nothing," I said. "Call me Sam."

"Okay. Call me Mr. Whelan. Everybody does.

My first name's Kennedy, but I hate it, so even my girlfriends call me Mr. Whelan."

"Sure," I said. "Mr. Whelan."

We were on the main street of Brookfield less than a minute later.

THIRTY-SIX

Brookfield—what I could see of it at twelve-thirty in the morning—was very small. A hamlet. Maybe thirty-five houses total, most of them whitish two-story Victorian. There was also a big brick Presbyterian Church, a Sunoco station, a grange hall, a small restaurant called Hattie's Brookfield Restaurant, and a tiny post office.

The village's main street was empty. There were no lights on in any of the houses, and only one streetlamp, a modern, expressway-type arc light on a long, curving aluminum pole that looked very much out of place in the village. It cast a wide, ragged circle of bluish light on the sidewalk in front of the grange hall.

"Kind of a bust," I said.

And Whelan, who had pulled the Chevette over so we were in front of the post office, said, "Abner Cray lives here somewhere, does he?"

I nodded. "Yes. Somewhere."

"But you don't know where?"

I shrugged. "I haven't a clue."

He chuckled a little. "Not much of a detective, are you, Mr. Feary?"

The LTD had pulled up five car lengths behind us. Its lights were off. I said to Whelan, "So what do we do now?"

"What *can* we do?" he answered. "We wait until morning."

"Here?" I was incredulous. "In the car?"

He jiggled with something on the side of his seat and the seat went back to a reclining position, which gave me a shudder, because his head was now where the woman in red's lap had been. "Sure," he said. "If you have to, you can sleep anywhere, Sam."

But I couldn't sleep, though I marveled at the fact that he could. He nodded off within seconds and—predictably, considering his asthma—began to snore reasonantly.

I got out of the Chevette, closed the door, and stood facing the LTD in the darkness.

It flashed its lights at me.

I sighed. "I'm sorry, my friend," I whispered, "but I'm afraid too much water has gone under the bridge. You're no fun anymore."

It flashed its lights again. I shook my head at it, turned, and walked up the street, toward the grange hall.

I expected that the LTD would follow me. It did. I heard its old gears mesh, heard that big engine pull it forward, and when I glanced back it was just passing the Chevette. It slowed and stopped a dozen feet in front of Whelan's car. Its gears meshed again, and it backed up slowly. I lifted my arm; I was going to yell, "Whelan, watch out!" but the LTD stopped, came forward, and halted five car lengths from me, just inside the circle of bluish light cast by the big arc lamp.

I strained to see the driver but saw only what I'd seen four of five hours before—someone hunched over the wheel, someone tall enough that the top of his head intersected the top of the windshield. And, as Whelan had told me, he was wearing a gray suit—a suit that looked achingly familiar. I saw others in the car, too—several dark shapes behind the tinted windshield, one in front, a couple more in back.

Surprising myself, I took three or four quick steps toward the car. I caught the driver off guard, I think, because he didn't put the LTD in reverse and begin backing away until I'd stopped walking. But I'd gotten close enough. I'd seen the driver.

Whelan had been right. It wasn't Art DeGraff.

It was the old man on the subway, the one that the woman in red had choked the friendliness out of, and when our eyes met, there on Brookfield's main street, he gave me a wide, gloating grin that said very clearly, "And now you'll get yours, Bozo!"

"Jesus," I whispered. "I'm sorry." I looked quickly away from those accusing eyes and into the back seat of the LTD.

Art DeGraff was there, in the middle of the back

seat, his body squashed into a fetal position, his huge black oval eyes in that long oval white face peering out from what looked like a form-fitting dark hood. It was a face that had anger etched hard into it, the way the bark of an old tree is etched with the furrows of age.

I froze. That face, that living mask of anger, knew that I had seen it.

I heard it scream as the LTD backed away, out of the glow of the arc lamp in front of the grange hall. It was a scream of awful and bitter recognition—*This is what I am,* it said. *This is the thing I have become. And now the world knows it!*

That was the first and last time I felt sympathy for Art DeGraff.

I ran back to the Chevette. Whelan was snoring happily when I got there. I figured he was safer with me around, or that I was safer with him around. I wasn't sure which. We were safer together, I knew that.

The LTD, which had backed down the street and into the darkness, took its position five car lengths behind the Chevette, lights off, and for a good half hour I sat turned in the seat so I could keep an eye on it. At last I decided that sitting like that was only giving me a pain in the neck. So I put my seat back and I fell asleep.

It was the smell of coffee that woke me. Whelan was holding a plastic cup of it near my nose. "Wake up," he said, "we got work to do."

I became aware of sunlight on me first, then of the sounds of people and traffic around us. I was also aware that I had a hell of a headache.

I sat up, leaving the seat back, and pressed my hands hard to the sides of my head. ''Dammit!'' I breathed.

''Take this,'' Whelan said, and he put the cup of coffee under my nose. It smelled good. I took a sip. It was very hot.

''He's in the Ford,'' I said, my gaze on the dark area below the dashboard because the sunlight was too bright.

''Art DeGraff?'' asked Whelan. ''No, I told you: the driver—''

''He's in the back seat,'' I said, sipped the coffee, then chanced a look around. People dressed for midspring—in jackets and sweaters and an occasional hat—were coming and going from Hattie's Brookfield Restaurant and a small general store called Pete's Groceries and Things, which I hadn't noticed the night before. ''What time is it?'' I asked.

''About eight,'' Whelan answered. ''Seven forty-five, actually.''

''Seven forty-five?'' I said, surprised that the whole town had, from the looks of things, been awake for at least an hour.

Whelan asked, ''What do you mean Art DeGraff was in the back seat?''

I nodded. ''He was. I saw him. He was sitting in the back seat, in the middle of the back seat.''

''Oh?'' Whelan said. ''When?''

''Last night. After you fell asleep.''

"Yes," Whelan said. "I see." Clearly his professional ego had been bruised. He, the hard-bitten former cop, had declared that Art DeGraff was not in the Ford, and he'd been proved wrong. "Well, it's not there anymore," he went on, and nodded at the rearview mirror.

I turned around in the seat. There was a green pickup truck behind us, a big yellow dog looking at me through its windshield, and, behind that, a black and gold Chevy Blazer. But no LTD. I turned back, sighed, sipped my coffee. "Good coffee," I said.

"I'll put it on your tab," he said.

"Now what?" I said.

"Now I get a sweet roll. You want one?"

I smiled at him. I was beginning to like him. "I'll pay," I said, fished my wallet out, and got a dollar from it. To my surprise, he took it.

"I'll be right back," he said, opened his door, climbed out—with several grunts and groans and wheezes—bent over, and looked back in. "They got raspberry and strawberry and prune, I think. Which do you want?"

"Raspberry's good," I said, and he nodded and lumbered across the street to Hattie's Brookfield Restaurant.

As I waited in the Chevette for Whelan to return with our breakfast, such as it promised to be, I hoped that Abner would pass by. After all, people who move to a small town, like Brookfield, often adopt its habits, become locals. Why move to a small town otherwise? So, because everyone else in town—or so it seemed—was up and moving about, starting the day's business, Abner should have been up, too. Maybe with his camera in hand, because Brookfield looked like a nice place to take pictures, a typical New England town, very picturesque. So I thought I'd see him wandering down the street, his gaze moving from here to there so he wouldn't miss the chance at a good shot.

But he didn't pass by, although a lot of other people did—couples, old people, young people, people in overalls, people in sports coats, people in hiking boots, people in sneakers, people who looked very purposeful and people who looked aimless, people with pets in hand, people with pets on leashes, people carting groceries home, people laughing and people frowning.

Lots more people, in fact, than should have been on the main street of Brookfield, Vermont.

It was as I was thinking this that Whelan opened his door, stuck his head in, and handed me a raspberry Danish wrapped in a napkin. "Nice little town," he said, and climbed into the driver's seat.

"Sure," I said. I sipped my coffee, munched on the Danish. "Awfully crowded, though."

"Yeah." He smiled a long-suffering smile. "Tell me about it." He took a bite of his Danish, chewed it, prepared to take another bite. "Fuckin' flea market," he said, the Danish poised near his lips. He nodded to indicate an area beyond the grange hall. "Over there." He took another bite of the Danish. "I guess it's an annual thing," he said as he chewed. "Just a bunch of junk if you ask me."

"That's why all these people are here?" I said incredulously. "Because of a flea market?"

"You'd be surprised how many people these things draw, Sam."

I took a bite of my Danish. I asked, "You can see them, Mr. Whelan?"

"See who?"

I nodded to indicate the crowds on Brookfield's main street. "Them. Those people."

"What the hell are you talking about, Sam? Sure I can see them."

"Good," I said. "I'm glad. It makes me feel better that you can see them." I sipped my coffee. "Tell me how you know about small-town flea markets, Mr. Whelan. I thought you'd put in forty years—"

He cut in, "At the NYPD? Yes. I did. But I also do a hell of a lot of traveling, Sam." He finished his Danish. "Anyway, like I was saying, I do travel. I get outa that freakin' city as much as I can, you know. Can't stand it there for too long, so I travel. Why the hell do you think I drive *this* damned lawn mower?" he asked, and answered himself, "Because it doesn't use any gas, that's why."

"I was wondering," I said. "You don't really . . . fit in it, do you?"

He grinned. "I'm not *fat,* Sam. I'm stocky."

"Gotcha," I said. I was enjoying the banter, the coffee, the raspberry Danish. I was even beginning to enjoy the crowds of people, now that I knew why they were in Brookfield.

The sunlight through the window glass was warming the side of my face and my shoulder—it had even taken my headache away. I leaned forward and looked through the windshield. The sky was an even pale blue, and all but cloudless.

Whelan nodded to indicate the post office. "They should be open at nine. That's when we'll find out where your friend is."

THIRTY-SEVEN

In Bangor, thirty years ago, my Aunt Greta told me that storms were really a giant old ''hausfrau'' sweeping out the old to make room for the new. Aunt Greta was in many ways a colorful and entertaining woman—''Lusty,'' my father used to say, which seemed to upset my mother. In my six- or seven-year-old brain, that giant old ''hausfrau'' was terribly real. I could see her. When storms came up, there she was with her awful broom, her long skirts, and her white bonnet (very much like the woman on the Old Dutch Cleanser cans), and, of course, of course, she was after *me*!

Eventually, I grew out of believing in the ''giant old hausfrau,'' though my feelings toward my Aunt Greta remained ambivalent. On the one hand, I thought the story, horrific as it was, was wonderfully entertaining, and on the other hand, it really did give me a scare—the genuine scare of insecurity and aloneness and fear that is somehow different from the scare we get on roller coasters and at horror movies.

I bring Aunt Greta and her hausfrau up now because sitting there, in Kennedy Whelan's Chevette Scooter, in Brookfield, Vermont, at 8:45 in the morning, I could tell that a storm was coming. Even though the sky was a flat, pale blue and the sunlight warm through the Chevette's windows. I knew a storm was coming because I have always had a sixth sense about such things; many people do. Maybe there was a ragged edge to the morning's pleasantness. Maybe it was a little *too* pleasant. Maybe the few clouds scuttling about had a tinge of gray in them.

I said to Whelan, "There's a storm coming."

"Sure," he said. He didn't believe me.

"I mean it," I said. "I have a sixth sense about these things." I set my empty cup on the Chevette's dashboard. "There's a storm coming."

He nodded at the cup. "You want more?"

"I could use it," I said. I was still feeling a little groggy from sleeping in the Chevette's bucket seat. "I'll get it."

"Good enough," he said, and nodded again at the cup on the dashboard. "Take that with you, okay? I like to keep the car clean."

"You bet." I took the cup, climbed out of the car, and headed across the crowded street toward Hattie's Brookfield Restaurant. I was halfway across the street, and picking up bits and pieces of conversation from the crowds around me—"*Eighteen* dollars for an *ash*tray!" . . . and "Guy must be out of his mind to be selling stuff like that at a *family* flea market" . . . and "Wouldn't mind settling here at all"—when I saw Abner.

He was coming out of Pete's Groceries and Things. He had a full bag of groceries in each arm and a look of desperation about him, as if the crowds that had invaded Brookfield planned to invade *him* next.

I stopped in the middle of the street. Someone jostled me; someone else, very annoyed, said, "Ex*cuse* me!" precisely the way Steve Martin says it.

"Abner!" I called.

He stopped. He glanced over at me. His look of desperation became a look of surprise and sudden panic. Then he bolted, his bags of groceries threatening to topple from his arms.

I looked quickly around at the Chevette. Whelan was rolling his window down and putting a new cigar into his mouth. "He's—" I called, and stopped. *No,* I thought, uncertain why, *I don't want him knowing*. But Whelan had heard me; he looked questioningly at me.

I held my cup high. "Cream?" I called.

He nodded.

"Great," I called, and walked very quickly to the door of Hattie's Brookfield Restaurant. I stopped there to let a few people walk in ahead of me, then I glanced back at the Chevette. Whelan was watching. He looked confused. I held the cup up again and smiled. "Cream?" I called; again he nodded.

I glanced in the direction that Abner had run. I saw

only the flea market crowds, and, fleetingly, a wisp of darkness at the horizon.

I went in. The restaurant was packed. At the counter, I got the attention of a young and schoolgirl-pretty waitress (like the ones that fast-food restaurants use on TV commercials) who said, "Be with you in a moment, sir." She smiled a flat, vaguely welcoming smile.

"No," I said, "I don't want anything. Do you have a rear exit?"

Her smile vanished, as if I had said something obscene. Then, quickly, her smile reappeared. "Oh!" she said. "Yes, sure we do," and she nodded toward the back of the restaurant. "Over there," she said, and turned to the person who'd stepped up behind me. "Be with you in a moment, sir," she said.

He said, "Just coffee."

I closed my eyes. "Nuts!" I whispered. It was Kennedy Whelan's voice. I felt his hand on my shoulder. He gripped hard—harder, I thought, than he looked capable of. "You're a real amateur, Sam," he said.

I shrugged. "You've got to start somewhere," I said. I hadn't turned to look at him.

"What do you do for a living, Sam?"

"Construction work, mostly," I answered. "I've done other things."

"Good for you, Sam," he said, sounding very paternal. "Stick to that, okay?"

"Sure," I said. "That's a promise." I looked at him. He was wearing a shit-eating grin, his cigar between his lips, and somehow he looked more robust, stronger, not the enfeebled, overweight, out-of-shape former cop with whom I'd shared the last ten hours or so.

Apparently he saw my confusion, because he said, "Yeah, Sam. I've got asthma. I've had it since I was a kid, and it gives me trouble every once in a while. Like last night. But, beyond that, my friend, I'm a real hale and hearty son of a bitch."

The waitress reappeared, gave us both her flat, vaguely welcoming smile, and said, "Now, what was it you gentlemen wanted?"

"Coffees," Whelan told her. "Both with cream."

"Coming up," she said, and went to fill the order.

I said to Whelan, "It was an act, you mean?"

His shit-eating grin grew bolder; he nodded gloatingly. "A pretty good one, too, wouldn't you say? Hell, it was the only way to get you back to the car. No way was I going to go chasing through the woods after you. Where were you going anyway, Sam?"

I sighed. "There were some railroad tracks—"

"Sure," he cut in. "I'll lay you odds you were going in the wrong direction."

I shrugged. "Probably," I said, and thought, *Jesus, you can't count on anyone, dead or alive*. It wasn't true, of course, and I knew it wasn't true. There were several people I could count on—Madeline, Abner, Leslie. They were predictable. They were what they appeared to be. I knew that as surely as I knew about storms and gravity. But there was always one person I knew I could count on without question: myself.

The waitress came over with the coffees in a paper

bag; she handed the bag across the counter. Whelan took it, thanked her, then said to me, "Let's go back to the car, Sam. You can tell me where Abner is."

We started out of the restaurant. "I don't know *where* he is," I said.

Whelan glanced critically at me. "You don't?" he said; it was almost a rhetorical question, as if he knew that I had told him the truth.

"No." I pushed the restaurant door open. "I saw him coming out of that little grocery store—"

"Did he see you?"

We stepped out of the restaurant, onto the crowded sidewalk. The sunlight was gone. "Yes," I answered. "He saw me. And he ran."

"Where to?"

I nodded toward the area beyond the grange hall and the spot where Whelan had told me the flea market had been set up. "There," I said.

We crossed the sidewalk to the street, Whelan using his bulk as a kind of courteous battering ram: "Excuse me, please" . . . "Excuse me" . . . "Coming through." He sounded like the archetypal New Yorker. He said to me, "And you didn't go after him, Sam?"

"I wanted to," I said. The street was alive with people now. *God*, I thought, *what if an ambulance or something has to get through?* "I wanted to," I repeated, "but . . . I guess I was having second thoughts about you, Mr. Whelan." We were at the car. I opened the driver's door; he got in. Before I closed the door, he said, "Why?"

"Why what?" I said.

"Why were you having second thoughts about me, Sam?"

I shrugged. "Instinct, I think."

He smiled at that, began, "Well, then, maybe there's hope for . . ." But he was cut off by a shrill, pain-ridden scream from the street.

THIRTY-EIGHT

Whelan clambered from the car, knocking the paper bag with coffees to the pavement, and looked quickly left and right over the top of the door as if uncertain from which direction the scream had come.

I pointed to my right, at a tight knot of people that had formed within the crowds clogging the street. "There!" I barked.

I heard another scream, a man. And a moment later, yet another. Whelan whispered, "What the *hell* is going on?!"

Something clattered to the pavement nearby. I looked. Fifty feet away, at the edge of the crowd, a woman in a light green dress stared blankly at the two halves of a waffle iron at her feet; within seconds, the crowd surrounded her and she was swallowed up by it.

Within the crowd, a man tall enough that his head was visible above it pleaded for order: ". . . be calm," he said, ". . . panic," he said, but most of his words were lost in the cacophony of screams and shouts and curses. Moments later, the crowd seemed to rise up and pull him down and he was lost within it.

Then, incredibly, over the space of only a few seconds, as if safety lay somewhere *within* it, the crowd formed itself into a huge seething mass. For a moment, there was stillness, quiet. Then that mass, that huge knot of people, moved like a tide in our direction.

Again Whelan said, "What the *hell* is going on?" There was fear in his voice now.

Some of the people at the leading edges of the crowd were facing toward its center and were backing toward us, arms wide, as if trying to contain it. Others were facing us—I remember a young man in a pink long-sleeved shirt who carried a mantel clock under one arm, reached wide-eyed for us with the other, and looked as if he were trying mightily to break into a run at the same time. But the crowd behind him, the crowd that was literally at his heels, made him stumble once, then again, and again, until, at last, he went down, that clock still under his arm, and the crowd pushed inexorably over him, into the front of the Chevette. Into the door behind which Whelan was standing. He started to move out of the way, but he was too slow—the crowd pinned him between the door and the frame. He tried to straight-arm the door; his face got beet red. Then the inevitable happened. He began to wheeze. His arms buckled, and the top of the door pinned him to the top of the frame, just below his neck.

Then the Chevette itself moved a good three or four inches in response to the crowd pushing against it. It was enough. It freed Whelan momentarily, and, using all the strength I could muster, I shoved at him; he burped loudly—for some insane reason, it made me smile—and he fell into the driver's seat. Half a second later, the Chevette's door slammed shut under the incredible weight of the crowd.

I bolted around to the rear of the car, climbed up onto the top of the car, and lay there with my hands gripping both sides of the roof as the car pitched and yawed and swayed in response to the tide of people pushing at it.

I saw the LTD. It was moving at a good ten miles per hour forward into the crowd. It was running people down by ones and twos and threes while the crowd itself tried—in vain because of its very mass—to get out of the way. And in a narrow path behind it, people lay writhing in their brightly colored spring finery, their flea market acquisitions—clocks, paintings, dolls, toasters, table lamps, puzzles—still tucked under their arms, or clutched tightly in dead hands, or smashed beside them on the street.

I yelled to the crowd surging around the Chevette, "Push it over, push it over!"—meaning the LTD—because I knew the crowd could easily do that if everyone joined in the effort. But it was, of course, a crowd of the panic-stricken and the fearful and the confused. It was not a collective intelligence, it was anti-intelligence, anti-rational, so it was doing exactly the opposite of what it should have been doing. And people were dying because of it.

"Push it over!" I screamed. "Push the damned thing over!" And the part of the crowd near the Chevette heard me above their own screams and shouts and curses. They heard me, and they put their bodies flat against the Chevette and began pushing against *it*.

"No!" I screeched, "goddammit, no!" But there were people on both sides and to the front of the Chevette—people who were now up on the sidewalk and falling through the big window at the front of the post office and jamming up against the mailboxes, people lying one on top of the other so they formed a human wall. The Chevette did not go over.

The LTD stopped.

The crowd continued to surge around me. I screamed, "It's stopped! It's stopped!"

Just as the first raindrops fell, the crowd began to disperse.

The LTD was thirty or forty feet away, at the center of Brookfield's main street, and because there was no glaze of sunlight on it, I could see through its windshield. I saw Art DeGraff first. He was where he had been the night before—in the middle of the back seat, his huge dark eyes in that hideous white oval face peering ratlike out at me. His anger was still etched hard into his skin, but he was wearing a grisly smile now. A smile of murderous satisfaction.

"Damn you!" I shouted over the squeals and screams

of the dispersing crowd. "Damn you, Art! May you burn in hell!"

And very clearly, his lips formed these words in response: "I have!"

I saw, then, people sitting so close to him that they looked as if they were propping him up. They were the Haislip brothers, Ryan and Trippe, from the restaurant in South Canaan. And like Art, they had wide, murderous grins on their mouths. And beside one of them, next to the right-hand passenger door, was the waitress, Florence, who was clapping her hands gleefully and looked as delighted as a five-year-old going to kindergarten for the first time. I remembered what Madeline had said: "It takes all kinds, Sam, to make a world." And, "People don't die, their *bodies* do." And, "You can know no one too well."

I was beginning to understand her.

Murder survived, it was true. Murderers filled up that LTD.

But love survived, as well. Because it was the survival of love that had brought me to this village. Love. And friendship. Abner's love for Phyllis. And the friendship Abner and I shared.

All of it survived.

All of it lingered.

Like leaves lingering through the fall and into winter.

And now the storm was coming, the monstrous hausfrau was coming to sweep away all that had to be swept away, all the lingerers and malingerers and murderers and lovers. She was coming to push them all on because, like petulant children, they had refused to go when it was time.

But there, in Brookfield, as I clung to the top of Kennedy Whelan's Chevette Scooter and the crowd dispersed, leaving behind the dead and dying in their bright spring finery, their bright *Let's go to a country flea market* hats and sweaters and scarves and skirts, I was certain that what was about to happen was only a spring storm.

How was I to know that it was going to be the same kind of storm that Abner had been sure was building in the air around the beach house? "You've got to go, Sam," he'd pleaded then. "You've got to go *now!*"

But he'd been wrong.

He had thought that his Phyllis was going to be swept away from him.

But he'd been wrong.

I took the first cold drops of rain square on my back, through my shirt.

And they *were* cold. They were very cold. Colder even, I thought, than an April rain should be.

It made me shiver, in fact. I climbed down from the roof of the Chevette and peered into the driver's seat, where Whelan moaned and wheezed rhythmically. I patted his suit pocket, got his inhaler, stuck it in his mouth, and squeezed. He swiped weakly at the air. "Sorry," I said. His eyes fluttered open, then closed, and he muttered something unintelligible. "It's raining," I said.

I straightened. I looked through the rain at the

rustic, pleasant, comfortable façade of a New England hamlet—the general store, the restaurant, the grange hall with its arc lamp. I could see faces in all the windows—the faces of the witnesses to tragedy. And I could see that each face was wearing the stiff mask of awe and disbelief and fear.

And I could see, beyond the grange hall, against a backdrop of black sky, a row of red and blue and gold and white plastic banners flapping crazily in the wind. And dimly, because it was nearly at right angles to me, I could see a big white sign which read "BROOKFIELD FLEA."

And because, I guessed, the LTD still sat big and dark and wet in the middle of the street, no one had moved to help the injured and the dying.

Whelan moaned a curse. I leaned over, glanced at him through the driver's window. Again his eyes fluttered open, then closed. "You okay?" I said, and though he didn't answer, his breathing was more regular, and I told myself that he was indeed okay. "Roll your window up," I said. He struggled feebly for a moment trying to roll it up, then wheezed, "A little rain never hurt anyone."

This is what I heard standing on the street outside the Chevette:

I heard the raindrops pelting against the roof of the car. Below it, Whelan's heavy breathing. And around me, on the street, the pleas and moans of the injured and the dying.

THIRTY-NINE

I could see into the LTD. I could see the people in it—the driver, the old man in the gray suit, the Haislip brothers, Florence, Art.

This is what I thought of as I watched them: I thought of Fizzies. Because that's what was happening to them. They were fizzing up, like Fizzies do in a glass of water. They were inside that big dark LTD and the cold rain was pounding on it, and they were fizzing up. All except Art.

Whelan moaned again; again he cursed; and then he said, "What's that noise?" I glanced at him. His eyes were open and he was trying to sit up, but he was having a bad time of it. I grabbed his hand and tugged. He sat up.

"Jesus," he said, "I'm all wet."

"It's raining," I said. "Are you going to be all right?"

"Sure," he said, sounding stronger now. Then, for the first time apparently, he saw the carnage on the street. "My God!" he whispered.

"I've got to help these people," I said.

In a wide circle around the LTD, some lay quietly in their spring finery, others writhed, others twitched as if in response to errant bursts of electricity. Some moaned, some begged "Please" over and over again. Someone, a young man, was saying, "Mama!" And a few—a man in a red spring jacket, a woman in gray overalls and a cream-colored shirt, a little girl in a frilly white dress, several others—were doing what everyone in the LTD, except Art Degraff, was doing. They were bubbling and boiling under that cold rain. They had their mouths wide open in a big "O" as if to scream, but no screams came out.

I looked at the LTD. It was empty. Except for a long, pasty white face and huge dark eyes peering fearfully out from the middle of the back seat. "Damn you!" I whispered at him. But he wasn't looking at me. His gaze was fixed, and unmoving, as if he were blind—it was the gaze, I knew, of a man who wants desperately to be dead.

Where do you start? I'd been in similar situations in Nam. Not often. Twice. After quick firefights, when I had to run from the injured to the dying to the dead, yelling "Corpsman, corpsman!" again and again.

But as I stood trying to assess this situation, as the rain lightened to a soft drizzle and the wind to a warm southerly breeze, I heard the wail of sirens at a distance.

I went over to a woman of twenty or so; she was closest to the Chevette. She was dressed in a pink halter top, a green, chic spring jacket, and black loose-fitting pants. She was lying on her back, with her arms thrown wide and her legs together, as if she were on a cross, and she clutched a white-faced porcelain doll in her right hand. She had her eyes open and she blinked every few seconds. I could see no blood.

I asked gently, "Where do you hurt?"

She took a quick breath. "I . . ." She stopped.

"Is it your back?"

She nodded a little.

The wail of sirens grew louder; I judged that there were three or four, and I was thankful for that.

I said to the woman, "Can you move your arms or legs?"

"No," she whispered. I caught movement out of the corner of my eye. I looked. Whelan was doing what I was doing, he was talking to one of the injured.

At Pete's Groceries and Things and at Hattie's Brookfield Restaurant, the doors opened and people moved tentatively onto the street. I called angrily at them, "Move, for Christ's sake!" It did no good. I called, "These people need help!" Still nothing. I couldn't blame them. They were trying to make sense of what they'd seen in the last five minutes, still trying to fit it into their structured view of the world.

But still I had to get them moving. "You assholes!" I yelled, "You dimwits! You knuckleheads!" It was enough. A few of them broke into a run and were soon attending to the injured.

The wail of sirens was very close now, at the edge of the town. I glanced toward the sound, saw the first of what would turn out to be a veritable army of emergency vehicles. "Thank God," I murmured. I looked back at the woman. She was smiling at me, a smile of quiet, painful amusement. "You're funny," she said.

It was very difficult for me to believe that I was actually seeing what I was seeing a half hour later. I was a couple of hundred yards south of the spot where the "Brookfield Flea" had been set up, in front of a bright white two-story house that had gingerbread under the severely peaked roof line and flower boxes sprouting some sort of small pinkish-purple flowers under the lower windows. Behind a white picket fence, in the well-manicured front yard, there were rosebushes trimmed back and even a pink ceramic birdbath.

I was seeing the names "CRAY/PELLAPRAT" in bold, black, hand-painted letters on the side of one of those tan rural mailboxes.

I found it very difficult to believe that Abner had actually put those names there, but it wasn't the work of genius to figure out why: He had put them there as his pronouncement of love and life and openness. What did he have to hide? Those names announced that he was living there with the woman he loved. He was tending his rosebushes, his flower boxes, his little lawn, his birdbath, and he and Phyllis were *happy* together.

"My God, Abner," I breathed, head lowered.

"Go away, Sam!"

I looked up. Abner was standing on his little open porch, hands on his hips and a look of grim determination on his face. "You're not welcome here, Sam."

I pushed the gate open and started toward him down the narrow fieldstone walkway.

"Don't come in here, Sam. This is *my* house," Abner warned as he backed away toward the front door.

I continued shaking my head. There was nothing I could say to him, and although I had no idea what I was going to do when I got inside, I knew that inside, into that house, was where I had to go.

"Don't you know that Art probably *followed* you here, Sam?" Abner pleaded.

"Yes, Abner," I said. "I know. But you don't have to worry about him anymore."

He guffawed. "You ignorant bastard."

"Maybe," I said, and started up the porch steps. He had his back to the front door now. He grabbed the knob, turned it, pushed the door open, and started backing into the house.

I saw someone behind him. Someone nearly as tall as he was, but, in the darkness beyond that door, someone who was visible only as a dark *presence* in the house. I was certain it wasn't Phyllis. I was certain that Phyllis had fallen to the same fate that the Haislip brothers and Florence and God-only-knew how many others in Brookfield had that morning.

I started across the porch. Abner backed further into the house so all I could see of him was his arm holding the door open.

I thought then, *If he really wanted me to go away, he wouldn't stand there holding the door open!*

"Christ, Abner," I sighed. And I lunged forward.

He threw the door shut at the same time. I slammed into it with my shoulder, then with the side of my head. The door flew open and crashed against the wall of the small foyer beyond. The foyer was empty.

I felt blood trickling down my cheek; I fingered it. "Dammit!" I whispered.

"Sam," I heard. The sound came from my right, from a short hallway that appeared to lead into a darkened living room. "You're not welcome here! Please go!" I heard anger in his voice. And pleading.

I started down the hallway toward the living room. I heard movement beyond, as of someone walking unsteadily across the hardwood floors there. I heard, too, a low shuffling noise, as if someone in slippers were trying to sidle across the same floor.

"Abner," I called, "you're my friend; I'm here to help you."

"We don't need your help," he called back, and again I heard pleading in his voice. "We have . . . each other!"

"We?" I called.

"Phyllis and me."

"But, Abner, the storm—"

"I sheltered her. I love her, and I sheltered her."

I was at the end of the hallway now. Before me lay a large living room, furnished with what looked like antiques from various periods. The only light was what streamed in through a pair of tall, narrow windows covered by lace curtains. These windows let copious amounts of light into half the big room and left the rest of the room in a kind of sugary darkness.

That's where Abner was, in that sugary darkness; in a doorway which led to the kitchen.

I could see the suggestion of his face, his eyes wide and his mouth moving as if he wanted to speak but couldn't think of the right words.

And Phyllis stood behind him.

I could see her head, her neck, her shoulders, the upper part of her breasts. I guessed that she was naked.

Abner's mouth stopped moving. Apparently he knew what I was looking at, because a nervous grin appeared on his mouth and he said, "She won't . . ." —another grin—". . . she won't keep her clothes on, Sam."

I could see her face more clearly than I could see Abner's, because she was a foot or so behind him, in light coming through the kitchen windows. It was the face that I remembered seeing at the beach house. But it was a face that was now at most the mask of beauty, a face that was the remembrance and imitation of beauty.

"I love her, Sam," Abner pleaded.

"Let her go," I said.

"I want to . . . to take her out, you know? To the store. To a restaurant. My Phyllis and me."

I started moving across the living room. Abner backed slowly away toward the kitchen. I realized then what the shuffling noise was. It was the soles of Phyllis's bare feet on the hardwood floor.

Abner babbled on, "I dress her up, you know—I dress her up the way she used to dress up. Sam, she's beautiful, she's really beautiful."

"You've got to let her go, Abner," I said gently, firmly.

"But she gets . . . angry, Sam." He stopped, seemed to think about that. His head lowered for a moment. Then he looked up and smiled as if he'd hit on the right word. "No, Sam. Not angry. She doesn't get angry. She gets *hot,* you know—like the clothes are too *hot*. I can tell. She doesn't say anything. She never says anything anymore. But I can tell."

I was halfway across the living room, and closer to him now, so I could see him more clearly. I could see that his shoulders were raw and naked, as if he'd been burned.

"Good Lord, Abner!" I breathed.

He knew what I was talking about. "It's nothing," he said. "Nothing. I had to shelter her from the storm, didn't I?" I got a mental picture of him huddling over her, protecting her from the awful, cleansing rain, the rain that even the roof and bulk of his house could not protect her from, but that his love could.

"Let her go," I said again. "She has to move on—"

He chuckled grimly, falsely. "And what do *you* know, Sam?! You don't *know* anything. I've lived with these people for two years, goddammit! Two years!" He had stopped moving. "And I *know* them,

Sam. I know they *move on*. Big deal. What do you think? Do you think it's like high school graduation or something? It isn't. Once they're gone, that's it, they're gone. I don't know where they go. No one does. So I'm sure as hell not going to let it happen to Phyllis. Not my Phyllis."

"Just, please, look at her, Abner," I said. "*Look* at her."

He smiled. "Yes," he said, without turning to look at her, "she's beautiful, isn't she?"

"She's dead, goddammit!"

Another guffaw. "We're all of us dead in one way or another, my friend—just because we can't get up and scarf down a Twinkie or think as clearly as we used to or—"

"She's *dead,* Abner! Phyllis is *dead*!"

"But, ah, you see, there's a difference, Sam, and the difference is, she *loves* me!"

I lunged for him.

FORTY

I think now, two months later, that he wanted me to do that. Because when I tackled him about the waist, he went down, and as we were toppling over into Phyllis, who toppled over, too, onto her back—and a long, foul-smelling gust of air, the smell of rotted wood, rose up from where she fell—Abner whimpered, "Help me, Sam."

And I remembered thinking that throwing myself on him was like throwing myself on a live grenade, which was a particular fantasy I'd had during my tour of Nam—throwing myself on a live grenade to save the lives of my buddies. (The chance never came up, thank God, because I wasn't at all sure how I'd have reacted. I think if there were a bunch of us and the grenade fell between us we'd all have sat waiting for the other guy to be the hero.)

Because there, in Abner's idyllic house in Brookfield, Vermont, I wasn't at all sure how he was going to react. He loved Phyllis, for God's sake, and I had come to take him away from her. I wasn't sure how he was going to react to that. Maybe he'd explode.

And I wasn't sure how Phyllis would react, either. She didn't react. She lay still, that foul smell—the smell of damp wood, the smell that had permeated the beach house—wafting over us and a continuous ragged kind of purring sound coming from her. After a few minutes, the purring sound stopped and she lay very, very still.

I pushed myself up from Abner so I was over him as if I were doing push-ups. I held his wrists with my hands and I hissed at him, "Let her go! Abner, let her go!"

His mouth moved. His eyes had a stark look of hurt and pleading in them, like a small child who has fallen and scraped his knee.

"Abner," I pleaded, "come back to us. Please come back to us!"

Again his mouth moved. He quivered a sigh. Then he closed his eyes, and he wept.

He's going to be the best man at my wedding next month. He tells me that he'll rent his own tux, thank you, that my taste in clothes is even worse than his, if that's possible. He also claims to like Leslie a lot, though, secretly, I think the two of them have a bit of a personality-clash problem. It happens.

Leslie buried her father in a little cemetery in Queens. He died during my trek from Manhattan to

Brookfield. She tried to call to tell me but, of course, got no answer. His death hit her very hard. When I came back, and for a month or so afterward, she broke into tears everywhere—in restaurants, at a movie, watching TV, whatever. And I don't know how many times I wanted to say something like, "It's okay, Leslie. Really. It's not as bad as you think," but for one, she wouldn't know what I was talking about, and for another, *I* wouldn't know what I was talking about, either. As I said several hundred pages ago, if I've learned one thing these past few months, it's what a really ignorant bastard I am.

Art DeGraff got hauled away, what was left of him. He could barely walk, couldn't talk, and was all but blind. No wonder. He had, after all, been kept prisoner in someone's wall for a year. I thought Kennedy Whelan would be all smiles while the troopers shuffled poor Art into their car and took his—Whelan's—report. But he wasn't. He was awfully glum. I guess it had been a pretty wearing day for him.

Madeline disappeared one fine morning, leaving everything behind in that room of hers, except Gerald's dirty softball. The day before she disappeared, she said, "I go where I'm needed, Sam. I'm not needed here anymore. Don't look so judgmental. Hell, there are lots worse ways I could spend my time."

And I suppose she's right. I suppose there really are lots worse ways to spend your time than helping to keep the traffic flow between this world and *that* one not only one-way but smooth, too, which is what she's chosen to do with her life. I suppose so.

But there are lots better ways to spend your time, too.

Abner's moving out of the beach house tomorrow. He rented a studio apartment in the West Village, using money another publisher advanced him to begin work again on a new photographic look at Manhattan. This morning, he collected a broom, a couple of pails, two boxes of Spic and Span, and a lot of gritty resolve, and headed out to the beach house. He says he wants to make it spotless, which will take some doing.

"My time will come eventually, Sam," he said. "So will yours. Until then, I think I'll do as much living as I can." From the fire in his eyes, I knew he meant it. And hell, if that fire dims, he'll have me around to kick his butt back into place.

After all, that's what friends are for.

ABOUT THE AUTHOR

T. M. Wright is the author of several previous horror novels, including *Strange Seed, The Playground*—published by Tor in 1982—and *A Manhattan Ghost Story*, published in 1984. Mr. Wright lives near Rochester, New York, where he spends much of his time feeding his cats, teaching, reading, and staying warm.

"Letters from admiring readers," he says, "are encouraged."